Guarding

My Heart

Guarding
My Heart

The My Heart Series, Book 1

Kathleen Nelson Tellish

Studio of Books LLC
5900 Balcones Drive Suite 100
Austin, Texas 78731
www.studioofbooks.org
Hotline: (254) 800-1183

Ordering Information:
Special discounts are available on quantity purchases by corporations, associations, and others. For details, contact the publisher at the address above.

Printed in the United States of America.

ISBN-13:   Softcover   978-1-964928-44-9
                    eBook   978-1-964928-43-2

Library of Congress Control Number: 2025907901

# DEDICATION

In loving memory of Katie and Kohl.

ACKNOWLEDGMENT

First, I would like to thank my husband, Gary, for always supporting my creativity, and for being my source of reasoning when I am ready to give up. Without you, there may have been days when I could have accomplished more writing and got more editing finished, but in the end, you are right where you need to be, which is right by my side.

I would like to thank my children, Jason Timmons and his wife Erin, Corey Tellish and his wife Nicole, Michael Tellish and his wife Kat, and my daughter Erica Timmons, for all the beautiful granddaughters and grand dogs who have made my life complete.

To my beautiful, talented granddaughters, Sage Tellish, Zoey Tellish, Rylie Tellish, Annabella Tellish, Hannah Timmons, and our sweet little Hazel Timmons, you are my inspiration for everything I do. You are my life and my heart, and not a day goes by that I don't thank God for each of you.

And finally, thank you to my readers.

Table of Contents

CHAPTER 1

Abbie woke up and felt a warm breath on her face. Grinning, she opened her eyes to a head of black hair hanging an inch from her nose. Before she had time to mutter the words, "Are you ready to start the day, my love?" A big wet tongue swiped slobber across her right cheek. Abbie sat up and gave Kohl a hug. Each day started the same way for them. His next move involved jumping up on the bed and throwing himself across Tom's stomach.

"Go ahead, Kohl," she encouraged him as he looked at her. "Wake up, daddy."

Tom got out the words, "I'm awake," as Kohl leaped onto the bed and hurled himself across Tom's middle. Tom let out a big grunt. "You are in so much trouble."

Kohl barked at him in response. Tom got up on his knees, and he and Kohl wrestled for the next few minutes. Abbie chuckled as she watched from the bathroom door.

She pulled on her bathing suit and rash guard and brushed her teeth. Tom and Kohl did this same routine every morning. She didn't know which one of them enjoyed the habit more.

Tom stood up and kissed Abbie good morning.

"I'm letting this knucklehead outside to do his business."

Kohl slid off the bed and followed Tom to the kitchen. Tom opened the door. "Here you go, buddy, and no chasing the squirrels!"

Kohl stared at Tom, huffed, turned, and ran outside and across the yard, looking for squirrels.

Tom laughed. Kohl was as gentle as they came, so the warning wasn't necessary. He just liked to listen to Kohl huff at him in response. He walked back to the bedroom, shaking his head.

"Something wrong?" Abbie asked.

"No. I often think how lucky we were to find him."

Abbie nodded her head in agreement. Kohl's past owners were moving to a smaller apartment and could not take Kohl because of his size. They turned him over to the local Newfoundland dog rescue shelter. The shelter's first call was to Tom, who was part of the rescue squad at the Coast Guard in Charleston, South Carolina. At four months old, the rescue staff believed Kohl to be the perfect addition to the rescue crew. They contacted the coastguard station, and Tom agreed to discuss the idea with Abbie and his commander. He would then get back to the rescue shelter with a decision.

Abbie and Tom searched the internet for information on Newfoundland dogs. They discovered that this breed was part of the working class and were known to be diligent workers but with a gentle disposition. Known as a Newfie, they are generally gentle giants. They are playful and love being around babies. They have waterproof coats and webbed feet that allow them to stay in the water for an extended period.

"Do we have enough room for him? And do you think he'll eat us out of house and home?"

Tom chuckled. "I read somewhere in the information they're big eaters, but only for a year or two. But we'll need to tolerate dog hair and slobber."

"I think we'll survive."

There were no regrets. Kohl was sharp as a whip, focused, and fit right into their little family. He showed love to everyone he met and enjoyed having fun.

After they brought Kohl home, Tom enrolled the two of them in classes to train Kohl in water rescue techniques. The station had never had a rescue dog before, but after discussions with his commanding officer, he received permission to try it. Newfoundland puppies undergo different training phases, and Kohl excelled at every single one. Graduating at the top of his class in basic and complex obedience, swimming, overcoming hesitation around water, and other complex rescue maneuvers, Kohl was a natural. Rescue training takes at least a year, but it was as though Tom and Kohl could read each other's minds, so Kohl graduated in just under ten months.

Kohl loved going to the guard station with Tom, and Tom's commanding officer was glad to have Kohl on board. The rest of the crew loved Kohl and bragged about the maneuvers he could do, and they loved it when he performed the basic puppy commands: sit, speak, lie, and roll.

Abbie was over the moon in love with Kohl. She was the first one Kohl greeted in the morning, and his slobbery kiss had become their routine. Abbie worked as a registered nurse (RN) at Memorial hospital and was glad to have Kohl as part of the rescue team. She hoped that Kohl's skills would reduce the number of drownings and near drownings they received at the hospital.

The rescue crews and hospitals in the area became busy in the afternoon hours. After hours of water recreation, which often included alcohol intake, people were tired and less able to make the right decisions for their safety. Abbie, Tom, and Kohl worked together to educate the public on water safety techniques. Abbie and Tom hoped that Kohl's influence on water safety might help the public become more aware of risks and outcomes.

While Tom was getting ready to go to the beach, Abbie made their coffee, filled their Yeti cups, filled Kohl's food and water dishes, and let the dog in from his morning routine. Then, they stepped out the door, grabbed their boards, life vest, towels, and paddles from storage, and walked the few yards to the water.

Abbie loved living on the beach. Purchasing a beach property was Tom's idea. As teenagers, the two of them spent hours at the beach, swimming, bike riding, and just hanging out. They both loved being near the water. So, when Tom suggested purchasing the beach house, they agreed to watch their budget to make their dream come true. After getting Kohl, they decided it was well worth the extra money, as Tom and Kohl often trained in the ocean, just outside their door.

Abbie and Tom sat on their boards to enjoy their first cup of coffee while Kohl frolicked in the water. One of Abbie's favorite activities was enjoying the sunrise and watching the sky turn from dark to light. Every sunrise was different, and she never tired of watching the morning sky. The waves, picking up reflection from the rising sun, calmed her. When she met Tom, they found joy in watching the sunrise together.

Abandoned at birth, Abby was sixteen and in foster care, at yet another foster home, when she met Tom. Her foster parents could not have children of their own. So, instead of adopting, they fostered older children who often had difficulty finding permanent placements.

Tom arrived one Saturday afternoon as Abbie was preparing for lunch. He said hello to her and introduced himself. They were inseparable from that moment.

Tom's parents died from injuries sustained in a car accident when he was fifteen. He'd been at multiple homes but could never fit in with the others. So, at sixteen, when he met Abbie, he planned to finish school, attend college, and join the Coast Guard.

Tom's arrival had been life-changing for Abbie. Finally, she found someone in whom she could confide. In their spare time, they explored Charleston and often hung out on the beach.

Tom spoke to Abbie, but she was so lost in thought that she did not hear him speak.

"Earth to Abbie. Are you okay?" Tom asked, bringing her back to the present.

"I'm great. I was thinking about the Wilson's and the day you walked into the Wilsons' house. Everything changed for me that day, and I would not be who I am or where I am without you and Kohl. I am in my favorite spot with my favorite guys."

Tom smiled at her response. It was always difficult for her to say she loved him. When they first met, Abbie was shy and standoffish. She had been with the Wilsons for six months when he entered the picture. Nevertheless, they got to know one another, and she trusted him.

"Am I your favorite guy? Or is it that sopping wet mess rolling around in the surf? He acts like it is his first trip to the beach."

Abbie laughed. "I love you both, but that mess is hard to resist."

The sun had risen, so they donned their life jackets, called Kohl so to put on his vest, and walked into the water. Abbie smiled, thinking about the first time she attempted to paddle board on the ocean. Tom warned her that it differed from paddling on still water. Of course, Abbie learned the hard way. She fell from the board multiple times, realizing she underestimated the power of the wind and waves.

Teaching Kohl how to ride the board was easy. As a result, he was better at keeping his balance and stronger at swimming in the ocean when he fell.

They enjoyed their early morning rides and took turns riding the waves with Kohl on their boards while visitors and locals watched. Once Kohl began water rescue training, Abbie was adamant that his time spent at home should be relaxing and fun. So, when the weather was decent, they stuck to this routine.

When they finished riding the waves, Kohl's routine was to jump off the paddle board, run around, and shake the water off his fur. Abbie tried her best to catch him and towel off the water this morning, but he was too quick for her. She knew he would not run away so she let him run. Abbie turned to help Tom gather their belongings and overheard a man's voice yelling at someone. She turned and spied a man and her dog facing one another.

"What are you doing? Hey, get out of here, you crazy dog. Get. Go."

She approached them. Abbie recognized the man as Dr. Alexander Montgomery from the ER where she worked, but as usual, he did not recognize her. Abbie stopped in front of him with her hands placed on her hips.

"I'm sorry. Is there a problem?"

Alex looked up and saw a tall, thin woman with curly hair pulled on top of her head. She released the hair tie at that moment, and her damp hair blew everywhere. She looked as wild as her dog.

"Is this your dog?"

Abbie nodded.

"Keep your dog under control. I'm wet from head to toe and covered in sand. Who lets a dog this size run wild? He's as big as a bear. He's going to hurt someone if he knocks them over," Dr, Montgomery warned her while attempting to brush water and sand from his clothes.

"I glanced at my phone to check a text message, and boom, water, and sand flying everywhere. I practically fell over him."

"Sorry! He must not have seen you."

Abbie turned to speak to Kohl. "Please apologize to the man."

Kohl refused to look at her and continued to stare at the man. Abbie repeated her request. Kohl huffed, turned around, then sat in the sand, facing away from Dr. Montgomery.

Abbie tried not to laugh. The doctor scowled at her with his hands perched on his hips.

"Kohl is always aware of everything surrounding him. He was goofing around this morning. I'm sorry he got you wet. We will try to be better at keeping this beast under control."

Abbie called him a jerk under her breath. She and Kohl turned to walk away.

"I heard you."

Abbie looked back over her shoulder.

"Stop texting while running, and you could see any hazards around you. I'll have him bark next time. It appears your hearing is better than your vision." She turned around, and she and Kohl walked away.

Dr. Montgomery stood with his hands perched on his hips and watched her walk away. Then, he brushed more sand from his clothes and ran off to finish his run.

"What was that?" Tom asked.

Abbie chuckled.

"Kohl ran out of the water, soaking wet as usual, and was shaking off water. He soaked that guy as he was running on the beach. That runner was Dr. Alex Montgomery from the ER. As usual, he did not recognize me. As I've said before, he is oblivious to everyone around him except for his patients. I told Kohl to apologize. He huffed at him and turned his back on him."

They both laughed. Kohl's bad habit was to huff when he did not want to do something he was told to do, and today, he did not want to apologize to the man he had gotten wet and turned his back to the man.

The trio returned to the house and started their usual routine of getting ready for work. Kohl dug into his food bowl while Abbie and Tom showered, donned their uniforms, and gathered their gear for the day.

Abbie's phone rang, and she saw Samantha's name on the screen. Sam was one of the four girls Abbie met during college. The "crew," as they called themselves, had become best friends, and while they did not live close in proximity, they called each other and remained inseparable from afar. Abbie grabbed her phone while pouring a cup of coffee and settled on the sofa to catch up with Sam.

"Hey, Abbie. Kohl and I are leaving now." Tom called from the front door.

"Hang on a second, Sam."

Abbie walked over to kiss her two guys goodbye.

"See you two later. Stop by the ER if you have free time. Love you!"

"We will," he said, giving Abbie a kiss.

Kohl stood on his back legs and reached out to Abbie for a hug. Abbie called Kohl's hugs her bear hugs because of his size.

"Love you, too, Kohl."

Abbie returned to her conversation with Sam as she watched them walk out to the truck. Kohl jumped in the back, and Tom opened the windows for him. Unfortunately, his size consumed the entire back seat. Tom had removed the seats when they got Kohl as a puppy, knowing his bulk might fill the entire space. She waved as they pulled out and blew Tom a kiss. He smiled and waved back.

"Sorry, Sam. I'm back."

"Did you spend time on the beach this morning, Abbie? The weather is glorious up here." Abbie sighed.

"Oh no, Abbie. I hate it when you sigh. What's happening? Are you and Tom okay?"

"We're good." She relayed the story of the altercation with Kohl and the ER doctor. Sam chuckled.

"It was funny," Abbie replied. "The problem is, I called him a jerk. I need to apologize to him. Even though he is an interim director, I don't want him to write me up for insubordination."

"If you weren't working, can he do that?"

"I don't know, but I won't give him the opportunity. He won't be here long and does not know my name. The problem is, we work together. Besides, Dana will give me hell for putting her in a tough spot if he insists on writing me up."

"I agree. Dana will not be happy if they force her to take disciplinary action. She can't show favoritism just because you are besties. Does he treat everyone that way? It is odd, don't you think?"

"I know. Part of his problem is that he is incredibly good-looking. Tall, dark hair, athletic, and add in intelligent, and you have the perfect recipe for a jerk that is used to getting his way because of his looks. I bet he's ridden that coat tail his entire life."

Sam was nodding her head even though Abbie couldn't see her.

"Oh, preaching to the choir, Abbie. I've dated that type way too many times, but I am not doing it again."

Abbie laughed.

"Oh, Sam. I need to go. I didn't realize how late it was getting. Talk to you soon. Hugs." she said as she dropped her phone onto the sofa to find her purse and stethoscope.

CHAPTER 2

After Tom and Kohl kissed Abbie goodbye and jumped into his truck, he opened both back windows and slid open the window facing the rear mirror. Kohl enjoyed riding in the truck. He enjoyed the breeze while looking out the windows.

His role as a rescue dog with the Coast Guard made him a celebrity in town. Every time the news stations ran a story of a rescue that Kohl took part in, his popularity rose. Tom had received so many cards and letters from victims he had saved that he started a wall with the correspondence.

Protecting the nation's ports, stopping illegal drug smugglers, marine environmental protection, and law enforcement was part of the coastguard's job. However, the proximity of the ocean and beaches made many of their calls rescue related, and even the locals forgot they oversaw other tasks.

Often, the survivors of one of their rescue calls stopped at the station and thanked everyone. Tom always offered to take a picture of them with Kohl. Then, he'd snap a second one with his camera and place it on the wall in the station.

Kohl ate up the attention. When riding in the truck with Tom, he loved looking for people to greet. Abbie had taught him to raise his paw and give a quick bark in response to the people who waved.

There were people everywhere this morning, which made their drive slow and treacherous. Tourists tried to cross the street wherever they chose instead of at the crosswalks. As soon as they caught sight of Kohl, they began waving and calling out to him. When they first got Kohl, he, and Abbie worried that his bulky, bear-like appearance and enormous head might intimidate everyone, but they were wrong. His size was one of his features that attracted the crowd.

If he and Abbie ran errands and Kohl tagged along, it would take them more time to complete their task. He drew crowds everywhere they went, and since they used him to educate the public on water safety, they always took the time to stop and answer questions. Of course, they still got questioned when they were out in public without Kohl, but the people did not tire of his sweet nature.

When they arrived at the coastguard station, Tom opened the truck door, and Kohl jumped out of the truck and ran toward the open station door to look for his friends, the crew members—after that, every day started with Kohl playing catch. But, of course, the crew enjoyed playing, too.

It was the start of the yearly regatta. Sailors from around the country gathered in the harbor. Today's schedule included a sailboat race. The boats raced eighteen nautical miles south toward Folly and Kiawah Island, then turned and headed back to Charleston Harbor. This year, one hundred thirty boats and five hundred sailors were competing.

The Regatta participants and race fans arrived along with their families and friends. They lined up on the beaches and coast for miles, eating, drinking, swimming, and overindulging in everything, including the sun. Local rescue squads were busy.

Beachgoers often underestimated the differences between swimming in a pool and swimming in open ocean water and ventured out when water conditions were less than ideal. Kids and adults entered the water without a single thought of changing tides, fast-moving currents, and waves, making rescue calls a frequent occurrence.

National Weather Service alerts had gone out earlier this morning about storms near Charleston but they had also cleared those warnings an hour ago. Tom hoped people would pay attention. The skies were cloudy, and the wind was gusting, but the regatta might go on if the weather did not get worse.

Tom entered the station to find Kohl chasing a tennis ball being thrown at him by a couple of guys on the crew. Knowing this would be a busy day, Tom needed Kohl at his best, so he commanded Kohl to rest in his crate. Kohl dropped the ball, huffed at Tom, and sauntered to his crate. The crew booed at Tom in good nature for making Kohl rest, but they understood it was essential for him to rest and the impact it had on their successful rescues. Kohl lay on his crate. He was asleep before Tom got the ball picked up from the floor. The crew stretched out on their bunks as well.

Tom worked at setting up crew schedules and completing paperwork piled on his desk. An hour had passed, and he stood leaning against the station door, watching clouds move in from the ocean. The weather was decent when the boats began arriving in the harbor this morning. Still, there had been intermittent rain and wind along with the periodic storm warnings announced, then canceled throughout the morning. Tom returned to his office to look at the radar. It showed a weather pattern that might develop into a storm before the race.

Less than five minutes after Tom walked outside, the National Weather Service issued yet another storm warning, and Tom became concerned. The warning urged boaters to stay out of the water, but the boats and people already in the water may have missed the warning, putting multiple boats and lives in danger.

Tom walked outside and looked toward the sky to check the conditions. His pilot, Kevin, was out checking the weather, too.

"What do you think, Tom? Are we in for a busy afternoon, or will this pass?"

"I was looking at the radar. The wind is blowing from two different directions, which might help the race participants if it stays calm, but if it picks up, we may get terribly busy."

Kevin agreed. "I just looked over the chopper, and it's ready to go. Everything we might need is on board, and the fuel is full. Let's just hope we don't need it."

"Isn't that the truth?"

Tom and Kevin stood outside watching the weather roll in off the water and were discussing local politics and events when a rescue call came in for multiple boats overturned in the harbor with multiple victims.

Earlier in the shift, they calculated the rescue needs and discussed the possibility of using the helicopter for quicker rescue, should they get a call.

Tom was glad they had that discussion earlier in the shift. Finally, Kevin and Tom decided it should be okay to fly, and Kevin ran and got the helicopter ready to take off. The other crew members grabbed their gear and headed to the chopper.

The sound of the alarm woke Kohl up, and Tom found him standing next to him. Tom donned his rescue swimmer gear, applied Kohl's gear, got them both in the helicopter, and belted in with the rest of the crew for a possible choppy ride.

Tom was thinking about the number of people who might need to be rescued today. With one hundred thirty boats scheduled for the regatta and five hundred participants, the local boaters anchored offshore to enjoy the festivities, and the weather, that number might reach close to one hundred.

Kevin took off and warned everyone on board that the ride would be bumpy. Within minutes, they arrived on scene. Examining the chaos, Tom and his crew prioritized the rescue needs. Tom estimated twenty people in the water. Nearby boaters were helping other boaters get out of the water. Finally, Tom and his pilot, Kevin, spotted a boat farther from shore. The Coast Guard had their rescue boats in the water, and Tom spotted other boats owned by the local hazmat team offering their services for the day

The boat farthest from shore, floated on its starboard side in the water. Tom noted three people clinging to the side of the boat. They all had a life vest except for one person. Tom wondered why anyone would choose to go boating without safety equipment. That man was having trouble staying afloat. So, Tom made him the first rescue attempt.

Tom instructed Kevin to position the helicopter near the man. Kevin maneuvered the chopper into position and lowered it, trying to hold it steady in the choppy wind. Tom instructed Kohl on his mission, released his belt, and Kohl jumped into the choppy water below to find his first victim.

Tom released his belt and grabbed the bar near the door as he prepared to exit the helicopter. A violent gust of wind tossed the helicopter, causing Tom to fall out of the door. As the helicopter spun and Kevin fought to gain control, the landing skid struck Tom's head, and he and the helicopter dropped toward the water.

People watching from the shore screamed. Kohl turned to look, watching as Tom and the helicopter fell. He paused his swim toward his victim. Torn between the mission Tom had given him and his need to check on his owner, Kohl looked around and saw a boat near the victim he was to rescue.

Charleston's local fire department had received the rescue call and had boats in the water. The lieutenant aboard one boat saw Kohl hesitate and shouted to him.

"I have this guy, Kohl. Find Tom. Go."

Kohl changed direction and swam toward the water where he saw Tom fall.

Kevin had gained control of the falling chopper and was hovering near the spot where Tom fell. Kevin wondered why Tom was not surfacing. His gear should have kept him afloat.

Kohl circled the area where Tom fell into the water, sniffing to pick up Tom's scent. As soon as he picked up his scent, Kohl began diving until he surfaced with Tom. Tom's life vest had come loose in the fall. It was hanging on his left arm. Kohl had Tom's right wrist in his mouth and was towing his lifeless body through the water. The drag of Tom's body was holding him back, but he swam as quickly as possible and searched for the closest place to get to shore.

The rescue personnel on shore yelled at Kohl and directed him to their location. Kohl started swimming toward help. The rescue crew waited on shore for Kohl. Fire and rescue personnel grabbed Tom from Kohl as soon as Kohl's feet touched solid ground, assessed Tom, yelled out, "Load and go," and started CPR as they ran with Tom and their gurney toward the waiting ambulance.

Kohl ran behind the gurney, and when they loaded Tom into the ambulance, he jumped in without direction or permission. Rob, the paramedic treating Tom, spotted Kohl sitting near the ambulance door.

"You can ride with us, Kohl, but sit and stay. Do you understand me?"

Kohl responded with a sharp bark, sat, and never took his eyes off Tom on the short ride to Memorial Hospital.

The paramedics worked on Tom during the ride to the hospital. They were so busy trying to save him that they did not alert the staff at the ER with their emergency management radio.

He had significant injuries from the fall. They continued CPR and pushed drugs to help stabilize his condition, but nothing worked. Tom had a large wound on the back of his head, but the ambulance crew did not know what caused his injury. Tom should have bounced back up in the water when he fell. They used rescue gear to keep rescue divers afloat should any problem arise.

"How much further?" Rob asked Burt, the driver.

"We're a mile from the hospital. I can't get these cars to move. There's nowhere for anyone to go."

"Move them over. We need to get there now. Do you know if anyone called Abbie?"

When Kohl heard Abbie's name, he let out a low growl. Rob reassured him that everything was okay.

"I'm hearing reports they are trying to reach her, but she is not answering her phone. She works the same shifts as Tom. She might be with a patient."

"I hope so."

Burt moved the ambulance, but within another hundred feet, traffic stopped again. Burt blared the siren.

Rob heard swearing coming from the front of the truck. He closed his eyes and offered a prayer to anyone who heard him. Then, he grabbed his radio and yelled into it.

"Find a police officer to open this road. We're at Calhoun and Ashley and can't get the ambulance through this traffic. This guy is tanking. I don't care what it takes. Bring a tank, if necessary, but find someone who can move these cars."

It took two minutes before they picked up the sound of the sirens. The police used bullhorns to get vehicles off the blocked streets. One officer used the bullhorn, and the others blocked the side streets. Burt overheard the officer screaming at people to get off the road.

"I don't care where you park. Park on the sidewalk or someone's yard, but get off the street, now!"

The police officers got traffic moved, and the road cleared. Burt laid on the siren and drove the short distance to the hospital. Rob looked at his watch. Had only eight minutes passed since they loaded Tom into the ambulance? He felt like he had been doing this for eight hours. Rob pushed more meds but was out of options.

He picked up the handset to radio his report to the ER and let them know they were en route with a traumatic cardiac arrest when he realized they had pulled into the ambulance bay. He let the radio fall from his hand. Never in his career had he felt so relieved. They unloaded Tom and ran through the doors, and Kohl ran right beside the gurney.

CHAPTER 3

Alex completed his run and started removing his shirt and shoes as soon as he stepped onto the porch. He did not want to drag sand throughout the house. Andy, his son, laughed at him as he entered the living room. Helen, his part-time nanny and housekeeper laughed as well.

"What happened to you, Dad? Did you fall in the sand?"

"Ha-ha, funny, Andy. I did not fall. An enormous dog ran from the ocean and about knocked me over. He was sopping wet and started shaking water and sand, and it flew all over me. That's why I am soaking wet and covered in sand."

"I swear he was as big as a bear. I yelled to him to stop shaking and go away. He stopped shaking but stood right before me and stared at me. His owner walked over to us, and she told him to apologize. Instead, he huffed toward me, turned his back to me, and sat in the sand."

"Really?" Andy exclaimed, laughing. "As big as a bear? Did he have claws, Dad? Maybe he had fangs, too. Did you look? And how does a dog apologize?" Andy asked as his seven-year-old curiosity and imagination ran wild.

"He didn't have claws or fangs. He was big and furry with an exceptionally large head."

"Did he have a name, Dad? Can we go back and find him? I've never seen a dog as big as a bear. Can we look for him, Dad?"

"We can't go this morning, Andy. I need to take a shower; then I'm going to take you to school. Ms. Helen was nice enough to fix your breakfast this morning, now finish it while I get ready for work, or we will be late."

"Do you know the lady with the dog, Dad? Can you call her?"

"No, Andy, I don't know the lady. We might see them on the beach one day."

"Are you sure we can't go today, Dad? It would be cool to see him. The kids at my school would think he's cool, too. Can we get a picture of him, so they believe me?"

"I'm positive we can't go today, Andy. So, finish breakfast, brush your teeth, and get your backpack for school."

Alex headed to the bathroom, removed his sand-covered clothing, and stepped into the shower. He thought about Andy's question. The lady with the dog might look familiar, but he couldn't place her. Perhaps he had seen her while running. Now that he thought back, he remembered thinking she was stunning.

Blue eyes that matched the ocean and curly blond hair lightened by the sun, which was blowing everywhere in the wind. And she had a nice tan. She looked familiar, but she was talking to the dog, asking him to apologize, and her voice and temperament distracted him from her looks.

Everything had happened so fast, and she and the dog were walking away and calling him a jerk. Her dog nearly knocked him over, and he was the jerk.

Alex shook his head. Maybe, he had acted a bit of a jerk. The sand and water would wash off his clothing. But it was her attitude that irritated him. And the dog had the same attitude as his owner. Her dog acted like a four-year-old child and reminded him of Andy when he stood with his hands on his hips, daring him to tell him again to do something he did not want to do.

I'm glad she thought the situation was funny. But who trains their dog to behave that way? An arrogant dog of that size could easily break someone's leg if he knocked them over.

Andy had often asked him for a dog, but his work schedule did not leave them time to train a dog. In addition, after the accident in Denver, he did not want to be near any dogs. Maybe if Andy met the dog, that would satisfy his need to own one.

Alex helped Andy into the car.

"Andy, I will try to find out who owns that big dog, but I can't make you any promises. But, if I find the owner, maybe we can meet him."

"That would be great, Dad." Andy smiled, clapped his hands, and let out a whoop.

Alex pulled from the driveway and was glad to see his son smiling on his way to school.

Alex arrived at the emergency room and went to his office. After checking the schedule to confirm staffing for the day, he walked to the medication room to review stock, then checked the triage, fast-track, sub-acute, and trauma rooms to ensure they had adequate stock to get them through a busy day.

Today was the local regatta. Dana, his Nursing Director, informed him they would be busy in the ER today. She said it was busy every year because of all the people in town. He looked at the patient intake board and saw the sub-acute rooms filled with patients who had sustained ankle injuries and sunburns. His nurse practitioners could manage these things, leaving him available for any bigger emergencies that might come through the door.

There were two other doctors today besides him, and they were expecting to be busy, too. Alex consulted with a heart patient in trauma one and reviewed labs that had come back in the abnormal range, so he recommended a cardiac consultation and a better diet. He helped put ankle splints on two patients and discharged two sunburn cases. Today, everyone needed to step up their game and help anywhere they could if they wanted empty rooms for fresh cases coming in throughout the shift.

Alex turned the corner, walked toward the physician's desk, and received the EMS radio call coming into the emergency room. Prepared to write the vital information on the incoming patient, Alex realized the ambulance was pulling into the bay. He caught the words traumatic cardiac arrest and crew before the doors to the emergency room opened, and the chaos started. The paramedics were doing CPR. Dana directed them to trauma three.

"What happened, and how many minutes has he been down?"

Rob, the paramedic, responded.

"He was in cardiac arrest when they pulled him from the water, and it took us eight minutes to get here because of traffic. He's with the Coast Guard rescue crew. When the storm blew in, it caused twenty boats to overturn in the harbor, and people fell from their boats and were trying to stay afloat in the water. Tom prepared to jump from the helicopter, and a severe wind gust knocked him from the chopper. The severe wind gust also caused the chopper to drop, and it spun, striking Tom's head with the landing skid. He fell into the water. We're not sure what he hit going in, but something ripped his rescue gear off his body. There has been no response. GCS is a three."

"His dog, sitting right here, was swimming toward another victim, but he turned and dove into the water repeatedly and searched for Tom. Finally, he surfaced with Tom and pulled him ashore by his wrist."

"What dog, Rob?"

"This dog, sir," Rob replied, pointing to Kohl sitting in the room's corner.

"Why is that dog in here? Get him out of here. This is trauma. Someone will trip over him and get hurt."

Alex continued to assess Tom, not liking his findings. CPR continued while the x-ray department's staff took quick head and chest x-rays, but Alex cringed at the results. This guy was in trouble.

Alex glanced up, noticing that nobody had moved. He looked around, stunned that nobody was moving, unable to make eye contact with a single person.

"What? What's happening? Huh? Does anyone want to inform me, or should I fire every one of you for letting an animal into my ER?"

Dana, the Director of Nursing for the ER, answered his question.

"He won't get in our way, but he won't leave Tom's side either."

"Have any of you tried?" Alex screamed. "Does he listen to anyone?"

"He listens to everyone. He's trained to take commands and rescue." Dana replied.

"Keep doing CPR. Get x-ray back in here, now. I need more films." Alex directed the assisting physicians.

"Let me show all of you how this works. Then, the next time one of you lets an animal into my ER, you will know exactly what to do."

Alex opened the door and looked at Kohl.

"Go. Get out of this room. Now. Leave!"

Nobody moved, and neither did Kohl.

Alex left the door open and walked over to Kohl. He pointed toward the door while looking straight at Kohl.

"Listen up, dog. There is the door. Go to the waiting room."

Kohl stared back at Alex, remained sitting, and bared his teeth.

"Does this dog bite?" Alex asked. Nobody responded.

"Drag him out if needed, but somebody needs to get him out of here now!"

"I'm sorry, Dr. Montgomery. Unfortunately, that's not possible." Dana replied.

"And why not?"

"Have you ever tried to move a hundred-fifty-pound dog that doesn't want to move?" Dana asked.

Alex looked confused. He looked at Dana, then toward the other staff members. Not one of them would make eye contact with him.

"Forget it. I do not know who's in charge here, but I think it's the dog, not me."

Turning to recheck Tom's vital signs, Alex sighed.

"I'm sorry. I know you are all friends with this guy, but there's nothing else we can do for him." Alex glanced at the clock on the wall. "Time of death, 11:37 a.m."

Alex turned to face the staff.

"Where is his family?"

"We haven't been able to locate his wife, Dr. Montgomery. We've checked the waiting room. Several people have tried to call her, but she is not answering her phone. Tom's coworkers have been calling, and they sent someone to the house, but she is not home. I have tried three times as well." Dana replied.

"That's great! Let me know when she gets here." Alex mumbled, slammed through the door, and stomped back to his office.

Kohl dropped his head and lay on the floor. The ER staff stooped down and spoke with him. They said they were sorry about his loss. They assured him Abbie would arrive soon.

Dana was alone in the room with Kohl. She stayed behind to straighten the equipment and clean up the mess thrown everywhere during their efforts to save Tom. Abbie should arrive soon, and Dana didn't want her walking into a mess when she arrived. And where was she? It was unlike her to be late. Dana remembered one paramedic saying they had gotten stuck in traffic, and they called for the police, who opened the road, allowing them to get to the hospital.

Dana walked to the gurney where Tom lay and spoke to him. She thanked him for his friendship and everything he had given to Abbie and Kohl.

They spent a lot of time at the house he and Abbie owned on the beach. When Tom left for basic training, Abbie had the place to herself, and she, Sam, Julie, and Kate, spent time with Abbie. Every night, they studied together. It was easy to study because they had the same healthcare classes. They would read each other's papers and make suggestions for corrections. Dana laughed when she remembered one of their professors asking if they shared the same brain.

They taught each other how to cook and produced amazing recipes. It was easier to cook at home and cheaper, too. In addition, it saved them time to run back and forth to the cafeteria. When Tom returned, they went to their apartments, but there was no notable change in their routine.

When they graduated, she and Abbie chose the local hospital. She liked Charleston and being near the beach. So, when Memorial hospital offered her a position in the ER, she said yes instantly. With Tom stationed in Charleston, Abbie chose Memorial and joined Dana in the ER.

Glancing at Kohl, Dana swore she saw a tear on his face. She walked over to him and sat on the floor beside him. Dana knew Kohl well. She remembered when Tom and Abbie adopted him and how proud they were of his ability to adapt to the water and the rescue dog life. The three of them, Abbie, Tom, and Kohl, were orphans. Abbie said the three of them found one another for a reason, and she agreed. Kohl was lucky to have such great doggie parents.

Dana and Abbie met during college and became fast friends. Samantha, or Sam as everyone called her, joined the group a couple of months later, followed by Julie and Kate. The 'crew' was what they called themselves and they were all in the healthcare field. Dana and Abbie became nurses. Samantha picked physical therapy. Julie chose pediatric medicine, and Kate, who they called the group's genius, studied gene therapy. She had to call them soon. When Abbie arrives and discovers the incident that happened to Tom, this crew will be the ones to help her through challenging times.

She spoke to Kohl about their fun on the beach and told him Abbie would be proud of him for attempting to save Tom. She talked about his rescues and bravery in saving people in trouble.

Kohl sighed. Dana knew he was terrified by what had happened to Tom. She expected Abbie to be terrified as well, but she and the rest of the crew would be there to help one another. They always did!

Dana needed to watch for Abbie to arrive. She was the person to tell Abbie what had happened. Dr. Montgomery was a stranger. He might threaten to fire her for giving Abbie the tragic news, but she didn't care. And if he found out about her next move, he would fire her anyway.

"Kohl, do you want to lie next to Tom?"

Kohl lifted his head and looked toward Dana.

"We'll need to be quick at this and keep it between us. Follow me." Dana directed Kohl.

He stood and followed Dana across the room while she grabbed a chair from the corner.

"Here's the plan, Kohl. I'll move the chair next to the gurney. You climb on the chair, then I will hold the gurney, and you can climb up and lie next to Tom's legs. Got it?"

Kohl let out a soft bark to acknowledge Dana's instructions and followed her instructions exactly.

"Perfect. Now you stay here until Abbie arrives." Dana instructed Kohl. "I have to go call the girls."

Dana bent to place a kiss on Kohl's head. She glanced back at him when she left the room. Working in emergency medicine taught her life changes within a heartbeat; this was a perfect example.

Dana had her hand on the knob of her office door when Dr. Alex Montgomery came out of his office.

"Where is that dog? He's not in another of my trauma rooms, is he?"

Not wanting to bear the wrath of Dr. Montgomery if he found out Kohl was lying with Tom, Dana replied, "I believe he left with someone," and closed the door to her office to make her calls.

She called Sam first because she was the closest. When Sam learned what had happened, she used her phone to conference Julie and Kate. They made plans to get to Charleston. Sam was running around her apartment gathering belongings as they spoke.

"Take your time, Dana. I can be at her house before you and Abbie complete everything in the ER and return to her house."

Dana wanted to stay with the rest of the group at Abbie's house. When Sam arrived, she would get items she needed from her apartment. Julie and Kate coordinated flights, and their flights would arrive late this afternoon.

They had their plan in place, and everyone got moving. Dana needed to get out of her office before Abbie arrived. She walked out to the nurse's station and watched the corridors for Abbie's arrival.

CHAPTER 4

Abbie tossed her phone on the sofa and searched for her stethoscope and purse. She grabbed her purse and noted her stethoscope was in its usual place, tucked in the outer pocket of her purse. She locked the back door, grabbed her purse from the counter in the kitchen, and locked the front door on her way out.

Abbie eased into traffic. It was bumper-on-bumper because of the regatta. She thanked all the tourists for causing the traffic to be at a crawl. Then, she saw a storm rolling onshore off the ocean, which would only increase the traffic mess.

She turned on the radio and turned it to a contemporary music station, hoping it might help pass the time while easing her anxiety about being late. If traffic didn't start moving in the next five minutes, she would call Dana to let her know she would be late.

A storm warning interrupted Abbie's music, and she heard sirens in the distance. She thought she could hear the coast guard helicopter and thought of Tom and Kohl. She wondered how Tom could train a dog the size of Kohl to jump from the helicopter into the open water, but Kohl trusted Tom and did as he was told during a rescue mission.

Traffic was at a dead stop, and she was going to be late. She reached for her phone in her purse and came up empty. She picked up her purse and searched again, realizing she must have left it lying on the sofa.

Tapping her fingers on the steering wheel, she considered going back for her phone, then finally gave up the idea as ridiculous. Backtracking would only cause her to arrive later. The problem was getting across the bridge because no alternate route was available. She would need to be patient until the traffic started moving.

Abbie sat back in her seat, took a deep breath, listened to the music, and tried to relax. There was no sense in getting worked up over something she could not change. So instead, she used the time to make her grocery list on a piece of paper she found at the bottom of her purse.

She was tapping her fingers again and glanced at her watch. 11:37 a.m., great, it was later than she thought. She flipped between stations on the radio, hoping to catch the news, but there seemed to be commercials on every station. She would try again in a few minutes if the traffic did not start moving. Maybe, the commercials would be over, and they would have something about the traffic and the mess she could not get around. There was probably an accident on the bridge.

She would never understand why people refused to slow down and let others ease in front of them to help keep traffic moving. How often had she had to give horrible news to family members because their loved one had died in a vehicle accident? So many were preventable, but the longer people sat, the shorter their tempers got, and everything turned into a colossal mess.

Traffic started moving at a snail's pace, but before long, Abbie pulled into the hospital's parking lot. She drove through the ER lot looking for a parking place but came up empty. So, she drove to the other lots, but the parking situation was the same.

She returned to the ER lot and spied a guy backing out of a slot. As soon as he backed out, the spot was hers. A guy in another car thought he would take her spot, but she blocked him from getting his car pulled in. She opened her door and walked to his car. She informed him she needed the parking spot because she was late for her shift in the ER because of traffic and needed the space. He nodded and backed up to allow her to pull into the spot.

"Well, that's one victory for today. Let's hope the rest of the day goes well."

She grabbed her things and ran from the car to the nearest door. People were everywhere. Abbie ran toward another door with access to the ER. When she made her way inside, she ducked into the Nurse's lounge, preparing to get a lecture from Dana for being late. She'd be honest with her and let her know she had been talking to Sam and had not been mindful of the time. Dana always talked to Sam, so she would need to admit her mistake.

Abbie took a moment to tuck her wayward curls back where they belonged. She liked her curly hair and wearing it loose, but it was not practical for work. Might as well put on lip gloss. She was most likely facing disciplinary action by Dana for being late on a day they knew would be busy. If that were the case, she would look great doing it. She grabbed two pens from her locker, closed the padlock, tied her sneakers, and looked in the mirror. Finally, she was ready to face whatever the day threw her way.

As Abbie exited the lounge, she spied Dana standing at the nurse's station, looking straight at her. "Great," Abbie mumbled. "I can't catch a break today."

"Hey, Dana. Sorry, I'm late. Traffic is horrible, and I forgot…."

"In my office, Abbie," Dana said without expression, trying not to break down in front of Abbie. Instead, she needed to keep her emotions intact until she explained what had happened to Tom.

"I'm sorry, Dana. Sam and I were talking, and I lost track of time. Then I left my phone on the sofa and couldn't call you when I got stuck in traffic." Abbie explained, following Dana into her office.

Dana sat behind her desk. "Take a seat, Abbie."

Abbie sat but wondered why Dana was so agitated about her being late. Her coworkers were late, and she told them to work on their time management skills.

"Abbie, I am not mad that you were late. I need to talk to you." She said as her voice broke, and a tear rolled from the corner of her eye.

"Dana, are you okay? Are you sick? Oh no, is it Julie or Kate? I just talked to Sam. She was good when I talked to her."

Dana stood up, walked around to the front of the desk, and sat down on the chair beside Abbie. She took Abbie's hand in hers. Then, unable to put it off any longer, she told Abbie about the accident with Tom.

"Abbie, it's Tom!" Dana said as tears flowed, dropping onto her lap.

Abbie stood up, then sat back in the chair.

"What are you saying? What's Tom?"

"There was an accident, Abbie."

Dana held Abbie's hand and told her everything.

"Stop, stop, Dana. Where are Tom and Kohl?" Abbie's voice was shaking. She leaned against the door, then slowly slid to the floor.

"Let me finish, Abbie, so you know how things happened. Kevin and Tom determined it would be safe to take the helicopter and the rescue boats. Unfortunately, one regatta participant boat was further from shore than any others. This guy was slipping under the water multiple times, and Tom gave Kohl the command to jump in the water and sent him after this guy. Tom unclipped his line and was preparing to jump when a severe wind knocked him out of the chopper. That severe gust of wind caused the chopper to whip around, causing the landing skid to strike Tom on the back of his head. He fell into the water. The helicopter fell, but Kevin quickly gained control, preventing further disaster."

"And where are my guys, Dana? Where are they?" Her voice rose, and tears started falling.

"Tom and Kohl are both in Trauma Three."

"I have to see them, Dana." Abbie picked herself up from the floor and reached for the door. Dana jumped up, as well.

"Abbie, wait." Dana reached for her hand and placed it over Abbie's on the doorknob.

"Tom came in via ambulance in traumatic arrest from the head injury. Kohl came in with the ambulance too. He's not injured but is frightened and wet. We did everything possible for Tom but ran out of options. I'm sorry it wasn't enough to change the outcome. I could not save him. I'm so sorry. Let me come with you, Abbie. I don't want you to do this alone."

Abbie turned, and Dana hugged her as tears ran from both of their faces.

"I need to do this myself, Dana. I need to assure Kohl that I'm not leaving him too, and I need to see Tom. What condition is he in, Dana?"

"All the damage was internal, Abbie. There is damage to the back of his head and a skull fracture. You won't see it if you are looking straight at him."

Abbie nodded her head.

"Who pulled Tom from the water?" Abbie asked. "I'll need to thank whichever crew member tried to rescue him."

Dana started sobbing. Abbie looked straight at her.

"It was Kohl, wasn't it, Dana?" Dana nodded.

Abbie opened the door and found the ER silent. She lowered her head to avoid eye contact with her coworkers or other staff present as she walked to trauma three, leaving a trail of tears in her wake.

Abbie wiped her face on her sleeve and pulled herself together before opening the door. She found Tom and Kohl on a gurney when she entered the room. Kohl opened his eyes and made eye contact with her but did not move a muscle.

Abbie walked over to where Tom lay. She reached out and touched him and Kohl at the same time. Overcome with grief, Abbie felt as though she couldn't breathe. Fearing she would faint; she bent over from the waist and took a few deep breaths. Hold it together for Kohl, she told herself, straightened up, reached over to stroke his head, and thanked him for finding Tom.

Abbie lost track of time as she stood by the gurney and talked to Tom and Kohl. Their little family had done so many fun things together, and she told them everything she could remember.

Kohl whimpered. She leaned over and kissed Kohl's head and Tom's. Her greatest fear when she and Tom married was that he might leave her. She never imagined that it would occur this way.

Sometime later, Abbie pulled herself together. She told Kohl to get off the gurney, and Kohl whined.

"Kohl, we need to go. Tom will be okay here by himself. My friends will take care of him while we are gone. We can trust them, and they know what to do. You are coming with me, Kohl. Now get off the gurney."

Kohl huffed at her. He used the same chair Dana gave him when getting up on the gurney to get back off the gurney. It amazed Abbie that Kohl could get down without dumping the two of them onto the floor. Instead, he laid his head on the gurney beside Tom's head.

"Kohl, we need to leave."

Kohl refused to move. Abbie walked over to him. Again, she stroked his head and reminded him Tom was with her friends. Kohl walked to the end of the gurney and stopped. He stood there, staring at Abbie. Finally, he turned his head, grabbed the sheet on the gurney with his mouth, and started pulling Tom toward the door, never breaking eye contact with Abbie.

"Kohl, drop it," Abbie said firmly to get his attention.

"We cannot take Tom with us. We need to leave. Drop the sheet."

He lowered his head and let the sheet drop gently from his mouth. Abbie was shaking. How was she going to do this?

"Come here, Kohl. I need a hug, and you could use one as well."

Kohl walked to Abbie, stood on his back legs, and placed his front legs on her shoulders. He threw his head back and let out a long, low howl.

Everyone in the ER, staff, and visitors alike, stopped in their tracks. Almost everyone was aware of the incident in the harbor earlier today. The crowd in the ER joined Abbie in sorrow.

Kohl's display of sorrow had struck the hearts of those who could hear him howling. Everyone within hearing distance stopped what they were doing. They said prayers, and people crossed themselves as the dog's howling seemed to go on forever.

Dr. Alexander Montgomery stopped in his tracks, and a chill ran through him. The patient's wife must have arrived, and that dog was acting up again. Mumbling to himself, 'I thought Dana said he left with someone.' Alex wondered if she had lied to him.

"How hard can it be to remove one dog from the building?"

He walked toward the trauma room and saw a nurse with the dog. They came out of trauma three. The nurse and the dog had their backs toward him. He did not know which nurse was walking with the dog and did not care if they were leaving the building. And where was this guy's wife? Surely, someone had found his wife by now.

"Nurse, I thought I was clear when I said the dog was to go?"

Abbie stopped, as did Kohl when they recognized the voice of Alex Montgomery.

They both turned and confronted the doctor.

"His name is Kohl. My name is Abbie. And we belong to that dead guy in trauma three named Tom. And don't worry; we are leaving."

Abbie enunciated each syllable. She wanted to be certain he understood every word she said. Before he uttered a word, the two of them turned and started to walk away.

As soon as she turned to face him, Alex recognized his mistake, realizing it was the same dog and lady from this morning, and she was in the same uniform his ER staff wore.

"Abbie, stop. Can we talk for a minute?" Alex asked.

Abbie threw her hand up to stop him from saying another word. Abbie and Kohl looked over their shoulders toward Alex.

"Really Montgomery? You've said enough for one day."

Kohl bared his teeth at Alex again, huffed at him, and together he and Abbie turned and walked toward the waiting room and Tom's coworkers.

Alex took a couple of deep breaths, then turned toward the staff who had watched the interaction between him and Abbie.

"Why didn't someone inform me the patient we were working on was the husband of one of my nurses?"

When nobody answered him, he continued.

"How can you stand in that room and let me and the other doctors work on him, and it never crossed your mind that I might need to know that information?" Nobody responded.

"I might not be what you were expecting from an interim ER Director, but I'm the one in charge, and for future reference, there is certain information I need to know about our patients and their families. If you aren't willing to share valuable information with me, then one of us needs to go."

With that, Alex walked back to his office, grabbed a bottle of water out of the mini fridge, slammed the door, and threw himself into his chair.

He contemplated his next move, grabbed his iPhone, looked up a phone number, and hit the call button.

"Hey, Peter, Alex Montgomery here!"

"Alex, nice to hear your voice. How are you?"

"Oh, I've had better days," Alex responded to Peter. "I was just wondering if you have any openings further up the coast. Something permanent! This wondering spirit needs to settle in one place. The interim gig worked while Andy and I tried to figure out how to get past Maria's death, but we are ready for something different."

CHAPTER 5

Abbie and Kohl walked toward the ER waiting room. She needed to face Tom's crew. As she approached the room, she heard people whispering. Tom's crew, commanding officers, and dozens of police, firefighters, EMTs, and paramedics were waiting for her. She became overwhelmed by the number of people. There were so many people lined up outside as well. Abbie noticed the local news station staff present, and she made an immediate about-face and walked back to the ER.

Dana was gathering her belongings when she noticed Abbie returning. Before she spoke a word, Abbie asked, "Where's Montgomery?"

The expression on Abbie's face told Dana this was no time for conversation.

"I'll get him, Abbie. Stay right here."

Dana knocked on Alex's door.

"Come in," Alex said. He was still stewing over Abbie's words to him. It was a repeat of her attitude from this morning.

Dana opened his office door. Her expression told Alex this conversation would not be pleasant, either.

"What do you need, Dana?"

Dana hesitated before speaking. "Abbie Foster is at the desk. She's asking to see you."

Alex shook his head. "She just got done dismissing me in the hallway in front of my employees. What could she possibly want now?"

"Believe me, Dr. Montgomery. She would not ask to see you if it weren't important. She is incredibly independent. She wouldn't ask for help if her ankle was hanging on her body by a tendon."

"Alright, Dana. I'll be there in a minute." Dana turned to leave.

"And Dana, when I ask about a patient, dog, or anything else occurring in the ER, I expect nothing but the truth."

"I'm sorry, Dr. Montgomery. It won't happen again." Dana realized she had been caught.

Alex rounded the corner to see Abbie and Kohl pacing in front of the nurse's station, and before he had the chance to ask what she needed, Abbie started giving orders.

"Kohl and I are taking Dana and leaving. I parked my car in the ER lot, but I can't use the front door to get to the car because there are so many people standing in the waiting room and outside the door."

"Somewhere in this building is a communications person. Locate her, and you two go out and talk to the crowd. And stick to the facts, Montgomery. You do not have my permission to release any personal information. Tom is a well-respected person in the community, and I will not spend my time correcting misinformation."

Abbie turned to walk away, then stopped. She turned around to face Alex.

"And see if you can find an ounce of compassion in that body you inhabit. Dana, Kohl, and I will wait in the back room. Text Dana when you are ready to talk to the press, and we'll use that opportunity to get to my car."

Alex turned and headed back to his office. She's lucky I don't fire her for that display. And I have compassion! What does she mean, no compassion? I'll show her compassion until it runs out of her ears, Alex thought, slamming the door behind him. And why was he slamming the door? Geez, why is she making my life crazy? The madness started early this morning between him and her dog, and it appears it will also end that way.

Alex opened his phone, found the number he wanted, and hit the call button. Sara from public relations answered the phone and said she was on her way. Sara was on the phone with her assistant when she arrived and had her assistant call the local news stations and put them on alert. In addition, she told her assistant to tell the Coast Guard Commander, who she understood was standing in her waiting room, along with the police and fire chiefs. Sara also asked her to contact the local weather person to get their opinion on how the weather had affected the events leading up to the accident and death of Tom Foster.

Sara and Alex worked quickly on a press release. Then, they walked to the waiting microphones to begin the press conference.

Five minutes later, Dana's phone beeped with the message.

"You're clear to go."

The three of them walked to Abbie's car unnoticed. Dana offered to drive, but Abbie refused, so they left the parking lot with Abbie behind the wheel.

Abbie pulled into the driveway and noticed Samantha's car parked next to the street. How had she gotten here so fast? Myrtle Beach was a couple of hours away. She glanced at her watch and realized it had been over three hours since she left the house earlier. Dana had alerted Samantha, Julie, and Kate. They had keys to each other's houses, so Sam let herself inside. Abbie looked over at Dana.

"Thank you. I'm so lucky to have you. I could never do this alone."

Sam wrapped Abbie in a big hug as soon as she entered the house, and the tears started again. Sam had listened to the news release on TV and hit the record button. Abbie might not be ready to listen to the news conference today, she thought to herself, but knowing Abbie, she would look for a copy when she found the time.

When everyone said hello, Abbie let Kohl outside in the backyard. She sat at the kitchen counter to start a list of the dreaded tasks she knew she had to complete. She found her iPhone and started reading the texts she had received in the last three hours. Dana and Sam had started the coffee and made light snacks. They encouraged Abbie to eat, but as they expected, she refused.

Neighbors began stopping by with food and drinks, so Sam directed Abbie to work from her desk in the master bedroom and told the neighbors she was resting. Within the hour, there was so much food that Sam and Dana began making plans to send food to the coastguard station.

Abbie finished her list, let Kohl into her room, and stretched out on the bed to rest. When she woke, she picked up Julie and Kate's voices from the living room. Kohl made his rounds to the newcomers, and Abbie did the same. Dana brought refreshments into the living room, and when Abbie peered into the kitchen and saw dish upon dish of donated food, she groaned.

Sam spoke up.

"Don't worry, Abbie. We've already contacted the guard station. They've agreed to accept food donations and are sending someone to pick up the food. People will be in and out of the guard station over the next few days, which will help keep the staff fed. There will still be enough to feed everyone here."

"Are Tom's funeral arrangements completed? Are there other tasks that need to be done?" Kate asked.

"It's taken care of," said Abbie. "The commander and I discussed the options, and we settled on one we believe will be best for the community's people."

"Okay, spill, Abbie. What's on the agenda?" Said, Kate.

"Sorry. We set it up to be a surprise for people in the community, and I want you to be surprised, too. I think you'll like what we have planned. The only thing I can tell you right now is that they will hold it on base for military members and their families, my family, which is you, invited friends, hospital, firefighter, EMT, and ambulance personnel. The community will take part as well. That information is to be released tomorrow evening before the funeral service. I have given the TV and radio stations permission to release the information on the evening news."

"I'm sure it will be lovely, no matter what you have planned," Kate said.

They sat and talked for the next few hours. Kate was currently engaged in an extensive research project, and Julie was preparing for the schools to open and the onslaught of sick kids from common bugs that got passed around when the school opened. So that would keep her busy for the next couple of months.

"If there's nothing else we need to do this evening, we can walk out to the beach and build a small fire. Then, we can have some drinks, and the five of us and Kohl can relax. Does that sound okay with you?"

Abbie smiled at her friends. "I would love to sit on the beach with you."

Alex came home from the hospital exhausted. It had been a mentally and physically exhausting day. It had been non-stop from the moment he walked in the door.

Andy was staying with a friend tonight. He grabbed a bottle of water and walked out to the porch to sit and watch the waves roll onto shore. The sun was about to set. He relished the quiet after the busy day but missed having someone to share in these quiet times.

Maria had been gone for about three years. He had not even considered dating again. His choice to take only interim director positions had him and Andy moving almost every year. He thought back to his conversation with Peter this morning and his offer to take the full-time Director of Emergency Department position that was open. They wanted to fill the position within the next two weeks. He accepted the offer on the spot.

Alex was restless now that the sun had set, and Andy was gone. Pacing through the house, he went over the day's events, trying to figure out where everything went wrong. He stopped pacing when he realized everything started this morning with the interaction between him and the woman with the dog.

Now, Alex realized why she looked familiar when she intervened between him and her dog. How had he gone from not knowing she existed at sunrise and having his life consumed by her at sundown?

He needed to let off steam. He was getting a tension headache. He went to the medicine cabinet for pain relievers and washed them down with the bottle of water he had grabbed from the fridge. What he needed was to go for a run. That might help relieve his stress. At this rate, he'd never sleep tonight. On top of everything that happened in the ER, his impulsive call to Peter and accepting the job added stress. He had to get his life together before it imploded.

Alex changed into his running gear and ran up the beach. Every step had him remembering how the day had started—one big sopping wet dog and a bossy, opinionated beauty. Hours later, she became a widow, and he could not get the day's events out of his mind, making him anxious.

Abbie Foster had suddenly lost her husband, forever changing her life. He had gone through a similar tragedy three years ago. An early December Christmas dinner with friends turned tragic. He and Maria, and Andy enjoyed an evening celebrating Christmas with friends. When the snow started falling briskly on that snowy Denver evening, everyone donned their coats, packed dessert to take home with them, and started driving home.

Alex would never forgive himself for looking at that text from one of the ER nurses. Maria was searching for a radio station playing Christmas music for the ride home when four-year-old Andy screamed, "Daddy, look at the dog!"

Alex looked up and saw a dog standing on the road. Not wanting Andy to see or hear him hit a dog, Alex swerved to miss him and started sliding on the icy, snow-covered road. He could not regain control of the car. The car slid and hit a guide rail, causing them to spin on the road. They hit the hill on the opposite side of the road, which caused them to flip back across the road, go over a guide rail, and tumble down a steep hill.

Alex shook himself from the image that often kept him awake at night. Maria did not survive the crash, and Andy was still in therapy, trying to recover his ability to walk. The doctors could not figure out why Andy lost his ability to walk. Instead, they chalked it up to trauma from the accident that they couldn't pinpoint. Andy had adapted to his wheelchair well, but Alex had not. Guilt ate at him daily for glancing away from the road.

Alex continued his run. He was ready to turn around when he noticed a fire burning a short distance down the beach. Alex picked up music playing over the sound of the crashing waves. Curious about who had an illegal fire on the beach, he continued to run closer, seeing the four women dancing and singing with wine glasses in their hands. When he went closer, Alex recognized Abbie sitting on a blanket in the sand, and of course, where Abbie was, her dog was with her.

He had overheard Dana mentioning to one of the other nurses she had to call the rest of the crew. These must be the friends she was referring to earlier today. Abbie did not participate in the dancing but sat with Kohl's head resting on her lap and sipping her drink.

How was it, Alex wondered, that she had flown below his radar? Was he so caught up in his miserable existence, unable to let anyone in, that he ignored everyone around him? Abbie had accused him of being uncaring, and she was wrong. He had dedicated his life to helping others. Or was she? Had he been so miserable that it had seeped into his daily actions, affecting everyone around him? Tomorrow, he needed to schedule an appointment with a therapist.

Alex turned around before anyone saw him. He didn't want another confrontation with the dog today. He knew he needed to apologize to Abbie. His behavior today was uncalled for, and she did not need him to complicate her life. He owed the ER staff his apology as well before he packed up and left for his next assignment.

Kohl's head popped up on Abbie's lap and he stared off into the darkness on the beach. Abbie looked around. She saw nothing that might have caught his attention. She saw a runner jogging on the beach. Nothing that should have alerted Kohl. The light from the fire seeped into the surrounding darkness. The man's silhouette looked familiar, but Abbie chalked it up to her exhaustion and turned back to her friends.

Abbie loved her friends and enjoyed having them with her, but she wanted to curl up in her bed and sleep. Instead, she knew she needed to lean on them this week more than she wanted to admit, so she sat listening to their voices as they sang and chuckled at the antics they called dancing.

CHAPTER 6

Abbie collaborated with Tom's commanding officer to complete the plans for the funeral service. Unfortunately, Abbie was not prepared to say her last goodbye to Tom.

Her friends answered phone calls and wrote thank-you notes to friends and neighbors for food and flowers. The only thing Abbie had to do was review and sign the notes. Then, they prepare light meals and let her and Kohl rest and walk on the beach to relax.

On the morning of Tom's funeral, Abbie took Kohl to the ocean. In the three days since the accident, Kohl refused to go in the water. Donning her suit and rash guard, she and Kohl slipped from the house so as not to wake the others. With coffee, paddle board, and safety gear in tow, Abbie walked to the water to check the temperature, but Kohl held back. Typically, he frolicked in the waves, but today he was not interested.

Abbie called him, but he sat on the beach and refused to move. Finally, Abbie gave up and walked back to where he was sitting. She laid her paddleboard on the sand, grabbed her coffee, and sat on the board. Kohl moved next to her but sat with his back to the water. Abbie urged Kohl to turn around and face the water. He ignored her request.

He sat on the paddleboard next to Abbie with his head on her shoulder, and Abbie put her arm around him, knowing he was also grieving. She told him stories from his puppy years and training days and described their fun times with Tom. She told him stories of the lives he saved and his impact on the neighborhood.

Abbie wasn't sure he understood what she said, but he looked relaxed and leaned into her as she talked. They needed to go in soon and prepare for the funeral. She was glad they had this time together this morning. They both need time alone.

Abbie wiped tears from her face. She never imagined saying goodbye could be so hard. So many times, she had tried to console grieving families in the ER and knew now that she lacked the maturity to understand their pain.

Today, Abbie was a different person. It had been a hard way to learn genuine empathy, but it was a lesson she needed to be a better person and a better nurse. She finished her coffee and watched the sunrise, then they walked back to the house, hoping they could make it through the day.

Abbie groaned when she remembered her behavior toward Dr. Montgomery yesterday. Sometime today, she needed to apologize to him. Her behavior was inexcusable and so unlike her. They needed to work together every day. If they could not mend their relationship, whatever it might be, they would put patients' lives at risk.

Abbie was unaware that as she watched the sunrise this morning, Kohl was baring his teeth at Alex Montgomery as he jogged past their spot on the beach.

Alex saw Abbie and Kohl on the beach again this morning. He wanted to stop and apologize to Abbie, but she appeared lost in her thoughts, so he continued to run. Today was the funeral. He didn't need to start the day on the wrong foot with Abbie.

Alex planned to attend the funeral today and hoped to catch her by herself to apologize. But how did he apologize to her dog?

Since the accident that killed Maria, he has had no time for dogs. It was his fault for not paying attention to the road. He looked at the text and changed so many lives in that moment. Reversing direction before Abbie saw him or the dog alerted her, Alex sprinted back to the house to shower and get Andy to school.

When Abbie returned to the house, she stopped on the porch to brush Kohl and trim his fur. She wanted him presentable for today's service. When Abbie and Kohl entered the house, everyone was awake, showered, dressed, and sat around the kitchen table, drinking coffee, and eating breakfast.

"Getting a shower. I'm covered in sand and dog fur." Abbie said to her friends as she let Kohl out the kitchen door. Kate had filled Kohl's water and food bowl, so it set him for this morning.

"Can one of you let him in when he's ready?"

"Absolutely," Julie responded. "Anything else you need us to do?"

Abbie smiled at her friend. "No. Thanks, Julie. But stay close. That's likely to change before long."

Showered and dressed, Abbie tried to tame her curls. Kate and Dana went shopping yesterday and bought her a hat with a widow's veil. At first, she balked at the idea of a veil but changed her mind when she realized it was an effective way to hide her emotions from the crowd.

Abbie gave the press permission to attend the funeral, with restrictions. She insisted the press not invade her privacy. However, she gave them leeway because the public was interested in hearing about the funeral events.

Deciding an updo should be the best way to hide her curls under her hat and widow's veil, Abbie twisted her hair into a low knot at the base of her head and pinned her wayward curls into submission.

Kate had coffee and toast waiting for her when she entered the kitchen. She accepted the coffee but shook her head, "No toast."

"Oh, yes." Sam and Julie said. "You need something light on your stomach, Abbie." Julie said, and Kate finished her sentence, saying, "You'll pass out or be puking your guts out before we get through the morning."

Abbie rolled her eyes. Everyone looked at Kohl when he let out a huff. "It's good to have someone on my side." Abbie smiled, took a small bite from her toast, and then poured another coffee.

The limo arrived, and everyone took the short ride to the Coast Guard base. Abbie's nervous stomach growled, and Dana reached for her hand.

"We will be right beside you. Just tell us what you need."

The Coast Guard station doors were up, and chairs were set up in straight lines throughout the bay. A small stage was set up with flowers surrounding the box that contained Tom's ashes. Above the stage, a video showed pictures of Tom and Kohl with the rescue squad throughout the years.

Tom's commanding officer asked Abbie if Kohl could stay on with the crew, but Abbie declined. Kohl belonged to her and Tom, and Tom was his trainer. Furthermore, Abbie was unsure what Kohl's reaction might be to the other crew members during a rescue, which could put lives in danger. If Kohl's reaction on the beach this morning showed how he might react in the future, his career would be over. Tom's crew offered to take over Kohl's training, but Abbie declined.

After the pastor had done his part, Abbie had asked three of Tom's senior crew members to speak at the eulogy. Near the end, Kohl was to receive recognition for his service.

Abbie sat in the front row, surrounded by her friends and Tom's commanding officers. Mr. and Ms. Wilson, Tom, and Abbie's last foster parents, were also in the first row. They had kept in close contact over the years and were devastated to learn of Tom's death.

Abbie waited for the service to begin and wondered how one death could change so many lives.

The funeral service started, and nobody noticed that Alex Montgomery had slipped in at the last minute. Tom's death shook Alex, but he couldn't make sense of why it was having such an impact on him. Was it the tragic way he died? Was it knowing the entire community was grieving? Perhaps it was because Abbie was one of his staff?

Alex attended other funerals since Maria died, but this was different. The events surrounding Tom's death and his staff's reaction prompted him to look for a permanent home. He and Andy needed a place where they could learn to live again.

Alex closed his eyes and prayed along with the other attendees. Near the end of the service, Alex watched Abbie and Kohl make their way to the stage. Alex was expecting Abbie to speak about Tom and his service. Instead, Kohl received the Coast Guard Distinguished Service Medal, presented to Coastguardsmen for meritorious service to the government in a duty of great responsibility. Tom received his award belatedly, and Abbie accepted it peacefully. Kohl received a standing ovation for his contributions to the coast guard, and there wasn't one dry eye to be found. He clung next to Abbie's side.

Abbie and Kohl followed the color guard and walked across the tarmac where the coast guard helicopter waited. Military service members, veterans. and friends and family followed. She carried a box with Tom's ashes as she and Kohl continued walking to the helicopter.

Kevin assisted them in to their seats in the helicopter and helped them get strapped in as well. Then, Kevin started the helicopter and hovered three feet over the ground while the twenty-one-gun salute took place and taps played. Abbie would be presented with the flag upon her return to the station. Then, under the command of the Admiral, Tom received a final salute from attending military members.

Kevin gave a thumbs-up sign to Abbie. She nodded, and the helicopter lifted off the ground and started a slow flyover along the coastline. Police and other rescue team members had locals and tourists move everything from the flight path, including cars, boats, and people, to allow Kevin to fly at an altitude of 500 ft and give the visitors and surrounding communities an opportunity to pay their respects.

The number of people gathered to say goodbye to Tom astounded Abbie. Everywhere she looked, there were signs with messages to Tom and Kohl. They wrote messages in the sand, and people held balloons to be released after the completed flyover. Kohl lifted his paw and barked at the crowds, knowing who they were. He looked at Abbie, raised his paw, and gave her one sharp bark, so Abbie lifted her arm and waved to the crowd.

Each one hundred eighty boats that signed up for the regatta took part in the flyover and lined up their boats in the water. The boats positioned themselves together to make a cross, and other boats formed the letters T and K. The last boats were positioned in the shape of a heart.

Kevin turned to ask Abbie if she was ready, and she nodded. Kevin climbed higher in the sky and began the flight back toward the guard station. Abbie opened a small box containing Tom's ashes, and with a nod to Kevin that she was ready, she released the ashes, as Kevin made a circle over the ocean and began a slow spiral toward the water. Kevin hovered above the water, and Abbie dropped a bouquet on Tom's final resting place. Kevin made the final route back to land while Abbie and Kohl sat together.

Alex watched the procession from the ground. He, too, had tears on his face. Although he had never met Tom and paid little attention to Abbie, he grieved with the public. Seeing Abbie exit the helicopter, Alex grabbed the opportunity to talk to her now. Her crew headed towards her, as well.

Abbie saw Alex walking toward her, and she wanted to speak to him. To let him know she was sorry for her behavior! Sam saw Alex before the rest of the crew, and they heard her mumble, "Oh, not now, Montgomery."

Abbie surprised her friends by holding her hand up to stop them from intercepting Alex. She sent Kohl to go with the crew. They stood watching.

Alex slowed to meet Abbie. She faced him with her window's veil still in place. God, she was lovely, Alex thought to himself, then berated himself for thinking such thoughts of a newly widowed woman. Alex spoke first.

"Abbie, I'm so sorry for your loss, and I need to apologize for my behavior on the beach and in the ER. I do not know how those behaviors originated, and I am terribly sorry. I also want you to know, I'm leaving Memorial."

"What?" Abbie replied. "What do you mean you're leaving? And I'm sorry, as well. My behavior was horrible, and I am embarrassed you saw a side of me that seldom surfaces."

Alex chuckled, and Abbie smiled at him. "We're like two storms crashing in the sky."

Abbie chuckled. "A couple of hurricanes might be a better description! I'm sorry, Montgomery. I mean Dr. Montgomery."

"You can call me Montgomery. I know how busy you are today, Abbie, so I don't want to hold you up any longer. Can we grab a cup of coffee next week before I leave? I need to give you the background on my lousy behavior and explain why I'm leaving. Somebody needs the entire story, or the rumors will spread as quickly as wildfire. I'm sure I deserve each one. Perhaps you can help keep the rumor mill in control if you know the truth."

"I'll take the time, Alex. I'm taking leave. Kohl and I need to figure out what comes next. Dana has my number. Just text me the time and place. I'm sorry we don't have the time to talk today."

Alex turned to walk away.

"Hey, Montgomery. Make sure it's outside and dog friendly. I won't leave Kohl alone for a while, so he'll join us."

Alex gave her a thumbs-up sign and groaned at the thought of facing that dog again.

Abbie entered the guard station, where lunch was being served, and looked around the room for Kohl. She found him sound asleep in his crate. She imagined the stress from the past few days had exhausted him. Normally, he slept in his bed at home in the living room, but since Tom's accident, he had been sleeping with Abbie every night. Exhausted, Abbie sat at a table set up for lunch. Dana and Sam joined her.

"Dana. Could you give my phone number to Montgomery, please?"

"Why?" Dana replied. "I thought you hated that man."

"I don't hate him, Dana. We apologized to each other for our behavior. He wants to grab coffee before he leaves to fill me in on his backstory. He thinks, it has been affecting his behavior."

"What do you mean before he leaves?" Dana asked, surprised. "Where is he going?"

"He didn't say, but he made it sound like next week is his last week here."

"How much time are you taking off?" Sam inquired.

"I'm not sure," she said. "I'm not sure what to do with Kohl. He won't even look at the water I tried to take him in this morning. While I drank my coffee, he sat on the paddle board with his back to the water and leaned on me. He's slept in my bed, which he has never done. We need more time together. I need to meet with Tom's attorney to review his will. I'll start running again while I have extra time. Kohl always likes to run on the beach so he can run with me."

"You two can stay with me for a while. Do you think a different beach will get him back in the water?" Sam asked. "If he still refuses to go into the ocean, we can try the therapy pool at Coastal."

"Oh, your boss will love having Kohl in his pool. He likes dogs almost as much as Montgomery."

"Hahaha." Sam chuckled. "We should do it just to see his reaction. I am curious, though, to find out Montgomery's story. I want to be the first you call after coffee with him next week."

"No, no, no. Nobody gets a first call. I'll set up a zoom call." Julie offered. "That way, we can dissect his life as a group."

Abbie shook her head, got up, and went to get Kohl. She was done interacting with people for one day and just wanted to go home and cuddle with Kohl. She said her goodbyes to the correct people, gathered her crew, and let the limo driver know they were ready to leave. The crew was quiet on the ride home. Finally, Abbie opened the door to the house, and everyone went to gather their things for their trip back.

Abbie let Kohl outside, changed out of her funeral clothes, and straightened things in the kitchen. When her crew left, she needed to list items that needed to be done. In addition, she needed to go through Tom's belongings and decide what to keep and donate.

Kate thought she should wait a while, but Abbie disagreed. Doing it now might help her come to terms with Tom's death. The last few days had been a whirlwind of decisions, and she had not had time alone. She needed the time to think and grieve and figure out how to be alone again.

Abbie's friends gathered in the living room. Even though Dana lived just a couple of miles from Abbie, she had wanted to be at Abbie's with everyone else, so she packed her things and stayed as well. One huge group hug had everyone teary-eyed again, but they separated, and each hugged Abbie, agreeing to the zoom meeting that Julie insisted was necessary to dissect Alex Montgomery.

Abbie closed the door and relished the quiet. She had put the teapot on to heat when they got home, made a cup of blueberry tea, and settled on the sofa. Kohl climbed up beside her, and they snuggled together. Tomorrow, they begin a new journey without Tom.

CHAPTER 7

Alex left the funeral and headed to the ER. It was silent when he arrived. So many people from the surrounding communities attended Tom's funeral, which might be why the ER was not a madhouse. Two patients were being treated for chest pain, and one was receiving treatment for a broken ankle from a roller-skating incident. The staff enjoyed the break and catching up on local gossip and family photos.

Alex received Abbie's phone number from Dana, and he found an outdoor café that allowed dogs, and it was the perfect place for him and Abbie to talk and for Kohl to terrorize him.

Alex was amazed at the number of people who stopped and spoke with Kohl today and wondered if he was the only one who did not recognize who this dog was or the impact he had on society. He returned to his office to search the internet for information on Tom and Kohl. He found a significant volume of information and wasn't sure where to start.

The original story he found discussed Kohl's first training and his success at becoming a rescue dog. There was story after story of how he saved lives. Time after time, swimmer after swimmer, he pulled them to shore or held them afloat until the rescue boat or helicopter plucked them from the choppy waters.

Someone started a fan page for him. Andy would instantly fall in love with Kohl after he showed him the page. There was an article that mentioned Abbie and Tom were aware of the page, but they were not associated with any of the information on the page. They were glad that the public was interested in his skills and asked that everyone learn water safety to help reduce the number of calls the rescue team received.

Dana had scheduled four days off to be with Abbie, but when she returned, he hoped she might answer his questions regarding Tom, Abbie, and Kohl. Alex shook his head.

Evidently, he had to have blinders on not to have noticed Dana or Abbie. One was as stunning as the next! Their entire group was comprised of the most stunning and elegant women he had ever met. They did not hesitate to put you in your place in a heartbeat. He learned the hard way that if you overstep the boundaries, they set for themselves, there would be consequences.

When the time was right, he'd share pictures of Kohl and Tom but now was not the time. Andy would be thrilled with the opportunity to meet Kohl, but Alex was afraid he might ask questions that could hurt Abbie's feelings. Alex decided they'd gone through enough of that for a while.

Alex walked out to the triage room. It was still silent. He and the nurse discussed the funeral. The entire hospital was mourning with Abbie. His blinders kept him from experiencing the everyday actions of his staff.

Another nurse joined them, and he asked after their families. They were busy mothers with families who spent their time off at the beach, running their kids to sporting events, doing laundry, and shopping, then starting the same routine over again.

Alex was hoping he could leave on time. He wanted to take Andy to dinner to discuss their move. So far, he has been okay with their frequent moves across the country.

He wanted to go for a drive this weekend to see houses and wanted Andy involved in the decision-making. This was going to be the first permanent home for the two of them in over three years. They managed everything on their own. Alex found Ms. Helen to help with Andy while he ran in the morning. She fixed breakfast, did light housekeeping, and picked up Andy from school when he needed to stay late at the ER.

Alex worried that their frequent moves might affect Andy's ability to make friends. The accident was his fault. So, he carried the guilt and responsibility of Andy facing life in a wheelchair. He attended his therapy sessions and did the exercises but made limited progress. He was a happy, polite, intelligent, and curious child, so Alex tried not to worry if there was no progress in therapy.

Alex picked Andy up from school and asked him to choose a restaurant for dinner. Andy's favorite restaurant served great burgers and had an arcade, as well. Alex enjoyed these types of places, too. He and Andy became extremely competitive but laughed over their competitiveness and always had a fun time. The loser got to pick the ice cream flavor for dessert. While they waited for their burgers, Alex decided it was a suitable time to discuss the upcoming move.

"Hey buddy, I wanted to let you know I accepted a new job."

"Did you get fired from your job, Dad?" Andy asked, his eyes as big as saucers.

"No, silly. They offered me a permanent position at a hospital two hours up the coast, and I wanted to get your thoughts on moving again."

"That's cool with me, Dad. The guys at this school are mean sometimes. They tease me because I'm in a wheelchair. They call me names, too."

"Andrew, why didn't you say something to me? I'm sorry that happened to you. I want you to tell me what happened."

He needed to call the principal and counselor tomorrow.

"Don't worry, Dad. Besides, we're moving now. Did you find a house? Where are we going to live? Do they have a beach? Can we live on the beach, Dad?"

"Let's take a ride up the coast this weekend. I'll get us a hotel, and we can look for a house, swim in the hotel pool, order seafood at an outdoor restaurant, and make it a fun guy's weekend away."

"That's an amazing idea. Can I pick the restaurant again? Do you have swimming trunks? Do you know where my trunks are, Dad? Can I play mini golf and search for shells at the beach? Will my wheelchair work on the beach, Dad?"

"Yes, Andy. I have swim trunks, and I also know where your trunks are. You can choose the restaurant and the mini golf. We will rent you a wheelchair that has gigantic wheels, so we won't get stuck in the sand."

"When do we move, Dad?"

"Soon. We need to find the house and complete the paperwork. I'll figure out what school you'll be attending, and we can do a drive-by, but I need you to tell me at once if you are getting bullied at this school. Andrew, bullying violates school policy, and I need to let the school know if someone is making you feel unsafe."

"I promise I will tell you, Dad." And Andy began with another list of questions.

Alex sent a text to Abbie with their meet-up information for coffee the following week. She responded that the café was a favorite place of hers and was looking forward to meeting him next week. Wow, Alex said to himself. I believe I did something right. If I can get through a cup of coffee without her dog terrorizing me, I will chalk that up as a momentous day.

Alex and Andy packed up the car on Friday afternoon and headed towards North Myrtle Beach. The realtor agreed to meet them Saturday morning to check out houses she thought might work best for them.

They completed their list of fun things as Alex promised. First, he checked the hotel pool. The water was clean and warm, and no one else was present when they were ready to get into the pool, and he helped Andy stay afloat while encouraging him to try kicking his legs in the water.

Andy tried but was not moving them enough to keep his head above water. They brought one of his favorite floats, and he enjoyed the freedom to move around the pool, and Andy exclaimed he had a fun evening.

They met with the relator on Saturday morning. The first house she presented to them was nice, and the location was great, but it was three floors, and it did not have an elevator. For Andy to maneuver the house, an elevator was required.

They looked at two other homes, and Alex thought they might have found the one. The house he liked had two floors and six spacious bedrooms, each with its own bath. There was an open kitchen and a separate dining room. A covered deck ran the length of the house. In addition, there was a ramp leading to the beach and an elevator for Andy. There was a large backyard if Alex ever got thc nerve to let Andy have a dog.

"I like this house, Andy, do you?"

"This one is great, Dad, but it's big. I counted six bedrooms. That's so many bedrooms. Do we need all these rooms, Dad?"

"Well, Andy, what if we meet someone nice one day, and we want to marry her and give you brothers and sisters? We might need those rooms. The showers are great as well. Since they are level with the floor, it makes it easier for you to take your showers without my help. This house will give you the independence to do things without me helping you. Do you think this house will work?"

"I can have brothers and sisters, Dad? This house is gigantic and has enough room for brothers and sisters. Hey Dad? Do you think we will meet someone with a dog? Remember the lady with the big dog? The one that got you wet the morning you went running. If we marry her, I can have brothers and sisters and a big dog. This house is perfect for a big dog."

"Andy, the lady with the big dog, lives near our old house. She works at the hospital where I used to work, and her husband recently died. She is a widow, and I am sure she is not considering getting married soon."

"I'm not sure I know what a widow is, Dad."

"A widow is someone whose husband or wife has passed away. The lady and her dog will be sad for a while, like how we were sad when your mother died."

"Does she have kids, Dad?"

"I don't think she does, Andy. Right now, she is incredibly sad. We might meet someone else who has a dog, but it might be a long time before the nurse I work with is ready to marry and have kids."

"I love the house, and I bet she will, too. Let's buy this big house. When she's ready and not sad any longer, we will have enough rooms for brothers, sisters, and a big dog."

"That's a good plan, buddy."

Alex was not ready to burst Andy's bubble. Someday soon, he needed to talk with him and help him understand we can't make plans for other people. But, for now, he'd let him dream.

Alex stood up and faced the realtor.

"Let's write up the contract. Andy and I both want this house. We may have different plans for the house, but I am not arguing with a seven-year-old."

"I hope your son's plans come true. If so, you will have one big, happy family."

Once Alex signed the paperwork, he and Andy went to the beach. They stopped and rented a beach wheelchair for Andy; the size of the tires amazed him. He talked nonstop about his chair, the waves, and shells that washed up on the beach from the recent tide. Alex packed a picnic lunch, and they ate on a blanket and watched the people swimming in the water.

Alex noticed the expression on Andy's face and offered to help him get into the water.

"Andy let's get in the water. I'll take you."

"I'm not sure, Dad. What happens if you drop me? Will the sharks get me, Dad? They have big teeth, you know."

"Andy, you will be safe. I will not drop you, and no shark is going to get you, either. It is a perfect day for a swim in the ocean. The water will be warm. I promise you will be okay."

Andy nodded his head, and Alex picked him up and walked into the water. Andy held tight to Alex when they entered the water. He was nervous getting in the water because he couldn't swim, but he realized his dad would not let anything bad happen. As usual, he asked question after question about the ocean and the waves.

Andy offered his opinion on sharks, and he and Alex laughed. They were in the water for thirty minutes when Andy shivered, so Alex said it was time to get out of the water and lay in the sun to get warm. So, they laid on their beach towels in the sun, discussing the house they had just purchased and how they might decorate Andy's room.

Alex needed a decorator. He was fine cleaning a house, but decorating was not on his skill list. Once the duo warmed up and dried off, they returned to the car and dropped off the beach wheelchair.

Returning to the hotel, they showered, dressed, and headed for dinner. But Andy was having trouble staying awake. The sand, water, and excitement exhausted his never-ending energy, and when Alex put him to bed, Andy mumbled out one more directive.

"Dad?"

"Yes, Andy?"

"Don't forget to call the lady with the dog and tell her we found the perfect house."

And with that, Andy was sound asleep. Alex shook his head. Tomorrow, he needed to discuss with Andy, the lady with the dog, and the house they purchased. In his young brain, wishing for something would make it come true, and Alex did not want him to continue to assume that his wish was going to come true. Alex kissed him on his head.

"If only it were that easy, Andy."

CHAPTER 8

Every day, Abbie worked to figure out what was normal for Kohl. She hoped that taking him back to the guard station might help him find normalcy again but taking him to the station increased his anxiety and nervousness. Abbie invited the crew to visit the house but knew that was unlikely to happen. Everyone had set routines, and adding a visit to Abbie and Kohl might be hard to fit in with their tight schedules.

Today was Thursday, and this was the day she and Kohl were to meet Montgomery for coffee. Abbie never exposed her past to anyone but was ready to share it with Alex. Unfortunately, Kohl disliked him, and Abbie did not know why. Kohl was an excellent judge of people's character, but she figured his judgment was off.

The café Alex picked was one of Abbie's favorites, and it always thrilled the owners to see Kohl. He drew so much attention from patrons and tourists, and when people were tired of admiring Kohl, most made their way inside to buy a coffee and a treat.

The owner refused to take Abbie's money because the attention they drew made the store so much money. Abbie always left the money she should have spent paying the check and gave it to the server. She dropped the money in the tip jar when they ordered from the takeout counter.

Abbie and Kohl woke up rested, and she looked forward to a good morning. There would be no moping around from either. It would do both good to get out of the house and do something familiar yet something that had nothing to do with the coast guard or the water.

The weather was warm today, and Abbie grabbed the new sundress from her closet that Tom had bought as a gift for her the previous month. Holding it up in front of herself, she smiled when she glanced in the mirror. Tom liked it when she wore dresses during their outings. He often saw her in scrubs and enjoyed looking at her in something feminine.

Abbie grabbed her purse and called for Kohl. After her coffee with Alex, she was going to stop by the attorney's office to go over Tom's will. Since she was his only survivor, the attorney said the paperwork was straightforward. Everything came to her, and it was a formality. She knew Tom had put the money he inherited from his parents into a trust to help preserve and protect any assets and decrease state and federal taxes.

Abbie tried to get Kohl into Tom's truck, but he refused, so they took her car to meet Alex. Kohl was avoiding the water and refused to get in Tom's truck, so she might have to consider selling it She seldom went anywhere without Kohl, so keeping the truck was a waste of money. She lowered the windows for Kohl, and he smiled at her as the wind whipped around him.

They arrived at the café. Abbie spied Alex at one of the outdoor café tables near the front corner of the patio. Alex stood and waved when she got out of the vehicle. Kohl noticed him and bared his teeth. Alex groaned. If this dog did not behave himself, this might be the shortest cup of coffee on record.

Alex helped Abbie with her chair, and Kohl stayed tight to her side. Finally, Alex took his seat and smiled at Abbie. Kohl huffed and turned his back, and Abbie had had enough of this rude behavior.

"Kohl, this behavior is unacceptable and not how you treat people. Stop with the huffing and turn around now."

Kohl obeyed Abbie and turned around and sat at her left side.

"Now, sir, shake hands with Dr. Montgomery and apologize."

Kohl peeped at her by shifting his eyes but not moving his head.

"Now Kohl."

Kohl stood, walked over to Alex, sat, and lifted his right paw to shake. Alex tried to keep from laughing but found this whole scenario amusing.

Alex took the offered paw, shook Kohl's hand, and stated, "Nice to meet you, Kohl."

Kohl gave a soft bark, lowered his paw, turned, and trudged back to Abbie.

"Now, lay and stay until I tell you to move."

Kohl lay on the ground, with his head on his front legs, and fell asleep.

Alex glanced at the menu but noticed Abbie did not pick up her copy. She knew what was on the menu and didn't bother looking at it because she knew what she wanted to order.

"Are you going to have something to eat?"

"Yes, but I have a favorite dish I always eat here, so I don't need to glance at the menu."

Lifting his eyebrows, Alex asked, "Are you willing to share your favorite dish?"

"Sure, shrimp pot pie. Oh, and sweet tea to wash it down."

They gave their server their order and resumed their earlier conversation.

"Alex, I am so sorry for Kohl's behavior. I have trained him well, but he is in his teenage years, and believe me, he can be as obstinate as a human teenager. I acknowledge we got off to a contentious start as well," Abbie declared, pointing back and forth between them, "but perhaps we can start over again?"

"That is a terrific idea, Abbie. I have had a week of fresh starts, and I will gladly include you in that category. How are you and Kohl doing?"

"It's been a tough week for sure, and we are still trying to find out what is normal, but Kohl refuses to get in the water, gets anxious if I take him to visit the crew at the station, refuses to get in Tom's truck, and won't walk in the door of the ER to visit either."

"I can't blame him. He has been through significant trauma, and while we can recognize his heroism, he can't. He only knows Tom is gone and is trying to avoid everything associated with him."

"Is there something that might help? I'm happy to help, but I bet Kohl is not willing to accept help from me."

"Contentious should be his middle name most days, but enough talk of him. He will stay curled up by my feet for a while. What brought you to Charleston?"

Alex explained his life in Denver, meeting Maria, marrying, and having a son, and the accident that took Maria's life and left his son in a wheelchair.

Abbie was so choked up when Alex stopped talking to take a bite of his food that it took a couple of sips of sweet tea to compose herself before she could speak.

"I'm so sorry, Alex. Is that why you take interim positions? To keep from getting too attached to anyone?"

"It's interesting. I had not considered that until your husband's accident, Abbie, but I believe you might be right. You looked familiar on the beach the morning when Kohl and I had the episode with the water, but I chalked it up to looking at the same people doing their same routines every morning."

"When Tom arrived in the ER, we were so busy working on him that I did not realize there was a dog in my ER until Rob, the paramedic, pointed to him. I told the staff to get him out, but they lowered their eyes and refused to look at me. I remember shouting at them and asking how hard was it to get a dog out the door. When nobody moved, I opened the door to trauma three and told Kohl to get out. He stared at me and bared his teeth."

"I threatened to fire everyone in the room. But, Jesus, Abbie, what type of idiot am I? No wonder Kohl and the staff hate me, but I swear this idiot is not who I am. It's who I've become through the grief and the running away, and I'm not even sure why I'm running. I'm a doctor. I'm supposed to be helping and solving problems. Not causing more! Can you ever forgive me for my rude behavior?"

"It's not me who needs to forgive you, Alex, and you don't need to be forgiven by anyone. You are a man grieving the loss of a spouse, and today, I understand how that feels. Last week was different, and I assumed you were aloof and a pompous ass. Today, I understand. Perhaps, we can stay in touch, and you can help me not become the same lost, grieving person you say you've become."

"I'd love that, Abbie, and will do everything I can not to let you get lost along the way."

"I will say, you must be the only person in town who didn't know Kohl. Of course, they knew he would never leave Tom's side, but they should have informed you of that fact. Was Dana in the room?"

"Yes, she was in the room. When we had tried everything the other doctors and I could think of, we realized there was nothing more we could do. I asked if his family was in the waiting room. They told me they were trying to reach his wife but were having trouble contacting her. Nobody told me you had arrived. You could not have been there long when I yelled at you in the hallway. As soon as you turned around, I recognized you from the beach. Next, you promptly told me who you were."

"After you walked away, I shouted at them again for not telling me that the wife of a prominent service member, whose life I could not save, was one of my staff members, and again, I threatened to fire everyone. I'm never going to be able to face them again. It's a good thing I'm leaving."

Abbie placed her hand over Alex's, providing comfort.

"Alex, it's not as awful as you are making it."

"Abbie, I have done everything to distance myself from everyone for the last three years. I put up a guard to not let anyone get close so that I wouldn't have my heart shattered again. However, after our incident in the ER, I realized that behavior was affecting everyone. I promise you I will change. I will do everything I can to help you, but I also need your help."

"And I promise to help you as well, Alex."

"Now, enough from me, Abbie. How did you come to live in Charleston?"

"I'll make this story brief. My mother abandoned me as a newborn, and they found me on the front stoop of the police department. The police officer took me to the hospital, where they estimated I was hours old. Unfortunately, the officers did not notice anyone dropping me off, and nobody came forward to claim me, so they placed me in child protective services."

"I was in and out of homes until I was sixteen. Historically, foster parents are often searching for a paycheck. I was alone, frequently cold, and hungry. I kept to myself and studied. The foster home I was in before the Wilsons took me in was horrible. I was lying in bed one night but not yet asleep when I heard the floor creak outside my room. I grabbed a pair of scissors I had used just minutes before off the nightstand and held them in my hand under the covers. The man who lived there was creepy. I often caught him staring at me. I considered running away, but that gets you in more trouble. He came into the room and sat on the bed. His wife was working late that night. As soon as he tried to lift my nightgown, I repeatedly hit him with the scissors. He ran from the room, but not before threatening to kill me. I gathered my things, including the scissors, ran to the bathroom, locked the door, and left through the bathroom window."

"I ran to the nearest neighbor, who called the police. They arrested him that night, and child protective services picked me up at the police station. The case worker told me they had a new set of foster parents willing to take older children and asked if I'd try them. The Wilsons took me in that night. They were kind. It took me months before I learned to trust them, but I ultimately recognized them as a loving couple I could trust."

Alex reached for her hand this time.

"Abbie, I'm so sorry that happened to you. I'm at a loss for words. I am grumbling about my life while you fought to save yours and survive."

"Montgomery, I won't lie. It was hard, but I survived!"

And Alex finally got it. Abbie's speech patterns changed when she felt the need to be defensive or if she was trying to make a point. She switched from calling him Alex and started calling him Montgomery; it was her way of proving she was in charge and knew what she wanted. A challenge of sorts. Now that he recognized this behavior, he might be better at helping her, as he promised.

Kohl stretched near her feet, and Abbie glanced at her watch.

"I've got to run, Alex. I need to stop at the attorney's office this afternoon."

"Thank you, Abbie, for agreeing to meet with me today. Lunch was great. I enjoyed getting to know you. I hope you can forgive me for being such a jerk."

Abbie cringed at the name she had called him on the beach.

"I enjoyed it as well. When do you leave Alex?"

"We leave on Saturday. Can I call to check on you before I leave?"

"Absolutely! I'm not going back to work for at least a couple of weeks, maybe longer. I need to figure out what to do with Kohl. Until that time, we are available."

Alex reached out to hug Abbie goodbye. She stepped forward into his arms. The hug lasted longer than either of them had expected, but her arms were right where he wanted to be forever.

He felt like a loving shelter to Abbie, and she never wanted to let go of him. As they pulled back from one another, Kohl let out a huff.

Abbie turned around to stare at him.

"I don't believe anyone asked for your opinion, Kohl."

Alex let out a laugh, wrapped his arm around Abbie, and walked her to her car. They received no more comments from Kohl.

Abbie pulled into the parking lot at the attorney's office. She let Kohl walk around before going into the lobby. If she remembered correctly, Mr. Walker had been Tom's parents' attorney, and Tom had kept him after his parents died.

Mr. Walker welcomed Abbie and Kohl and offered Abbie something to drink. She accepted a bottle of water and settled into a chair at the conference room table. Abbie smiled. This was a massive table for the two of them, but there was room for Kohl to lie under it. Abbie wondered if Mr. Walker had assessed the space Kohl needed and decided the conference room size gave him room to move. If so, it was an excellent decision.

"Abbie, how have you and Kohl been since I saw you at the funeral? It was a lovely service, and we are so proud of Tom and Kohl's contributions to the community. Unfortunately, Tom's death will leave a hole in the people's hearts."

"Thank you, Mr. Walker. We appreciate everything the public has done for us as well. Kohl is having a tough time adjusting to Tom being gone, so I plan to take time off to help him adjust. Then, when I return to work, I will find someone who can keep him during the day."

"Abbie, did Tom ever discuss with you any of his financial information?"

"No, Mr. Walker. He told me that his parents had left him money when they died, but he never mentioned the amount of money he received. We used around ten thousand when we bought the beach house and a few thousand more when we did renovations, but we both had good incomes and lived frugally."

"Were you aware that his parents were single children to single children?"

"Tom mentioned that when I met him. I was living with the Wilsons. He said that was the reason he was in a foster home. He had no aunts or uncles, and he did not want to impose on his friends' families. So, he suggested they find him a decent foster home, and he came to the Wilsons right after he turned sixteen."

"We both worked after-school jobs, so we didn't see each other every day even though we lived in the same house. If we were both off on the weekend and did not have any homework or test to study for, we often took our bikes and rode throughout the city. Ms. Wilson always made us lunch, and I had a basket attached to my bike. We'd load it up and head out for the day. We spent time on the beach, and Tom taught me to paddle board in the ocean."

"When he turned eighteen and was getting ready to enlist in the coast guard, he suggested we find a modest house on the beach. He had to get through basic training and would be gone for weeks, and I needed to finish school, but the Wilsons and family services were okay with the arrangement, such as: if I checked in at least three times a week, kept my grades up, and did not miss any school."

"That appears to have worked out fine. I managed Tom's trust as well, so when he wanted money for the house, renovations, and other minor items, we discussed the details before I approved the expenditures."

"Tom told me he had a Trust, but I thought he had just used the wrong term. He said they didn't leave him much. I assumed a trust required a significant sum of money?"

"Abbie, Tom, and his parents are wealthy. Mr. and Ms. Foster's parents were wealthy, as were their parents. Tom has left everything for you. Please read this document, Abbie, and there are a couple of others I will need your signature on. If there's something you don't understand, let me know. Once you are sure you understand everything, we will sign the documents, and I will have my assistant witness and notarize them, and she will give you a copy of the documents."

"Thanks, Mr. Walker. That sounds good."

Abbie accepted the document, opened it on the table, and started reading. Then, she reached for her water bottle, took a drink, and choked on her water.

"This can't be right," Abbie exclaimed and stared at Mr. Walker.

"It's right, Abbie." Mr. Walker assured her.

"I'm not sure I know what all those zeros mean. What figure are we talking about, Mr. Walker?" Her hands were shaking, and she was ready to vomit.

"I'm going to be sick. There must have been a mistake. Who has this much money?"

"Dear God in Heaven. Forgive me, Mr. Walker."

Abbie pushed her chair back, and Kohl stood up. Kohl watched Abbie to ensure she was okay and moved to her side, ready to place himself in the path of anyone who might want to harm her.

"You have that sum of money, Abbie. There is enough to take care of you for the rest of your life. And to care for any future children, grandchildren, and their children."

"I can't. It's too much. This belongs to Tom's family, not me." Abbie exclaimed, taking another sip of water as she paced back and forth in the conference room.

"Abbie, look at me for a minute." Mr. Walker said, trying to get her attention. She was as white as a sheet.

"You are Tom's wife. You are the only family member left. It belongs to you. If you can trust me, as Tom and his family did, I will help you manage your funds."

Abbie stared at him and wondered if he was speaking another language. She sat on a chair near the door, ready to flee, stood up again, then whipped her head around to face Mr. Walker and glanced at Kohl. She walked to the window and studied the cars moving about on the street.

"What am I supposed to do now, Mr. Walker?"

Abbie was having difficulty holding back her sobs. Kohl whined, and she realized she needed to pull herself together.

"The first thing I need you to do, Abbie, is to sign the documents. I'm going to suggest that you leave the money in the current trust account. One document transfers the money to your name and will be available as soon as you sign it. It will help if you take the time to digest the events that have happened today. The money will be there for you. You don't need to move it unless there's something that you need, and I will be happy to transfer any sum you wish."

Abbie stared at Mr. Walker.

"We need to go home, but I'm not sure I can drive right now."

"I'll get you a car, Abbie, or I can drive you myself. Someone will drop your car off at your house.

"It might be best if you drop me off, but Kohl will not fit in your car. Can someone follow us in mine?"

"Sure, Abbie. Give me a moment to get that arranged."

Then, she asked, "Can we stop on the way home and get a bottle of wine? I need a glass of wine while I figure out who my husband is and what I am supposed to do next. Do you have any family history on him?"

"I do, Abbie, and I will have my assistant email it to you promptly. Do you prefer red wine or white wine?"

Abbie stared at him again. He must be thinking she had lost her mind.

"Is a bottle of each asking for too much? Apparently, I can afford it."

And with that, she picked up her purse, told Kohl to follow her, and turned toward the door.

"Thanks for the ride, Mr. Walker. We'll wait for you in the lobby."

CHAPTER 9

Mr. Walker drove Abbie while Kohl rode home in Abbie's car, which his assistant was driving. Unfortunately, he was too big to fit in Mr. Walker's car, and Abbie did not want to take the chance on Kohl getting his seats dirty or leaving fur and drool. He walked Abbie to the door and waited until she unlocked the house.

"Here is your wine. Drink responsibly, Abbie. Is there a friend you can call to discuss the events of the afternoon or anyone who can be with you this evening?"

"I don't think I should tell anyone about the money yet. Kohl and I will be fine. I'll do the things normal people do. Clean the kitchen, do laundry, cook, and I might even clean the toilet. Then I will read the documents your assistant will send me so that I can figure out who my husband was and where those zeros came from."

Abbie stopped talking for a second. "Please tell me; it's not the mob."

"It is not the mob, Abbie. They were legitimate business owners who made good and invested well."

"I'll decide that for myself. And thank you again for the ride home and the wine. I'll call you later this week to see what is next, and I appreciate you, Mr. Walker, and I trust you to help me with the zeros."

"You are welcome, Abbie. Take care. I'll see you soon. Call me with questions."

Abbie did precisely what she told Mr. Walker she was going to do. She cleaned the kitchen, fed Kohl, did laundry, and even cleaned the toilet. Then, still restless, she poured a glass of white wine and settled on the sofa with Kohl.

Abbie needed somebody to talk to; her crew was not the ones she wanted right now. So, she grabbed her phone and sent Alex a message.

"You busy?"

Abbie tapped her fingers on the sofa while waiting for Alex to respond, causing Kohl to get up and move to the floor.

"No, just taking inventory of what needs packed next."

"Are you too busy to call me?"

"I can call. Give me a second."

Abbie's phone rang, and she picked it up on the first ring.

"If you're too busy, I understand. We can talk later."

"I'm good, Abbie. Andy is staying with a friend before we leave on Saturday. What are you doing this evening?"

"Do you like wine, Alex?"

Alex chuckled at her question. "Yes, I do. Do you like wine, Abbie?"

"Do you want to come over for a glass of wine?"

"Umm, what's going on, Abbie? Are you okay?"

"There're zeros, Montgomery. Way too many zeros. I'm not sure what to do."

"Abbie, how much wine did you drink? Did you have anything but wine this evening?"

"No, Montgomery. I only had one sip of wine. I want to drink more, but I prefer not to drink alone. That's where you come in, Montgomery."

"I see."

"Listen, Montgomery; I am not drunk. I am not hallucinating or delusional. But I need somebody to talk with tonight. Dana, Sam, Julie, and Kate won't understand. They'd pack their things and rush to stay with me again. Are you free?"

"I need your address, Abbie, and I'll be there in a few minutes. Is there anything you want me to bring?"

"Yes, bring your stuff, Montgomery."

"What stuff, Abbie? Are you sure nobody drugged you?"

"I'm sure, Montgomery. Your overnight stuff in case we drink too much, and you can't drive home. Listen, when I explain the zeros, you'll need wine and most likely more than one glass of wine, so bring your stuff."

Abbie gave Alex her home address and promptly hung up on him.

Alex started to ask her another question and realized she had hung up the phone. He ran through the house, gathering his stuff. He was worried. Something had happened this afternoon. She was perfectly coherent at lunch, but now she was talking like she was high, drunk, or drugged. He stopped what he was doing and sighed. *I forgot to ask her if she had fallen and hit her head. Why didn't I ask if she had had an accident?*

Alex put her address into his phone and grabbed his car keys. The directions pulled up onto the screen, and Alex started laughing. She was a two-minute walk away, and he ran right past her house every day and did not realize she existed until last week.

He locked the house on his way out and walked the short two-minute distance to Abbie's. He rang the doorbell and heard Abbie approaching the door. Before she opened it, he heard her talking to Kohl.

"That's Montgomery on the other side of the door. You will behave yourself, or I'll put you in your puppy crate. Do you understand me?"

Kohl gave a soft bark to acknowledge her and stood beside Abbie as she opened the door.

"Hey, Alex. Thanks for coming. Did you bring your stuff? Kohl promises to be good, so you won't need to worry about him acting up tonight. If he does," she turned and looked at Kohl, "I'm putting him in his puppy crate."

Kohl whined and walked to the other side of the room.

"I brought my stuff, Abbie. Are you okay? Did you fall and hit your head? Did someone mug you this evening, Abbie?"

He realized he sounded like Andy with the questions he was asking her.

"White or red, Montgomery? We are going on a mission, so let's get the wine to get started."

"How many glasses of wine did you drink this evening, Abbie?"

Abbie turned and picked up her wine glass from the coffee table.

"This is the same glass I poured before I called you, Montgomery, because I was waiting for you. Didn't I tell you I prefer not drinking alone?"

"Yes, I remember what you said. I'll take a glass of the white you are having."

"That's good, Montgomery, because we have one bottle of white and one bottle of red."

She poured his wine, and they sat on the sofa facing each other.

"Abbie, could you start from the time we left lunch and tell me everything you did, so I can understand where we are and where we need to go from here?"

"I need you to explain the zeros."

"When Kohl and I left you, we drove straight to Mr. Walker's office. He's Tom's attorney. He was Tom's parents' attorney, as well. I remember Tom mentioned him, but I didn't remember that until today."

"Mr. Walker wanted to know how much information Tom gave me regarding our financial position. I was confused. What financial position? Tom was a guardsman, and I'm a nurse. He told me his parents had left money that became his upon their death. Tom withdrew ten thousand dollars for the down payment on this house and several thousand more to do renovations. We worked hard, lived frugally, and saved money every month. Mr. Walker told me to read the documents his office had prepared."

Alex noticed Abbie's hands shake, and she took a long swig of wine. Alex reached out for her hand and told her to keep going.

"I started reading the document, Alex, and took a drink of water and started choking. There were all these zeros. I don't know the total. There was just zero, after zero, after zero. I couldn't think! I told him there had been a mistake, that the money belonged to Tom's family. He said I was the only family left. Tom was the only child of parents who were only children of only children. How does that happen, Alex?"

"I do not know, Abbie. Keep going," Alex prompted her.

"Who was I married to, Montgomery? He was aware of the money. He had a trust fund. Now I have a trust fund that used to belong to Tom, and since he died, those zeros belong to me. All the money in that fund! All the zeros, Alex."

Abbie stopped talking and looked at Alex.

"Abbie, try to stay calm. We'll figure this out. Does the attorney have any information on Tom's family?"

"I asked if Tom's family were part of the mob. Mr. Walker said no and emphasized that they were businesspeople who did good and invested well. His assistant is sending information for me to read."

"Alex. What am I supposed to do with all those zeros?"

Abbie picked up the wineglass and drained every drop.

"How many zeros were there, Abbie? Could you be overestimating the number?"

"Billions, Montgomery. Hundreds of billions if I'm counting correctly. What does someone do with all those zeros?"

"Abbie, you do not need to do anything right now. The money will stay in the trust fund. Have Mr. Walker transfer money to your checking account when you need money. Pay off this house, car, or bills, and take time off work. Certainly, you don't need the paycheck. You must be extremely careful who you tell about the money, Abbie. People will try to take advantage of you."

"You're the only one who I've told Alex. I'm not telling anyone else, but if something happens to me, somebody else needs to know what to do with the trust fund. I'm not sure why, but I trust you. Don't break that trust, Montgomery. I need someone on whom I can depend."

"I will not break that trust, Abbie. This is between the two of us and Mr. Walker. That's it! We need to keep you safe."

"I need more wine, Alex. Do you want another glass?"

"What both of us need is food, Abbie. Let's order and have the food delivered."

He reached for his phone to place the order. "Pizza or Chinese?"

"Really, Dr. Montgomery? Those are our choices? Did they offer nutrition classes in med school? There's an excellent plant-based restaurant just a couple of miles from here. Somewhere here is a takeout menu. Let me see if I have it in a drawer in the kitchen."

She walked toward the kitchen, and Alex heard her mumbling about cardiac disease and CPR.

"Great!" He exclaimed aloud. "If I plan on spending time with her, Andy and I will be forced to give up our bachelor ways. Also, I should remind Ms. Nurse that she's consuming alcohol and a plant-based diet, which is not healthy either."

He decided not to mention it tonight. But, after the day she had, it entitled her to a couple of glasses of wine.

They placed their food order, and while waiting for the food delivery, Abbie grabbed her computer and returned to the sofa with a bottle of red wine. She filled their glasses, and Alex considered telling her to slow down, but he kept his thoughts to himself.

Abbie sat beside him on the sofa, tucked her legs under her, and continued sipping her wine. She was about to find out who the person was that she had trusted enough to marry. If she wanted a couple of drinks, he'd make sure she stopped before she got sick, drunk, or both.

"Here, Montgomery. You open it and read the first few paragraphs. Then, if it's not too awful, hand it back to me, and I will read it aloud, so we both will know his history. But that food better hurry, or I'm going to be drunk."

Alex accepted the computer from her and started reading the document but found little information related to Tom's family history. He forwarded through a couple more pages, but still no details.

"I don't think you are going to be happy with this, Abbie."

"What? Why? What did you find, Montgomery?"

She grabbed the computer out of his hands, scrolled back to the first page, and started reading. Looking over at him as though this was his fault, Abbie started on a rant.

"There's nothing here. How can anyone not have a family history? Well, wait. I can understand that part because I don't have a history to talk about either, but how do you get this much money with no history? Montgomery, is this as crazy as it sounds? Who are these people? Why did Tom not tell me? He has a history because he attended school. He lived in a big house. His parents died. There should be newspaper articles. Montgomery, we need to start over with our search. What is Mr. Walker trying to hide?"

Just then, the doorbell rang.

"I'll get that, Abbie. You grab the plates and silverware. Let's talk through this again while we eat."

Alex placed the containers on the table and placed a serving of each item on their plates. Both dug in at the same time.

"Okay, Abbie. You won. This food is great. You chose two meals today, and both were perfect."

"Your turn to pick next time, but you better up your game, Montgomery. And it bothers me that you didn't answer my question. Were you even required to take a nutrition class in med school?"

Alex acknowledged he did, but he was too busy studying and exhausted from lack of sleep to remember much more than trying to figure out how to survive the chaos of the next day in med school.

Abbie took a bite of food, held her fork in front of her face, and stared. She turned it back and forth as she studied it from every side.

"What are you looking for, Abbie?" Alex glanced at the wine bottle to see how much she had drunk from the red wine.

"I bought this fork at Walmart, Montgomery. How much do you assume I paid for it?"

"I'm not sure, Abbie. Five dollars?" He said calmly, unsure where she was going with this line of questioning.

Abbie rolled her eyes.

"Less than a buck fifty, Montgomery. Do you think he didn't care that he had all that money, or maybe he felt I wasn't worth it? Poor girl, abandoned at birth, raised in foster homes, tossed from one place to another. Why spend money on someone he felt was beneath him and the zeros in that bank account?"

"Abbie, let's take Kohl and go for a walk on the beach. We both need fresh air. It might help us clear our heads and burn off the alcohol. It's a pleasant night, and the moon is bright. The exercise will help you sleep better tonight as well. I'll clean this up when we get back. We need a break from the zeros and the doubt swimming around in your brain right now."

Abbie laid her fork on the table, drained her wineglass, grabbed a jacket, and called Kohl for a walk. Closing the door, she reached for Alex's hand and began walking up the beach.

Alex held Abbie's hand as they walked. How did this seem so normal, he wondered, when just last week, she was grieving over the tragic death of her husband, a local hero who everyone loved, including her.

Alex had put a plan together to make long-needed changes for himself. Then, finally, he saw himself in someone else's eyes as she called him out on his behavior and treatment of others around him. Finally, he understood what grief could do to someone and watched Abbie's reaction to everything that had occurred since Tom's death.

Abbie was quiet as they walked, and Kohl walked beside her but never ventured near the water. Tom's death had affected him as well. Abbie's concerns he may never return to the water were valid.

Despite his training, Kohl could not save the one person he loved. Growling and showing teeth were not typical behaviors shown by Kohl or his breed but most likely was a reaction to those he didn't know or trust. So not only was he guarding himself, but he was also guarding Abbie.

Abbie stopped walking and turned to face Alex. She remained silent as a single tear slid off her face. Alex pulled her in for a hug.

"Thank you, Alex. How is it that after just a few days, it feels like we've known each other for a long time, and the husband I was married to for several years is a stranger?"

"I'm not sure why that happens, Abbie. Let's head back to the house so you can get a solid eight hours of sleep. I'll stay at your place if you need something during the night. Tomorrow, I need to pick up Andy and finish packing. If you've got nothing better to do, you could give me a hand, and Kohl and Andy can keep each other company."

"That sounds good to me. I need something to keep me from thinking of those zeros, and Kohl could also use a new friend."

CHAPTER 10

They returned to the house, and Alex cleaned the kitchen as promised. Abbie closed and put away her computer. She had enough for one week and was tired of talking about money, funerals, and families she didn't know existed. Alex asked Abbie for a pillow and blanket, and Abbie stared at him.

"For what, Montgomery?"

"Not important. I can sleep on the sofa without a pillow or a blanket."

"You are not sleeping on the sofa, Montgomery. You can take one side of the bed. Kohl will lie between us, and believe me, he will not let you get anywhere near me. You'll possibly find yourself on the floor by morning, anyway. He has a habit of slowly pushing you out of his way while you're sleeping. He never slept in a bed before Tom died. Now, he assumes he owns the whole thing. I am going to need to fix that behavior, as well."

"Abbie. I'm not sure if that is a good idea."

"Listen, Montgomery. I'm tired and probably a little drunk, and I don't think it is a good idea to have all these zeros floating around either, but here they are, and until I can get used to them, I need your help. I trust you to do the right thing. So, suck it up and try to keep your place on the mattress or lose to the dog and end up on the floor."

Alex wanted to respond, but she had consumed too much alcohol, and he did not want her to think he was laughing at her.

"Is life as your friend always going to be a battle, Abbie? Because I don't like to lose."

"Not likely, Montgomery. But it will keep you on your toes."

Alex awoke the following day to the aroma of coffee and found himself still on the mattress and considered that a victory. He opened his eyes to find Kohl staring at him.

"Dear God, Kohl. Shouldn't you be up chasing squirrels or something by now?" Alex murmured and heard Abbie laughing from the doorway.

"You might have been lucky enough to be the receiver of a big wet, slobbery kiss. That's how he wakes me up. I got a reprieve this morning. He was more concerned about you. So, thanks, Montgomery. At least I realize you're good for something."

Abbie walked over and handed him a large cup of steaming coffee.

"Peace offering, in case my dog kept you awake all night."

Alex sat up on the side of the bed.

"Thanks, Abbie. He didn't bother me at all, but I appreciate the coffee. Can I take the cup with me? I'm going to head home. I want to run and take a shower before I pick up Andy. After I get back, I will text you my address. I want to wait until the last minute to tell him about Kohl. He'll be so excited. Andy has been asking for a dog for years, but with our nomad lifestyle, it was not at the top of my list. He'll love spending time with him, even if it is only an hour or two."

Alex gathered his stuff and hugged Abbie.

"That sounds like a good plan, Montgomery. Thanks for everything yesterday. Kohl and I will see you soon."

Alex ran, showered, and picked up Andy.

"What are we doing today, Dad?"

"Can we go to the museum and then for lunch? Or maybe shop for decorations for my new room? Let's go to the movies, eat candy and popcorn, and later we can go for pizza." Alex sighed, knowing Abbie's response to Andy's idea.

"I have a surprise for you, Andy, but you must be patient for a couple of hours. No questions, Andy! Just patience. Can you do that? There are things I need to get done today before the movers come on Saturday, but I promise you, you are going to love this surprise."

"Okay, Dad. But can we still get pizza later?"

"I'll take that under consideration."

"What is a consideration, Dad?"

"It means we might get pizza for dinner if you are patient and are good with the surprise, and I get my stuff done for the move on Saturday."

"I'll be good. But I'm not sure I can wait long for the surprise."

Abbie walked into Tom's office and glanced around when she received a text on her phone. Alex had sent his address, and Abbie plugged it into her phone and laughed. A two-minute walk away. He never mentioned the short walk over here last night, and she did not pay attention this morning when he left. Instead, she sent him a laughing emoji, and he responded.

"I know. I laughed when I plugged your address in last night, but zeros surrounded us, and I forgot to mention I walked. Eighth house on the left."

The office would wait, she decided. She turned out the lamp and closed the door. She gathered Kohl's things, and they strolled up the beach. They located Alex's house, walked up the sidewalk, and knocked on the door. Alex answered the door, smiling. Andy rolled up behind Alex, eyes wide when he spied Kohl and sat there speechlessly.

"Andy, I want you to meet Abbie Foster and her dog, Kohl. Abbie and Kohl, this is my son, Andrew Montgomery."

"Nice to meet you, Ms. Foster. Your dog is so big."

"Nice to meet you too, Andy, and you can call me Abbie. Kohl is looking for a new friend, Andy. Are you available?"

"I sure am, Abbie. Can I pet him?"

"Kohl, Andy would like to be friends. Do you want to be friends with Andy?"

Kohl let out a quick bark, walked over to where Andy sat in his wheelchair, sat down, and lifted his paw to shake hands.

"That's so cool."

Andy took Kohl's paw. "Nice to meet you, Kohl. Do you want to play ball?"

Kohl glanced at Abbie for permission. Abbie nodded her head, and Kohl barked once. Abbie pulled Kohl's ball out of her pocket and handed it to Andy.

"He loves to play Andy, but sometimes, he doesn't realize when it is time to take a break. You will need to tell him what you want to do. If he doesn't understand, just find me, and I will help him understand."

"Thanks, Abbie. Come on, Kohl, let's go play ball." And the two of them took off toward the backyard like they had been friends forever.

Abbie entered the house to find boxes everywhere.

"What's the plan here, Montgomery?"

"I planned to pack and mark boxes with the stuff we would need first: coffee, breakfast, and bathroom items. I'm packing a couple of suitcases with clothing and toiletries for the first few days. That should cover our first night in the hotel and the first few days in the house until we can unpack boxes."

"That makes sense. Let's start in the kitchen. Go through your morning routine and everything you use, place on the island. Then reevaluate for snacks, lunch, and dinner, and don't forget about can openers, knives, and serving spoons. When we are done, we'll move to the bathroom items."

A short while later, Andy and Kohl came in for a drink and a snack, and Abbie pulled Kohl's treats from her purse. Andy was in awe of Kohl's size but had a wonderful time playing with him. Next, Andy asked if they could watch a movie together, and Alex got them set up. Before long, Andy and Kohl were fast asleep.

Alex and Abbie made the rounds in each room, which impressed Alex with their progress. Since she arrived, Abbie had not mentioned the zeros, so Alex took that as a successful day. When Kohl and Andy woke up, they all went out on the porch to relax and watch the waves. Kohl had brought his ball outside and dropped it in Andy's lap.

"Dad. Did you take pizza under con, con? Ugh. What was that word again?"

"Consideration."

Abbie peered at Alex.

"I told Andy that if he promised to let me get work done and not ask too many questions before his surprise got here, I would consider pizza for dinner."

"That is a great idea, Andy. What do you like on your pizza?"

After discussing what everyone wanted and Alex placing the order, Andy and Kohl returned to the living room to finish watching the movie they had started earlier. Abbie and Alex settled back on the porch.

"So, tell me, Ms. Foster. When Andy asks for a pizza, it's a great idea, and when I ask for pizza, I get interrogated about the classes I had in med school. What's up with that?" Alex leaned toward Abbie with raised eyebrows.

"Simple, Montgomery. You're not a seven-year-old boy who is as cute as the dickens and loves my dog. He gets what he wants within reason. Keep helping me with the zeros, and things may also change for you."

"I'm not cute?"

"No, you're not!" Abbie paused long enough to cause Alex concern.

"You are a very handsome, intelligent doctor, Montgomery, who stepped up when I needed a friend. That might get you a pizza someday, but with Andy, those enormous eyes and that charming smile will do it every time."

The pizza arrived, and everyone dug in. Abbie had ordered a couple of slices without sauce or other toppings so that Andy could offer Kohl a couple of tastes as a treat.

"What's on your agenda for tomorrow, Alex?" Abbie inquired.

"Not much. One more pass through the house to make sure I did not overlook anything, and we should be ready for the packers and the movers. What's on your agenda?"

"Nothing of any significance on mine, either. The weather is supposed to be great tomorrow. I'd like to take Andy and Kohl to the zoo."

"Great idea, Abbie. Andy loves the zoo and will be delighted that Kohl can go, too. I assume there is no problem getting Kohl in?"

"No problem. The staff at the zoo are aware of who Kohl is, and with his training, Kohl ranks higher than most service dogs. He doesn't bark at anything, so he doesn't scare the animals, and the other visitors love watching him. People may recognize him and offer their condolences for Tom. We need to make sure Andy understands what happened and that he will be okay with all the attention and chaos that occurs when Kohl is in a public setting. Andy will get tons of inquiries about Kohl's breed, behavior, size, and weight, so I will fill him in on the simple stuff before we get there. In addition, I'll help him out if he gets questions he can't answer. Is he ready for all this, Alex?"

"Abbie, Andy loves to question everything. You may be the one who's not prepared for tomorrow. Let me get him, and we'll walk you and Kohl home. But don't mention tomorrow, or there will be no sleeping in this house tonight."

Abbie and Kohl woke up early the next morning and walked on the beach. Kohl was still avoiding the water, so Abbie walked closer to the surf today to force him to get his feet wet, but with no luck, Abbie turned back toward the house. There was always tomorrow.

Abbie and Kohl walked to Alex's house, and they all tried to pile into Alex's car, but Kohl was too big to fit in. Andy found this hilarious, and his laugh caused Abbie and Alex to laugh. Abbie walked back to her place and got her SUV. Once again, everyone piled in and got settled. She handed Alex the keys to allow her time to catch Andy up on Kohl's statistics. Andy asked question after question, and Abbie answered every question. Finally, Alex glanced over at her and smiled.

"Are you ready, Andy? Any questions for me?"

"I'm ready! Are you ready, Kohl?" Again, Kohl let out a soft bark, and again, Andy giggled.

"Everyone will think Kohl is your dog, Andy. So today, Andrew Montgomery, I grant you custody of Kohl."

"What does custody mean, Abbie?"

"It means that if someone asked if he's your dog, you are allowed to say yes."

"That's so cool, Abbie. I have been asking Dad for a dog, but he keeps telling me no. Thank you, Abbie."

"You are welcome, Andy. Now, let's have a good day at the zoo."

Alex pushed Andy's wheelchair, and Kohl walked beside Andy. Not over three minutes after they entered the zoo, Kohl had drawn a sizable crowd of people, and Andy answered every question Abbie had prepared him to expect. Alex had not heard Andy laugh this much since Maria died.

Alex reached for Abbie's hand. "How do I thank you, Abbie? I've not seen him this animated since his mother died. He's still a happy child, but I've missed this instantaneous laughter."

"It's not me, Montgomery. It's Kohl that's bringing out that laughter. He's at his best when children are involved and genuinely loves people. What you are witnessing today is his breed, but he also has a remarkable personality."

"Remind me of that remarkable personality the next time he bares his teeth at me."

Abbie grinned.

"Are you saying you don't like my dog, Montgomery?"

"I love your dog for bringing laughter back into our lives, Abbie. And he'll adjust."

Abbie's phone rang, and Julie's name was on the screen.

"Excuse me, Alex, I need to take this call."

"Hi, Julie. What's up?"

"Hey yourself, Abbie. I was calling to find out if you are available for a Zoom call this evening. Everyone else is good. Just checking with you."

"We can do it if it is after 8:00 pm. Would that work?"

"Yes, that works. Everyone else will be free then as well. What have you been up to this week? And what's all that noise in the background?"

"I'm at the zoo with Kohl," Abbie responded, leaving out that she was with Alex and Andy.

"You remember how excited everyone gets when he is out in public?"

"Sounds like fun! I'll let you go, so you can keep that situation under control. Talk to you tonight." And Julie hung up without Abbie needing to reply.

"Everything okay?"

"Everything is great. That was Julie. Nobody has talked to me for a few days, except for a rare text here and there, and they want a zoom meeting tonight. We do that to stay connected."

Abbie decided that Andy and Kohl had enough interaction with the crowd, and she explained to the crowd that they needed to let Andy make his rounds at the zoo. Andy waved to everyone to who he had been talking with and turned to Abby.

"Is it always this way when you take Kohl places? People were asking me questions nonstop. Kohl likes people. Do you think he likes people, Abbie? That was so much fun. Can we do it again one day?"

Alex and Abbie both laughed at Andy's interpretation of today's events.

"If you have fun today, we'll do this again. Kohl had fun, too. Thanks for joining us today, Andy."

"I'm having a blast, and Kohl is, too. Can we look at the elephants and get a snack? The elephants are my favorite."

"Yes, we can. I love elephants too, Andy. Let's go, Montgomery. We have elephants to find."

They spent the afternoon leisurely observing the animals, ordered lunch from the concession stand, ate next to the flamingo viewing section, and returned to the elephants again before loading everyone back into the SUV.

Andy chose a local burger joint for dinner with outdoor seating at Alex's prompting so that Kohl could join them, and he talked non-stop through dinner about the zoo and how he and Kohl had fun. He could barely hold his eyes open on the way back to the house. Alex scooped him up and walked him to his bed. Abbie and Kohl waited on the front porch. Abbie sat in the rocker and watched the waves roll in while Kohl promptly fell asleep at her feet, exhausted as Andy.

When Alex emerged from the house, he glanced at Kohl, who was snoring, and smiled.

"I guess they both wore themselves out. Abbie, I don't know how to thank you for today. Andy had an amazing day."

"I wanted to thank you, Alex. Kohl had a good day as well. I haven't seen him this animated since, well, since he soaked you with water last week." Abbie laughed.

"Oh, you find that funny, do you?" They both laughed.

Abbie stood to go and woke Kohl.

"Can I leave my car here, Alex? It might be easier for him to walk home than get his tired body up in the SUV."

"No worries, Abbie. You can get it tomorrow."

Alex pulled Abbie toward him for a hug, and Kohl let out a huff.

"Will he get used to me? If I'm going to be your friend, he and I need to come to terms with what's huffable."

"Is that even a word, Montgomery?" Abbie asked, chuckling.

"It is now," he replied, and Kohl huffed again.

Abbie and Kohl walked home. She filled his food and water bowls but suspected he'd go right to sleep. He and Andy had fun today, but he had not had this much exercise or excitement for days and was sound asleep.

CHAPTER 11

Abbie fired up her computer, poured a glass of wine, and logged into the zoom call. She enjoyed looking at everyone again, even if only via zoom. Abbie redirected the call to everything other than herself. There were two subjects she wanted to avoid. Tom's will and the time spent with Alex.

She listened to everyone discussing jobs and the latest project Kate was engaged in, but the conversation turned in her direction when Sam asked how the coffee meeting with Dr. Montgomery went and what subjects they discussed.

"It went well. We discussed Tom's accident and everything his team tried to save Tom's life. But unfortunately, Alex said that due to the injuries' severity, there were very few options."

"We talked about his previous jobs and family. He lived in Denver with his wife and son. One evening, they attended an early Christmas dinner with friends, and it started snowing. The hostess packed up their dessert, and they started home. The roads became terrible, and their car slid over the guardrail and tumbled over the hill. His wife died in the accident, and his son has been in a wheelchair since that night. He stayed in Denver for a brief time, then sought temporary interim positions because the memory of the accident haunted him."

Julie, Dana, Sam, and Kate talked at once. Each offered their opinion of why Alex upped and left their home and why he would drag his son across the country.

Abbie let them voice their concerns. The friendship that was developing with Alex puzzled her, and she wanted to avoid getting into the fact that her husband of seven years was not who he presented. Once she had the facts about Tom and his wealthy family and how she became the sole person to inherit the astronomical sum of money, she'd fill them in on what had occurred. But, for now, those subjects stayed between her and Alex only.

They asked how Kohl was doing, and Abbie filled them in on his refusal to get back in the water. Julie asked if she and Kohl had fun at the zoo, and the conversation shifted in a different direction. Abbie discussed the zoo, leaving out the information about Alex and Andy.

As they were wrapping up their call, Abbie's phone pinged with a text. She glanced at her phone and smiled at the message from Alex. Sam caught the glance and smiled.

"Abbie. Who is texting you?"

"A friend!"

"What type of friend, and who is this friend? That glance and smile are pretty telling, Abbie."

"I do not know what you're talking about, Sam. It's a friend. Do you know what a friend is, Sam? A friend is someone like you, Dana, Julie, and Kate. Just a friend. I have friends other than you four. I'm allowed to have over four friends."

Abbie groaned. She realized she had made too much of Sam's remark. How did she get herself out of this mess she created?

There was silence in the group.

"Things are going on that I'm unable to tell you right now. Tom is not who he portrayed himself to be, and I'm so angry

I can't think of what to do next. His attorney is trying to help me find information so that I can sort this out. Unfortunately, I had to confide in someone that didn't know Tom or me well. I needed someone who could be objective. Besides Tom's attorney, my friend is helping me search for information and is trying to help me stay sane through this mess. It would help if you didn't assume I don't trust you, but I need someone who will not take sides. You know Tom well, and you will be as shocked as I am once I explain everything. I promise to tell you when I have more information to share, but for now, you need to trust me on this one."

Kate spoke up next.

"Abbie, we are your best friends. We will help you through everything, but you need to be honest with us. Are you in trouble because we can help?"

"I'm not in trouble, Kate. This mess is complicated. I trust the four of you with my life, but I needed a neutral person. Someone who doesn't know Tom or me. Someone who can look past my anger and help me try to sort out the position Tom has put me in with his lies and deception. This has been tougher than you might imagine. Sometimes I'm glad he's not here because I'm angry with him. I am angry with myself for having those thoughts. I am unsure what my reaction might be if I had to stand face-to-face with him. Can you accept that for now?"

"That's a lot to comprehend," Dana said. "How was he so deceptive and us not recognize any of it? We are good at being able to read every one. So, if something slips by one of us, the other catches it."

"I am aware of your stealth radar. And before your imagination runs wild, Tom did not have another wife or wives, and he did not have children with anyone else, so remove that thought from your brains. In addition, he did not belong to the mob. I received a definitive no to that inquiry."

"You assumed he belonged to the mob?"

"Oh, Abbie, this subject is getting serious." Said Sam. "Has he been hiding from the police? Do you think he is wanted for criminal activity? If that's what's going on, none of us knew him."

Julie chimed in next. "Do you think his parents really died in a car accident? We've read of people dying in accidents, and the police find out someone cut the brake line."

Kate spoke up next. "We could always do a DNA or Ancestry test, Abbie."

"Kate, I don't think a DNA test is necessary. If you relax for a moment and give me time to do my research, I will have answers for us."

"If you need help, Abbie," Sam said. "I am available for you, and I'm sure the others are as well."

Abbie nodded her head. "I love each one of you more than you realize. When I need your help, I will call you. I am going to drop off now. I'm trying to go through Tom's things and desk, which is an emotional job."

Abbie hung up the phone. She glanced at the text message again that Alex had sent. Whew, she nearly blew that one. Sam is always so observant, and she is quick to call you out on things.

Instead of texting Alex, she pushed the call button. Alex answered after one ring.

"Hey. Everything okay?"

"Everything is good. I'm getting ready to undertake Tom's desk and need to hear a voice of reason before I delve into his den because I'm not sure if I'll find any more surprises."

"I know what you mean. I surprised myself with the things I came across when we packed my stuff. I'm unsure where it came from or why I kept it."

"Let's hope Tom was better organized, or you may have to come searching for me in the morning. Anyhow, I'm going to get started, but I wanted to say good night, Alex. See you in the morning."

"Good night, Abbie."

Abbie walked into the office. She glanced around to decide where to start. The office was modest but neat and well-organized, as Tom had organized the books in alphabetical order on the shelves. She'd donate the books according to the subject and send everything that pertained to the rescue squad to the guard station, and the rest would be donated to the library.

Abbie peered at the piles of books on the desk and was happy with her progress. She stopped to get a bottle of water and got her step stool from the closet so she could reach the top shelf. The middle shelf had one book turned backward. She got curious about why it was backward, and she turned the book around to look at the title but could not read the words.

The book looked old. Abbie stepped off the stool, placed the book on the desk, and planned to call Mr. Walker on Monday to ask if he knew a book appraiser. As she continued, she found more old books on the shelves and added them to the pile on the desk.

When she got to the shelf with only new books, she laughed. Tom had a habit of researching everything, so it did not surprise her that he had also researched their dog. Those she'd keep! She gathered them in another pile, walked them to her bedroom, and put them on top of her dresser.

Abbie checked on Kohl to find him still asleep. Andy provided excellent company for him. Nothing like a child to keep you occupied and your mind off your problems. Not only did it work for Kohl, but it also worked for her.

Abbie emptied drawers of office items and files. The papers that she found were from the bank. So, it surprised her when she found a receipt for a safe deposit box. Mr. Walker did not mention a safe deposit box. She added that to her note for the call to him on Monday. He might know how to get access to the box.

She gathered the garbage, put everything into a bag, and took it to the trash bin. She had made progress today. Work remained, but she promised to help Alex tomorrow and needed sleep.

CHAPTER 12

Abbie got up early on Saturday morning to make a treat for Alex and Andy. Today was their moving day. She had talked to him last night and offered to help keep a sense of order in the day's chaos. So, she knocked at the door at 7:00 am, and Andy answered the door.

"Is someone in this house moving today? I have a big treat for anyone who is moving today."

"I'm moving today, Abbie, and so is Dad."

Kohl barked and stood by Andy's side.

"Well, let's eat breakfast then, so we have the energy to move this stuff." Abbie proclaimed as she closed the door and walked to the kitchen.

She smelled coffee, and Alex held a large to-go cup of coffee in each hand.

"Caffeinated or Caffeinated? It's the only choice for this morning."

"I choose caffeinated. It is the perfect accompaniment to the carbs hiding in this pan."

Alex took a big breath, and his mouth watered.

"Yum. Do I detect cinnamon?"

"Yep, and I brought disposable plates and forks as well. So, let's eat before the movers get here, and the chaos begins."

They sat around the table, and Abbie asked Andy about his new house.

"Well, it's enormous and has six bedrooms, so if my dad meets someone and she wants to marry us, there will be room for sisters and brothers."

Alex choked on his coffee, and Abbie grinned.

"It's on the beach Andy continued, so we can see the sunrise and go swimming when the weather is warm. Also, it's near my dad's hospital, so he can pick me up at school, or I might ride the bus sometimes."

"That sounds perfect, Andy. I love seeing the sunrise in the morning, and sometimes Kohl likes to play in the water while I drink my coffee. Did you realize Kohl can ride with me on the paddleboard?"

"No way, Abbie! Can you visit us and bring Kohl, so I can see him ride?"

"If your dad says it is okay for us to visit. Kohl likes to show off in the water."

The movers arrived and started loading the truck. Alex sent Andy and Kohl to the backyard to play ball while he and Abbie monitored the rest of the packing. They stopped for a bottle of water and took a seat on the porch.

"Do you realize, Montgomery, that you've told me you are moving up the coast, but we've never discussed what town?"

"North Myrtle Beach, Abbie. A friend of mine helps find physician staff for hospitals around the country, and I called him right after our run-in at the ER the other day. I decided it was time to change and take a permanent position.

"Andy is at the age now where I need to get him to a location where he can make friends and a school where the teachers recognize him. We've been nomads long enough, and the house is big enough for him to maneuver around in his chair and not get stuck in tight places or need to ask me for help constantly. His bathroom has a curb less shower, so he can also be more independent there."

"Brilliant plan, Montgomery! I'm going to miss my new friends." Abbie reached for his hand.

"Promise to keep in touch and help me with the zeros."

"I promise. How are you with decorating, Abbie? That house is enormous, and I need another opinion on decorating. It's not my niche. Andy has asked me to take him shopping for decorations, but where do I start? Are you up for the job?"

"Oh no, Montgomery. That's not my niche, either. Haven't you looked at my house? It resembles a lazy beach nurse with dog hair added in and slobber to bring it to the next level. It's a losing battle between the hair and the slobber."

Alex did not respond right away. He appeared as though he was weighing his options, but what he was doing was trying to find a legitimate way to ask Abbie to come up for a visit. He had gotten used to talking to and seeing her these past few days, and Andy enjoyed playing with Kohl.

"You should look for a designer, Alex. I'll call Sam. She used one when she moved here years ago. You should hire a cleaning company as well. If that house is as big as Andy said, you'll need help."

"You're right. You will visit though, won't you, Abbie? Andy is going to miss seeing Kohl. I'm going to need to rent your dog for the weekends."

"I'll arrange for you to rent him, Montgomery, but he's an expensive dog. Do you realize how much food he consumes, which means he leaves me enormous gifts to clean up in the backyard? Your decorator will need to calculate the slobber that goes everywhere, including the ceilings, walls, floors, and whatever else is in its way when it goes flying."

"Noted. I'll look for one with that specialty." He took out his phone and pretended to make a note.

"Find a home decorator who specializes in dog slobber. Done!"

Andy and Kohl were exhausted after playing in the backyard. Finally, Abbie offered to take them to her house. Without interruptions, Alex could keep up with the movers. Andy said it was a fantastic idea and started clapping. Kohl joined in by barking, indicating he was also happy with the plan.

They walked on the beach toward her house. She found pushing Andy's wheelchair in the sand was a chore.

"Do you have an electric wheelchair, Andy?"

"No. My dad pushes me in this one. He's strong, and he doesn't mind."

Abbie got the two playmates settled with their lunch, and Andy asked if he could watch a movie with Kohl. So, she turned on the movie, and they climbed up on the sofa, and within minutes, they were asleep.

Abbie took out her phone and snapped a couple of pictures, then got her computer out and started looking for electric wheelchairs and a chair made to move in the sand. She was shocked by the price. How do people afford this equipment? She'd place a call to Mr. Walker on Monday and have money transferred to her checking account.

Andy and Kohl were awake and back outside, playing. Alex had sent a text telling Abbie he would be free in the next 30 minutes, and he'd be by to pick up Andy. So, Abbie sat outside with Andy and Kohl while she waited for Alex.

People on the beach stopped to talk to Andy and his dog, and he turned to smile at Abbie. Kohl sat next to Andy and had his head on Andy's lap, and Andy talked to him while gently petting him. Abbie snapped another picture and felt the pictures might be perfect for Andy's room. Tomorrow, she would look for a place to have them blown up and framed so that Andy could feel like he had Kohl with him, even when they were not together. She took photos at the zoo and one while they were sleeping. He would have a collection for his wall.

Alex appeared on the porch way sooner than Abbie was hoping. She hated goodbyes and wanted to put this off if possible. How had she become so attached to these two guys so fast? She offered Alex her shower and dinner, but he declined.

"We need to get on the road, Abbie. It's not far, but it's been an emotional day and not likely to get better."

He took her hand and pulled her out of the chair, and they wrapped their arms around each other.

"Abbie, I can't imagine going more than a day or so without seeing you, and I will bet you that Andy will be crying for Kohl by Monday."

"I'll need your address. I ordered something for Andy and his room and need to have it delivered."

"I will send it to you soon. And thanks for thinking of him, Abbie. Are you going back to work soon?"

"No. I've decided to take two or three months off to research Tom's family. I am still angry with his deception, and Kohl is still avoiding the water. He's a rescue dog. He needs to be in the water to stay sharp and in shape."

"Would it help if the two of you were away from this location? The new house is right on the beach. If Andy goes in, perhaps Kohl would follow Andy."

"That might work, but he's being stubborn. Let's wait a little while, then try. He needs to go in the water because he wants to, not because I am forcing him."

"Andy, we need to get going. Come, give Abbie and Kohl a hug."

"Do we have to, Dad? Can Kohl come with us? He's my best friend. Can't Abbie and Kohl stay at our big house? There's room for them to stay with us."

"Andy, we can't just take Abbie and Kohl. They live here, and Abbie works at the hospital here in town. She can't just leave. We need to get moved in; then they can come to visit."

Abbie hugged Andy.

"Thank you, Andy, for being Kohl's friend. We can't live with you, but we can visit. I am glad you and your dad are my friends as well. Your dad promised to help me with an enormous project, so we will see you soon."

Andy wrapped his arms around Abbie and held on tight. She picked him up to hug him tighter. Abbie felt Andy's tears sliding down her neck. She kissed him on the cheek and told him he was the best friend ever.

Alex took Andy and walked toward the car. Kohl and Abbie followed. Alex settled Andy into his seat, and Kohl jumped in to lick the tears from his face. Abbie ordered Kohl out of the car, but he huffed at her and licked Andy's face until Andy started laughing. Alex pulled Abbie to him again, and both had teary eyes. Finally, he kissed her on the forehead.

"Text me tonight and let me know you made it to the hotel. Are you going to the house tomorrow?"

"I'm going for a couple of hours. After that, I need to check in at the hospital to check my schedule. They promised me most weekends off."

Abbie got Kohl out of the backseat. Alex kissed Abbie again and got in the car before he couldn't walk away. Abbie waved as they drove away, hoping this was not a goodbye forever.

CHAPTER 13

Abbie woke up the following day with Kohl standing over her. She missed this usual routine and was glad he might be getting back to normal. She put on her bathing suit and rash guard, grabbed the paddleboard and coffee, and walked to the beach. Kohl sat beside her while she drank her coffee. She prompted him to play in the water, but he huffed at her, and she told him there would be no huffing. He stared back at her. She shook her head and was determined to work on his behavior.

She finished her coffee while the sun rose and snapped a couple more pictures she might use for Andy's room. After she and Kohl finished their morning routine, she got her computer fired up and began the search for Tom's relatives but kept coming up empty.

She called Mr. Walker's office and left a message with his assistant to transfer funds. She asked his assistant if there were any additional records on Tom. When she heard the word no, she was furious with Tom and was considering a way to spend every single penny of the money to spite him and his ridiculous secrets.

Abbie wondered how long it would take to spend that amount of money and decided she would be dead and gone before she spent every cent. To whom would she leave the money? She needed to start looking at organizations that deserved donations.

Struggling to determine his intent to hide the money, Abbie assumed he wanted to ensure their marriage worked before informing her of his family's background and inheritance. What made her even angrier were the years that passed with no mention of any family history.

Abbie also needed to accept part of the responsibility because she did not ask about his family. When she had searched for a couple of hours with no results, she gave up and turned her attention to finding a wheelchair for Andy.

A search on the internet provided a list of medical supply companies that would deliver. She chose a local company and called the number posted on their website. The owner provided information about the size, battery options, and daily ease of use for a seven-year-old. It needed to be lightweight to lift and store in the car and easy to fold up.

Once they had decided on one that would work, she asked about a motorized beach wheelchair. Abbie imagined Alex would have room in the big house to park both chairs. So, she asked for a big red ribbon on both chairs and a card that read:

"Andy, I hope these chairs give you the freedom to roam the hallways at school and the great sandy beach at your new house. Kohl and I hope to spend time on the beach with you. Love, Kohl and Abbie!"

The next item on her to-do list was to find a local frame shop. She searched and located one four blocks from the house. She and Kohl needed to get out of the house, so they walked to the frame shop and spoke with the owner.

He recognized Kohl and told Abbie he was sorry to hear about Tom's death. Abbie told him she had a friend who moved to a new beach house, and she wanted to give his son pictures of him and Kohl. He helped her pick the best ones and asked about the room's décor. Abbie laughed, saying she did not know about the decor. Finally, they settled on neutral gray frames. The shop owner asked about the delivery, but Abbie said she and Kohl would deliver them in person.

Abbie and Kohl strolled through the streets and did window shopping. They stopped for lunch, then took a walk on the beach, and when they returned to the house, Abbie was restless and missing Alex and Andy. She planned to reach out to Alex later to see if he wanted help unpacking.

Before the end of the day, she wanted to find pet therapy programs at the local hospitals. She was going to broach the subject with Alex to get Andy involved. With him in a wheelchair, the children might be more open and trusting to the pets, especially large dogs such as Kohl. The kids always loved him, and that would give Abbie and Kohl something to do during the day.

Abbie's phone pinged, and she looked at the screen. "Missing you," she read from Alex and replied, "Missing you and Andy as well. Do you want help unpacking?"

"Never turn down help to unpack. I'll call you later."

Abbie's phone pinged again. This time, Sam asked if Abbie wanted to come up for the weekend.

"I'll let you know later this evening. I have a couple of projects in the works. Waiting on a callback."

"Is one project your new friend? The rest of us cannot imagine what Tom did, but we are behind you one hundred percent."

"We will talk soon, and I'll let you know what we are doing this weekend."

Abbie wanted to finish going through Tom's desk. Alex had interrupted the last time she started going through the drawers. So far, she had found nothing else, only pencils, papers, old receipts, and pictures that someone had taken of the three of them on the paddleboards.

It took two hours to open all the drawers, look through everything, shred the old documents, and sort the books remaining on the shelves. She leafed through the pages. About midway through one book, she noticed a folded piece of paper and hesitated before reading it. Why was she feeling guilty for reading Tom's stuff? He had not considered her feelings. If so, he would have told her about his family. She was the only one left, so he could hide nothing from her any longer.

Her phone rang, and Alex's name appeared. She placed the piece of paper on the pile of books and a paperweight on top of it so it would not get lost. She would read it later.

"Hey, Alex. How's your day going?"

"Good. I am trying to get familiar with the new building and staff. Andy is at the home of a doctor who works here. His son is about the same age as Andy, so that gives him someone to hang out with and me a little more time to settle in."

They talked about their day, and Abbie asked again if he needed help unpacking.

"Do you want to help? That is a big job, Abbie."

"I don't mind at all. I'm not sure what to do with all my empty time. We can discuss things over a glass of wine. Kohl would love to see Andy again, and since I will be at the house unpacking, Andy can stay with Kohl."

"If you are sure! It would be best if you didn't think I only want you here to work. I want time to relax with you as well. The truck is supposed to be here in the morning. Andy and I are going to meet them at the house."

"Kohl and I will hit the road early, and when I get there, you can head to the hospital. I'll unpack and make dinner, and you can spend the evening searching through the closets and cupboards to find out where I have put everything, or you can relax on the deck with me and a glass of wine."

"Wow, tough decision, Abbie. Let me figure out what I want to do, and I'll let you know."

"Don't ponder for too long, Montgomery. I may be gone by the time you decide. I'm going to grab a room at the hotel in town."

"Why would you do that? I have six bedrooms! Even Kohl could have his own room if he wants, but I bet we will find him in bed with Andy."

"If you're okay with us staying, I'll bring an air mattress and everything we need. I don't want to put you out, and I don't want Kohl drooling all over your new place."

"The last time I checked, I was a doctor, Abbie, which means I can put up with pretty much anything. A little slobber will not scare me off. And by the way, I remember someone making me sleep in bed with her and a big dog instead of sleeping on the couch. So, you're welcome to sleep in my bed. I'm sure Kohl will be our divider. It will be a tough decision for him, though. You or Andy! Wonder who will win?"

"Got it, Montgomery. Tell Andy we will see him in the morning. Better yet, don't tell him. Let's surprise him. Good night, Alex."

Abbie spent the rest of the evening packing her belongings to take to Alex's house. She would call the frame shop tomorrow and have them deliver the pictures to Alex's address instead of picking them up. Tom's office would have to wait until another day.

Andy was such a great kid. Alex was fortunate. Abbie wanted to be there to see the expression on Andy's face and made a note to check with the wheelchair company. She was hoping they would deliver those while she was at the house. Andy would have much more freedom with these electric chairs, and Kohl could still walk beside him. In addition, the beach chair would allow him to roam the beach and play with friends without struggling to get through the sand.

CHAPTER 14

As promised, Abbie and Kohl arrived early, and Andy opened the door. "Surprise!" Abbie proclaimed. Kohl barked at Andy three times as his greeting. Then, the two of them took off for Andy's bedroom, and Abbie could hear him explaining to Kohl where everything was going and the plans he had for decorating.

Abbie had called a local cleaning company last evening and was thankful she was able to hire cleaning staff at the last minute. She could sort boxes and put stuff away once they cleaned each room. She made coffee and made a list of things that needed completion first. Allowing someone else to clean the house saved her and Alex time.

Once the rooms were clean, Abbie made the beds with freshly laundered linens. Next, she set up the bathrooms with the necessities and moved to the kitchen.

Late last night, she prepared a pan of lasagna, and in a bit, she would put it in the oven. Then, Abbie opened a bottle of red wine to let it breathe, made a salad, garlic bread, and with a couple of last-minute finishing touches, and she would have dinner ready.

Andy and Kohl had been busy the entire day playing and putting toys away in Andy's room. Abbie oversaw the closet and dresser and put a note on her to-do list to have the rods lowered so that Andy could choose clothes by himself and put the clothing away once laundered.

FedEx delivered the frames, but she wanted to wait for Alex before letting him open his gift. Abbie had everything she needed to hang the frames and put that task on tomorrow's list.

Abbie was pleased with the progress they had made today. She broke down the boxes to put in the recycle bin and chuckled when the container was full. She had emptied more boxes than she had realized.

Andy and Kohl napped for a couple of hours, and when they woke up, the three of them decided to go outside to sit on the deck and enjoy the pleasant weather while they waited for Alex to get home and for dinner to be ready.

Andy was so excited about everything in his new room. Abbie asked if he remembered his room out in Denver. Andy said he did not. What he remembered, though, was the accident that took his mother from him.

"Abbie, I was sad when my mom died. It was my fault, Abbie, and I need to apologize to my dad, but I'm not sure how to apologize."

"Andy, that accident was not your fault. Your dad told me what happened, and none of the events leading to the accident had anything to do with you. So, why do you think it was your fault? You were young, Andy. Maybe, you don't remember everything that happened?"

"I remember, Abbie. My mom was searching for Christmas music, and my dad looked at a text on his phone. I saw a dog in the middle of the road and yelled for dad not to hit it. He swerved to miss the dog, and the car spun and fell over the hill. I remember nothing after that, Abbie."

Abbie lifted him from his chair, walked over to the rocker, and placed him on her lap. Andy was teary but not crying. They cuddled in the chair as Abbie talked to him and told him stories of Kohl's rescues and living on the beach.

Abbie heard Alex come in, and she asked him if he wanted her to speak to his dad. Andy nodded yes and sat on her lap and continued to cuddle.

Alex found them on the deck in the rocker, Andy still on Abbie's lap.

"What's happening? Are you two okay?"

"We're okay, Montgomery. We wanted to sit quietly and talk about the things we did today. I have dinner ready. I need to toss the salad; then we can eat."

Alex saw Abbie murmur something to Andy, but Alex did not intrude on their private conversation. Andy nodded his head, and he reached out to Alex. They took their seats at the dining room table, which Abbie had set with good plates and silverware she had found, and lit candles, too.

"Are we eating a fancy dinner, Abbie?"

"Yes, we are, Andy. We are celebrating your fancy new house."

Andy and Abbie both giggled at the same time.

"Wow, this looks great, Abbie." Alex declared as he looked around the house.

"How did you get so much done in one day?"

"I called in a favor at a cleaning company whose owner I took care of in the ER one evening. He said to call him if I ever needed cleaning done. I realized I could get more done if someone else cleaned, and all I had to do was empty boxes and put things away. He had a client cancellation and was happy to send his crew."

"We completed so many tasks today. We made the beds with fresh linens, and Andy put his clothes and toys away. Tomorrow, I will call someone to lower the rods in his closet so he can reach everything from his chair. That will give him more freedom to make his own choices."

"I agree, Abbie, and the place looks great, but I don't want you spending your money. Tell me what you need, and I'll take care of the finances."

"The cleaning was supposed to be a surprise, Montgomery. I am not asking you to pay for something that ruins the surprise. But I have another gift for Andy tonight after dinner. I believe you will both love it."

Alex took her hand and raised it to his lips.

"Thank you for always being so kind, Abbie. That means so much to both of us. Now, can Andy and I dig into this amazing-smelling lasagna before I die of hunger and never get to taste it?"

"Sure, my Montgomery men, go for it."

After dinner, Abbie walked to her car, where she had hidden the pictures that were delivered, and walked back to the living room, where Alex and Andy were impatiently waiting for Abbie.

She sat next to Andy and handed him the first wrapped photo. He ripped the paper from the frame as though it were Christmas morning. Paper was flying everywhere. Kohl sat watching as Andy's eyes got big at the sight of him and Kohl at the zoo. He turned to Abbie.

"That's so cool, Abbie. Are these two gifts also pictures of Kohl and me?"

"I guess you better open them up, Andy."

After every scrap of paper settled on the floor, Andy wrapped his arms around Abbie.

"Thanks, Abbie! I love the pictures. I didn't notice when you took these pictures. Kohl, did you see the pictures of us?"

Kohl let out an excited bark and walked over to Andy. Andy gave him a big hug as well.

"We could hang these in your bedroom, Andy, if that is where you would like them to hand."

"Great. Dad, can you get my chair from the deck, please? Kohl and I need to decide where to hang these."

Alex got his chair and let Andy and Kohl go to his room. He sat beside Abbie and took her hand.

"I love that you are such a kind, generous woman, Abbie. Andy is over the moon. The pictures are amazing. Thank you from both of us."

"Alex, I don't want to ruin the evening by saying this, but you need to talk with Andy about the things that happened on the day of the accident. We were sitting on the deck talking, and out of nowhere, he told me the accident was his fault. I asked him why he felt he was responsible. He said he yelled at you because the dog was in the road and made you swerve the car, which caused the accident. He said he was afraid to tell you but permitted me to talk to you."

Alex dropped Abbie's hand.

"What prompted that, Abbie? What were the two of you discussing?"

"Nothing much. We were sitting on the deck watching the waves, discussing how nice it was to live on the beach. I asked Andy if he remembered how he had his room decorated when you two lived in Denver. He said no. Not over two minutes later, he started telling me things from the accident."

"He was sad and teary-eyed, so I picked him up, and we sat in the rocker together. A tear slid from his cheek and down my neck, but after a moment, he was better, and we rocked in the chair while I told him some of the things Kohl likes to do. That's when you walked in and found us sitting together. I'm sorry, Alex, it must have been my question regarding his room decorations in Denver."

Alex stood up and started pacing across the living room.

"My God, Abbie. What type of father am I not to have noticed how much he must have been suffering? He was young, and I was unsure how much he understood. He missed his mother, but after a while, he didn't ask for her much. Occasionally, he mentioned her or things he remembered us doing together, but he had never said one word about the accident. I'll talk to him right now."

Abbie stood up as well.

"Don't go right now, Alex. He and Kohl are having a wonderful time with the photos. Let him enjoy his time with Kohl. It might be best if Kohl and I left, so you two can have the privacy you need to discuss the accident and his mother."

"Don't go tonight, Abbie. Andy and I will talk this weekend when we have time to relax and not rush through that conversation because I need to leave for work, or he is off to school. So, let's see what those two are up to and see if we can get the photos hung before they go to sleep."

Abbie smiled at Alex.

"No worries, Montgomery. I have everything we need to get that accomplished."

"I'm sure you do. I'm beginning to realize how resourceful you are, and I can never assume what's coming next."

Andy told his dad that he and Kohl had decided where the photos should go. Abbie agreed their ideas were great but suggested they line them up on one wall and make a gallery.

"What's a gallery?"

"A gallery is another name for a wall where you hang photos. We can add other ones whenever we want."

"Andy, I'll look for photos of your mother. Would you like to add those to the wall?"

"Really, Dad? I would love to put her photos up with mine and Kohl's, and I'd like to add photos of you and Abbie, too."

CHAPTER 15

Alex and Abbie sat talking on the deck. Kohl and Andy fell asleep together again. Abbie was yawing, and Alex reached for her hand.

"Let's get you to bed. We exhausted you from doing more than needed, Abbie. Tomorrow, leave the house and relax and enjoy the beach. Andy will be in school, so you'll have the entire day to do something interesting."

"Sam lives not too far from here. Did I mention that, Alex? She works at the physical therapy company associated with Coastal Hospital. But I did not mention that I would be in town, so she'll have questions. A list of questions."

"Oh, knowing that crew, I'm not sure I'm safe when they are around."

"Montgomery, I'll sleep on the air mattress tonight."

"No, Abbie. You are exhausted. You will sleep in the bed tonight, and I'll take the mattress."

Abbie considered the offer and gave in.

"Okay, you won. I am too exhausted to fight about who's sleeping where, but both of us will sleep in the bed. We are adults, Alex, and should be able to sleep in the same vicinity and not have problems."

"There will be no problems from me, Abbie."

Both fell asleep quickly. Abbie woke around 1:00 am, wondering where she was. The room was dark, and she did not know if Kohl was with her. When she rolled over, she met up with another person. Frightened, she suddenly remembered falling asleep at Alex's place, and Kohl was sleeping with Andy. She got up and walked to the kitchen for a glass of water. Returning to bed, Alex reached out for her hand and asked if everything was all right.

"I'm fine. I woke up and I didn't realize where I was, and I couldn't find Kohl."

"Come here," Alex murmured. "I'll keep you safe."

Alex pulled Abbie toward him, and she snuggled up next to him. He kissed her neck, and shivers ran through her entire body. Both laid still for a minute, then Alex reached out to turn her toward him. He brushed her long, curly hair from her face and kissed her. Abbie wrapped her arm around him and sighed. Moving closer, Alex kissed her lovingly, and Abbie enjoyed the feel of his kiss and the comfort of being in his arms.

Abbie realized she'd never had these same feelings with Tom in all these years together. Oh God! What had she been missing, and what was she doing? Abbie wanted to weep. Never had she experienced such sensations! Caught up in the moment, Abbie moaned and wrapped her legs around Alex.

"Abbie, if you want to stop, tell me now."

Abbie kissed him and moaned with pleasure.

"Not in this lifetime, Montgomery!"

Alex and Abbie caught about thirty minutes of sleep before it was time to get Andy up for school. Alex got up, showered, and dressed. Abbie stirred.

"Go back to sleep, Abbie. I'll let Kohl out, fix his food and water, and get Andy to school. Call Sam and have a good day. See you later."

He leaned over and kissed Abbie goodbye.

Kohl crawled onto the bed, but Abbie was too tired to get up and lay there, remembering the night with Alex and smiling. Before she got too involved with Alex, she needed to find the underlying cause of Tom's deception.

Who was he, and why did he not tell her about his family? Indeed, there was a friend somewhere who might recognize him and would help her find more information.

Perhaps, she'd do one of those ancestry tests with his DNA. She would discuss that with Samantha today, and Kate would have suggestions.

She would get a call set up with the rest of the crew and tell them what she had discovered so far. Second on that list was to spill her guts about Alex, but she wasn't quite ready to tell them everything. Third, she and Kohl would also need to return to their own place. Fourth, Andy and Alex needed time to talk about the accident and Andy's memory of what had happened. That would need to be between the two, with no interference from Abbie or Kohl.

Abbie rolled over to see Kohl staring at her.

"Are you missing Andy already, Kohl? Me too! Let's get up and call Sam. We can spend time with her for a while today."

Kohl barked in response, and Abbie reached over and gave him a big hug.

"Time to get this day started."

Abbie got out of bed, showered, sent Sam a text, and made plans to meet around noon at Sam's house. She and Kohl had a couple of hours before meeting Sam, so they went to the beach for a walk. She walked a short distance into the water, but Kohl still refused to get in. All her efforts to coax him to get wet or play ball failed.

She gave up, and they continued up the coast. She threw the ball, and Kohl would chase it and bring it back to her. People they passed during their walk stopped Abbie to ask Kohl's breed, which always led to additional questions. She gladly answered their questions. It was time to head over to Sam's, so they returned to Alex's house, and she gathered her purse and snacks for Kohl and got into the car.

Sam saw them pull into the driveway and met them outside. Kohl trotted to her, and Sam hugged him and Abbie.

"I figured it would be easier for us to talk here than at a restaurant, so I made our lunch. It's nice today, so let's eat on the patio. What do you think, Abbie?"

"That is perfect. I would have stopped on the way over and brought something, though. Why didn't you give me a call, Sam?"

"My treat today!"

Sam reached into the fridge for the food she had prepared. She had laid out the patio table with plates and silverware, and they filled their plates while Kohl settled on the patio in the shade to take a nap.

"What are you doing in Myrtle Beach, Abbie? I assumed you were busy trying to tie up Tom's estate."

"Everything has gotten complicated, Sam. I'm not sure where to start."

Sam looked at Abbie and realized there would be more to this story than Abbie was letting on.

"Spit it out, Abbie. There is no judgment for anything the five of us do. If you are in trouble, we are always here for you."

"I'm not in trouble, Sam. I discovered Tom was wealthy and had been hiding information from me."

"How wealthy are we talking, Abbie? Your emphasis on the word wealthy makes me guess it must be significant."

"The word significant does not even touch it. When Tom's attorney handed me the paperwork to read, I choked on my water. I was close to having a panic attack. There were all these zeros, Sam. I've never seen so many zeros in someone's bank account as were in that document. I was so angry with Tom for not telling me. And not that I cared about the money, but that he was hiding things from me. Who was I married to, Sam? Who was this guy that I assumed was my best friend?"

Sam took Abbie's hand.

"What do you need from us, Abbie? We are always here for you."

"There's more, Sam."

Sam raised her eyebrows, and Abbie continued.

"Don't be angry, but I called Alex Montgomery. I had lunch with him three hours before when this news broke that day, and I panicked. I was embarrassed to call you and the others. Here I was, the wife of a fake who had lied to me and all of you. I wanted someone to talk to who wasn't friends with Tom or me and hoped he would not judge me." Abbie laughed before continuing.

"He asked me if I was drunk or had been taking drugs and how much I had to drink. I asked him to come over to the house. We sat on the sofa and talked. Then we had wine. Well, I had more of the wine than he did, and Alex watched me act like a crazy person who did not know what she was doing."

"Days after I buried my husband, I found out he had lied to me about who he was, and I did not know he was fooling me all these years. So now, here I sit, a new billionaire widow, two weeks after I buried my lying husband, falling in love with another man."

Sam stopped her fork midway to her mouth and set it down.

"Abbie, did I hear you say billionaire and falling in love with another man in the same sentence? We have more to discuss, Abbie. I bet it's the stress of everything that has happened. How did you meet someone, and what makes you assume you are falling in love? And what amount of money are we talking about, Abbie? I have so many questions. I'm unsure where to start."

Abbie took a drink of water and looked over at Sam.

"Hundreds, Sam. Hundreds of billions. Who has that kind of money? Alex and I have talked and decided I need to ignore the whole money thing for a while. I spent money buying Andy a couple of new electric wheelchairs. One for everyday use and a specialty one for the beach, but that's all I have bought for now."

"Abbie, you need to back up a bit. "Who is Alex? and—Dear God, Abbie!" Are you talking about Dr. Alex Montgomery? And who is Andy?"

Sam stood up.

"I'll be right back. I've got to get my phone. I can't take all this in by myself. We need to call the others."

Sam sent a 911 request to the other ladies of the crew and returned with her phone. Abbie heard everyone already talking over each other. What a joy this is going to be!

Abbie considered getting up and walking out on all the craziness her life had become in such a brief time, but she took another sip of water and braced herself for the onslaught. The next half hour involved Abbie trying to answer all the questions they threw at her. She barely had time to answer before Sam asked the next one.

"So, what's next, Abbie? What are your plans?"

"I have no plans, but I have ideas. I've investigated Kohl becoming a therapy dog, but he will not get back into the water. He won't even put his feet in it. He runs away from the waves if the water gets close to his paws."

"Abbie, have you considered training him to become a water therapy dog? I'm not talking about him taking water therapy. However, he may need a dog whisperer to help him overcome his fear, but a dog that helps others during their water therapy."

"Where do you come up with this stuff, Sam?"

Sam rolled her eyes, and Abbie tried not to laugh.

"Julie, let me remind you, I'm a therapist. Part of my responsibility is to look for new therapy options like you and your colleagues look for new findings in pediatrics. I remember reading something in a professional journal. I'm going to do more research, Abbie. Then, we might be able to work with Kohl. He loves kids, which might also help him deal with losing Tom."

"Thank you all for wanting to help, but I don't believe there is any quick answer to getting Kohl back in the water. I'll try to find a pool owned by someone who will permit us to go in the water, but who wants a human size pile of fur swimming in their pool?"

Kate spoke up next.

"Let's forget about Kohl for a moment and get back to Abbie. Where are you staying while you are in Myrtle Beach, Abbie? Is there a pool at the hotel where you are staying? Perhaps, they will let you use their pool?"

"I'm staying with Alex – he doesn't have a pool. I'm sure he would let us use it if he did."

There was dead silence on the phone. Sam stared at her with her mouth hanging open.

"Oh, Abbie," Dana said. "This is worse than we imagined. Was this thing with Alex going on before Tom died? How were you able to hide this from all of us?"

Abbie was furious at the accusation.

"Listen up, Dana, and the rest of you, too. Nothing was going on with Montgomery before Tom's death. I've told you what prompted me to call him that night instead of all of you. Don't any of you feel betrayed by what Tom did? In all honesty, can you tell me you expected something like this from him because if you tell me yes, you have not been honest with me for years?"

No one spoke up.

"I'm waiting for an answer from every one of you."

Abbie's raised voice alerted Kohl, and he jumped up from his nap and walked over to Abbie.

"Everything is okay, Kohl."

Abbie laid Kohl's head on her lap and stroked his head to help keep him calm.

"Abbie, none of us suspected anything like this from Tom. All of this has shocked us, but we need to figure out what we do next."

"I don't have a clue what's next, Julie. I'm staying with Alex again tonight and going home tomorrow. Alex needs time alone with Andy this weekend. I offered to help them settle in at the new house, but they need to get used to it without Kohl and me. Andy and Kohl are inseparable. And we all need space to manage the suddenness of this new relationship."

They acknowledged as a group that Abbie and Kohl going home was the right idea and agreed to a group call the following week.

Sam got up and hugged Abbie.

"I'm sorry all this is going on. But I want you to understand that we are all fine if you are ready for a relationship with Alex. He must assume we don't like him, but we will follow your lead on this and get to know him if that is what you want."

"We will figure this out, but for now, be patient and let me get through all the muck that has settled on me. I am heading back to the beach to tempt Kohl again with the water. After that, I'm having dinner with the Montgomery men and going home tomorrow."

Abbie and Kohl took their walk, then waited on the deck for Alex and Andy to get home. She chose burgers on the grill and fries for dinner. Andy loved burgers, and Abbie had made toppings for him to choose from. Andy and Kohl headed outside to play as soon as they got home.

Alex came home, entered the kitchen, and made a beeline for Abbie. He wrapped his arms around her, picked her up, and sat her on the kitchen counter. She wrapped her arms and legs around him. He kissed her neck, crossed her jawline, and devoured her lips. He reached under her shirt and ran his thumbs over her breast. Abbie groaned and leaned into his hands. Abbie realized Kohl and Andy had returned to the house and moved Alex's hands to her waist. Now, it was his turn to groan. He kissed her again.

"I'll see you tonight, Ms. Foster."

Abbie grinned and kissed him back.

"All of me?"

"Yes," he replied. "Every single inch!"

Abbie jumped down from the counter before Andy saw her.

"You better keep that promise, Montgomery."

When dinner was over, Abbie and Alex played board games with Andy. After the games, Alex helped Andy with his shower and tucked him and Kohl into bed.

Alex leaned against his bedroom door and called Abbie. She smiled, got up, turned off the lights in the house, and joined him in the bedroom. Abbie locked the door behind her and nonchalantly stripped her clothes off on her walk across the room.

She had not felt this sexy in a long time. One look from Alex had heat coursing to her core. She wasn't sure how this had happened, but she would not pass on this opportunity. Alex picked her up again and deposited her on the bed. As promised, he explored and kissed every inch of her body, and Abbie returned the favor.

"Abbie, I don't understand why any of this is happening to us, but I am overwhelmed by the feelings I have when I am with you."

Abbie kissed him passionately and rolled on top of him.

"Let's see if I can overwhelm you with this, Montgomery."

They slept less than they had the night before. But since it was Saturday and Andy would sleep in, they showered together, dressed, made coffee, and made plans for the following week.

Abbie sipped her coffee while Alex made pancakes.

Kohl sauntered out of the bedroom. Andy was close on his heels. She let Kohl out and asked Andy about his classmates.

"They are nicer than the ones at my other school, Abbie. They don't tease me because I'm in a wheelchair. I told them I was in an accident, and they asked me questions about it. I told them my mother had died in the accident and that I miss her. I told them about you, too – Abbie and Kohl. They all want to meet Kohl. They say it's cool that he can pull people out of the water and pull a whole boat of people, too. Can we take him to school one day, Abbie?"

"I can call the school and talk to the principal. Do you have a show-and-tell day at school? If so, I can help you put pictures together and show them to everyone, and they can also meet Kohl."

"That would be great, Abbie. I will ask my teacher next week, and I'll ask dad to call you when I have an answer." Abbie hugged him.

"That sounds like a great idea, Andy! Kohl would love to go to school and show off for you."

Abbie started gathering her and Kohl's belongings.

"Abbie, where are you going?" Andy asked.

"Kohl and I are going to our own house for a couple of days. You and your dad need to spend time at your house with only the two of you, and I need to take care of things at home."

"But this can be your home, Abbie, and Kohl's, too. Dad, tell them they don't need to leave."

Alex got up and walked over to Andy.

"Andy," he said. Abbie and Kohl have their own house. I love having them here as much as you do, but they still need to go to their own house and take care of things there. We will see them again soon." Alex reminded him. Andy pouted.

"That's not fair. Kohl and I are best friends. He enjoys being with me. He sleeps with me and keeps me safe. I don't want him to go home."

"Andrew!" Andy felt he was about to get into trouble with his dad.

"This is not up for discussion. Abbie and Kohl are leaving, and if you don't want me to send you to your room before they leave, stop the pouting, and hug them."

Andy did as he was told, excused himself, and went to his room.

Alex walked Abbie and Kohl to the car. He kissed Abbie goodbye and opened the door for Kohl. Kohl got in, huffed at Alex, laid down on the seat, and turned his back to him.

"Looks like they are both mad at me."

"They will both get over it, Montgomery." Abbie kissed him again, started the car, and drove home.

CHAPTER 16

Abbie grabbed the mail on the way into the house and moved from room to room, opening the windows to bring in the fresh air. She considered Sam's suggestion on the drive from Myrtle Beach. *I wonder if using a pool might be the way to get Kohl back into the water.* She'd do research today and make notes on water therapy. Kohl loved people, and she was not letting him back in the water with the coast guard crew. Tom was his partner and trainer, and with Tom gone, it left Kohl alone. If she could train him for therapy, he would do an excellent job. He loved children and adding them to the equation would be perfect for Kohl.

Abbie poured a cup of coffee, grabbed her computer and a notepad from her office, called Kohl to follow her, and they got comfortable on the porch, so she could research water therapy.

She read article after article, and the more she read, the more intrigued she became. Her hand was flying over the notepad as she wrote ideas she wanted to run by Sam. Water therapy was excellent for adults and helpful for autistic children, senior adults, and animals, such as dogs and horses. However, she had not stopped considering the wide-ranging benefits available to such a diverse group of people and animals.

Abbie grabbed her phone and called Sam.

"Hey, Sam! I've been researching hydrotherapy this morning, and you might be onto something. Is there any place nearby with a baby pool that might let me use it to get Kohl into the water? Kohl might not be as afraid of the water in a baby pool. Any thoughts?"

"Hey Abbie, school is in, which means the neighborhood pools are not being used as often. So, you may convince one of them to let you try. I am going to stay here tonight to catch up on the paperwork. I don't have a baby pool, but we have one that has a gradual slope. That's what you need. The problem is, you will need to make another trip up here when you just made that drive this morning."

"That is not a problem, Sam. It's less than two hours. Besides, what else do I have to do? Kohl has enough room to stretch out in the SUV, so he couldn't care less. Are you sure you will not get in trouble for letting us try?"

"Nobody else will be around, Abbie. My last appointment is at 3:00 pm and should only take forty-five minutes to an hour. After that, it is fine with me."

"That's perfect. See you later this afternoon, and remember, dinner is on us."

"Great, Abbie! Can't wait to see you two again."

Abbie made hotel reservations and packed a couple of days' worth of clothes and Kohl's water gear. They'd leave after lunch, but she wanted to continue her research. A plan was coming together in her head, and she wanted it down on paper before she forgot the details.

Abbie and Kohl pulled up in front of Sam's therapy building. It was not yet four o'clock, so the two left to take a walk and wait until Sam's last appointment left.

As usual, they stopped along their walk to answer questions on Kohl's breed and let people pet him. When Abbie noticed

Sam's last appointment leaving the building, she and Kohl said goodbye to the people admiring Kohl and walked over to the pool building. They entered the pool room and called out to Sam. She came out to greet them, and Kohl made a beeline for her.

After hugging Abbie, she said, "Let me try with him first, Abbie. He's so used to you and Tom and the water, which might be part of his hesitancy."

"Go for it, Sam. He might cooperate if we can make it look like we didn't have this plan. I put my suit under my clothes before we left the house. If he goes in with you, then I will get in, too. I brought his ball to make it a game for him. He loves to chase the ball in the water. I'll try whatever it takes, and I have a ton of questions for you at dinner tonight."

Abbie tossed Kohl's ball to Sam.

"Hey Kohl, want to play ball?"

Kohl looked at Sam and wagged his tail, and she threw the ball in the far corner of the room, and Kohl chased it and brought it back to her. She and Abbie wanted to keep this first session laid back so that Kohl did not suspect that he was being forced into the water. They discussed the therapy department and how the rest of their crew was doing as she continued to throw the ball for Kohl.

She moved to the front of the pool, but this time when he brought the ball back to her, she dropped it, and it rolled into the water.

"Awe, shucks, Kohl. I dropped the ball."

Sam paused for fifteen seconds, then said.

"Hey, Kohl, can you get the ball for me?"

Kohl looked around and spotted the ball in the water. He looked over at Sam and hesitated.

"Go ahead, Kohl, get the ball."

Sam and Abbie talked while watching his movements. He took a couple of steps, then bent over to sniff the water.

Sam said to Abbie, "He should only smell chlorine. Today's appointments have been standard therapy, so nobody has been in the pool."

Kohl stood and looked at the ball floating in the water. Abbie watched him look toward her, so she turned and looked out the window. This was Sam's turn to interact with him, and she did not want Kohl to think he had to wait for a command from her.

Abbie stood with her back to him and heard Sam ask him again to get the ball for her. Abbie turned her head and watched Kohl take another few hesitant steps. Finally, the ball was right at the edge of the water, and he snatched it up with his teeth, turned to Sam, and trotted out of the water. Sam continued to throw every third or fourth ball into the water so that Kohl needed to enter the water to retrieve the ball.

Abbie removed her outer clothing, put on her rash guard, and entered the pool. Kohl watched her wade out to the middle of the pool. The pool's depth was only four feet, so Abbie stood there and continued to watch Kohl and Sam play ball. Then, she swam back and forth across the pool and noticed Kohl watching her.

Kohl took a break from chasing the ball. Sam filled his water bowl. Abbie smiled, swam toward him, and sat at the water's edge. She reached out to him and tried to coax him into the water, but he didn't move. Abbie was not concerned. He had made more progress today than they had done since the accident.

Kohl took a long drink from his bowl. He sat at the water's edge. Abbie had his ball now and tossed it back to him. He caught it but refused to swim back to her to drop it. Instead, he released it into the water and used his nose to push it toward Abbie. Abbie praised him for trying to return the ball. Small steps were what she was expecting, and she refused to push him to do more. Abbie exited the water and dried off with her towel. She grabbed a microfiber cloth out of the bag to wipe the water from Kohl and hoped they would make more progress the next day.

Abbie and Sam agreed on the restaurant for dinner, and Kohl followed Abbie to the car. She loaded their equipment and headed toward the hotel. Kohl napped at the hotel while Abbie showered and dressed for dinner. She did more research on hydrotherapy programs and looked for apartments that allowed dogs. If they were going to spend time up here working with Sam, it would be nice to have their things and not have to keep packing and unpacking their equipment.

Abbie looked at her watch. She had not heard from Alex since leaving his house this morning. He often sent her a text during the day. So, it must be a busy day for him. She reflected on a typical Friday in her ER, remembering that they could be quiet or non-stop the entire day.

Abbie did not miss working every day. She missed seeing Dana every day, but she had been working since she turned sixteen and was enjoying this unexpected break. Now that Tom had left her the trust fund, working was a choice, but she felt she was too young to sit around and do nothing. Once she got Kohl back on his feet and found someone who could care for him while she worked, she might consider getting back on the schedule.

As she was scrolling through the list of apartments, her phone pinged with a text message from Alex.

"Hope your day is going well. Busy here. Missing you. Talk later?"

"Miss you, too. Thinking about last night. Kohl and I are in NMB. I spent time with Sam in the therapy pool today. Kohl made progress and got his paws wet. Woo-hoo! Sending our love to Andy. Later is good with me, too."

"LOL! Last night is the reason I'm so distracted today. If everyone is lucky, they may survive."

"Great, Montgomery. Get it together. What are you? Thirteen? LOL!"

"I'm all sorts of things since I met you. Just trying to figure it out."

Her phone pinged again, but it was Sam. "Leaving now. Be there soon."

"Leaving as well."

Sam chose a restaurant on the inner coastal waterway within walking distance of the hotel. Abbie picked an outdoor table and ordered drinks and appetizers while she waited for Sam.

Sam arrived, and they ordered and settled back to enjoy their drink. Abbie approached Sam with her idea.

"Sam, I've been reading up on the hydrotherapy you mentioned the other day. Can you tell me where I might need to take Kohl to get him certified? Or is there such a thing as therapy dogs?"

"What role do you imagine he might play in the therapy, Abbie? There are diverse types of therapy, so we need to figure out where to start."

"Well, since he is such an excellent swimmer and trained in rescue techniques, I imagined him assisting children in the pool. They make a vest that the dog wears, and the children wear a vest as well, and they can hold the handles on his vest and learn to move their little legs. From what I've read, the water gives them more freedom to move and experience less pain and provides a better range of motion to their joints. Another article discussed how dogs could work with autistic children and teach them to swim. Older adults can improve their range of motion as well. Is it possible for Kohl to do this work, Sam?"

Sam laughed in response to Abbie's questions.

"Kohl can do whatever we teach him to do, Abbie. He has made incredible rescues over the years. I don't know if any of us realize what he can do. The question is, where do we locate a pool for this therapy you envision?"

Abbie laughed at Sam's question.

"I do not know. I was hoping you had something in mind. Could we work to put a proposal together and present it to the hospital board? If I can get Montgomery on board, he can also talk to other physicians. I'll do the research and put together a list of risks. We can do this list of benefits together since that is where your ability lies."

"I'll make phone calls to other facilities. I'll start with a list I can find on the internet. We can tag Dana, Julie, and Kate. As Julie's skill is children, she should know about pediatric therapy. Kate can be our research guru. She is always at the forefront of new meds, technology, and whatever else those brains she spends time with can conjure up out of nowhere. When I talk to him, I'll run it by Alex tonight and get his opinion from a physician's view."

"That's a good place to start, and since you are the one who is not working right now, you can do the typing and setting up meetings and such. So, between that and the certifications Kohl might need to work on, that should keep the two of you busy while we figure this out."

Alex called just after Abbie and Kohl got back to the hotel.

"Hi, Montgomery. How are you? Did your patients survive despite your teenage brain?"

"Listen, Ms. Foster. Get in the car and come over here, and I will show you I am not a teenager with teenage thoughts or actions. And by the way, why are you at a hotel and not over here?"

"I wanted to give you and Andy the time and space to talk about the accident and his mother without Kohl and me interfering. And it was obvious, you were not happy with his reaction when we left last night. So, it might be good for everyone if we stayed at our place, at least for a day or two."

"When I called Sam earlier today, she offered her therapy pool to tempt Kohl into the water, so I booked a hotel for a couple of days. Andy is getting attached to Kohl, and I want to ensure he knows his boundaries. He needs to remember we are still two separate families, Alex. He's too young to understand the complexity of our sudden friendship or the grief Kohl and I are both working through, but we need to make sure we do that for him. If our relationship doesn't work out, he will be sad and need to grieve another loss. I can't and won't do that to him."

Abbie heard Alex sigh.

"I agree with what you are saying, Abbie. The same thing has been on my mind as well. We just fell into this relationship, and I don't want this to end either, but both of us are aware we need time to learn more details about one another, and we both need to make it through this grieving business, or this will never last."

"I am considering getting an apartment up here, Montgomery. If I do, you and Andy can visit us, which might help him understand that we still need separation in our lives, but we don't have that two-hour drive between us if we decide to do something together. Does that make sense?"

"Complete sense, Abbie. Are you selling the beach house?"

"No, Montgomery! Remember those zeros? Well, they keep growing, so I need to spend money. I feel like a fraud. Every day, I worry that someone will take me to jail for stealing money I didn't know existed."

"At least you have bail money, Abbie, and you need to relax. Nobody is going to come along and take it from you. But it might be nice to find out who the money maker was in the family."

Abbie mentioned the therapy program to Alex and asked his thoughts on how to write the proposal. He gave her sound advice and thoughts on how to put the budget together. Before they hung up, Alex had a question.

"Are you close enough to sneak out in the middle of the night and come over here? My bed is so empty without you." Alex sighed.

"Oh, Montgomery. Could you not tempt me? I am close enough to do that, but we agreed that's not what we need right now."

Alex agreed but still wanted her by his side.

CHAPTER 17

Alex asked the mothers on his staff where the best shopping places were, and two mothers with young sons quickly gave him the best spots. The following day, he and Andy left early to stop for breakfast. As they pulled into the restaurant's parking lot, Andy spotted Kohl and Abbie surrounded by a group of people waiting outside for tables.

"Dad, look. There's Abbie and Kohl. Are we having breakfast with them? Did you and Abbie plan this for a surprise?"

Alex smiled and shook his head at the same time.

"No, Andy, I did not plan this as a surprise. Abbie and Kohl are going to be surprised to see us."

Alex helped Andy out of the car, and Andy started calling for Kohl. Abbie heard someone call Kohl's name. Kohl's head whipped around, he barked and took off across the parking lot. Abbie ran to keep up with him when she spotted Andy and Alex.

Kohl met Andy's chair, and Andy threw his arms around him. Kohl started licking Andy's face, which caused Andy to laugh uncontrollably. His laugh was so contagious; the crowd was laughing too. Alex wrapped Abbie in a hug.

"I'm sorry, Abbie. We did not mean to interrupt your breakfast this morning. Andy spotted Kohl as soon as we were pulling into the lot."

Abbie laughed again.

"No worries, Montgomery. We had no plans. We went out for a walk this morning and stopped here. Of course, we got caught up with the crowd. Our table should be up soon. You should join us."

Alex shook his head.

"No, Abbie! This is your weekend away from us. We will get our own table."

Abbie tilted her head.

"Montgomery, you better be prepared to separate the two of them because I'm not taking the blame for that one."

Alex looked around and shook his head again.

"Nope, I'm not going there either."

The hostess called for Foster, a party of four, and Andy clapped and let out a whoop.

"When did you tell them that there were four of us?" Alex asked.

"I didn't, Montgomery, but even a blind person can tell there's no separating the two of them this morning."

They sat at an outdoor table and placed their orders. Abbie ordered two pancakes without butter and syrup so Andy could give Kohl a treat. It was rare that Kohl got people's food, but the occasional pancake from a seven-year-old wouldn't hurt him.

Abbie asked Andy what his plans were for the day. Andy filled her in on the plans and asked Abbie to join them on their shopping trip, but she declined. She told him she was looking for a house or an apartment for her and Kohl and that she had appointments to look at a couple of places. Andy got confused.

"Why are you doing that, Abbie? Dad and I have six bedrooms, and you've been staying with us. Are you leaving us, Abbie?"

Abbie felt like her heart was breaking.

"No, Andy. I am not leaving anyone. Kohl and I need our own place for a while. Also, instead of driving up from the beach every time we want to do things together, I want to find something closer."

Abbie looked at Alex for his okay to continue explaining to Andy why she was getting her own place.

"Andy, your dad and I have not known each other long, and it's best if adults take things slow and get to know each other very well before they live in the same house. I was helping your dad, and you move. Your dad had done me a favor, and I was doing one for him. He said it was okay if Kohl and I spent a few nights at your place instead of driving back home when we were so tired from unpacking. But now that unpacking is done, you and your dad need to get used to your new house alone."

Andy's eyes got teary.

"Are you mad at us, Abbie? I don't understand."

Alex started to intervene, and Abbie stopped him.

"No, Andy. I am not mad at you. Can you remember when your mom died, and you were sad?"

Andy nodded his head.

"Well, my husband Tom died, and I have been sad, Andy. But spending time with you and your dad has helped me not to be so sad anymore. I love being with you and your dad, and so does Kohl. But I need to learn how to live independently, the same as you and your dad needed. It's okay for us to spend time with you, but we can't stay every day."

Abbie reached for his hand.

"I know this is difficult for you to understand, but I promise you, you will still be able to spend time with us, and Kohl will get to spend time with you. I know it's not what you want, but do you understand that we can make that work for now?"

Andy nodded, and Abbie bent over and kissed his cheek as the server brought their food.

"Hum, look at that. Someone sent pancakes for Kohl. Can you help him with those, Andy? He will scarf them like a little piggy if I hand him the plate."

Andy laughed and cut up Kohl's pancakes. Alex took Abbie's hand under the table.

"Thank you! He and I still have things to discuss, but this helps. I did not want the responsibility to fall on you, Abbie."

Alex squeezed her hand.

"Happy to help, Montgomery."

They finished their breakfast, and Andy hugged Abbie.

"Thanks for letting me feed Kohl, Abbie. That was fun."

"You are very welcome, Andy. I bet Kohl had fun, too." Alex hugged Abbie and kissed her on the cheek.

"We are going to get our shopping done, and I will check in with you later."

Abbie kissed him on the lips and smiled at him. How was she going to stay away from him?

"We should find a sitter for Andy and Kohl and spend quality time together."

Alex smiled back at her.

"I know exactly what I want to do when we are together."

Abbie laughed.

"I bet you do, Montgomery. I bet you do."

Abbie and Kohl met the realtor. The realtor wanted her to view two small places on the beach. One was for sale, and the other was being offered on a monthly lease.

It was rare for a beach house to come on the market, and it was usually condominiums that were for sale. Abbie was looking for a place with a ground floor with access to a backyard, making it easy to let Kohl out and for Andy and Kohl to play.

She settled on the rental, which was renovated and airy. With three bedrooms and two baths, it would be perfect if Andy wanted to spend the night. There was also storage space, which meant she could bring the paddle boards if Kohl ever got back in the water. She signed the rental contract and planned to move in tomorrow, but they needed another trip to their house to pick up supplies and mail. So, she logged into the USPS website and set up a mail forward to decrease the trips to Charleston and send her mail to the rental, but they had everything they needed for the next few days.

Sam was waiting for them when they arrived back at the pool, and they started playing ball with Kohl. He ventured further into the water, which made Abbie happy about the direction they were going.

Abbie told Sam about the new rental while they played ball with Kohl. There was a call with the rest of the crew later this week, and they needed to plan a girls' weekend at the new place.

Abbie heard her phone ping with a message and got out of the pool to look at her message. It was a message confirming the delivery of the new wheelchairs she had ordered for Andy.

Abbie was eager to see how he liked them and to watch him roll along the beach with newfound freedom. The beach chair had wheels that reminded her of the wheels on the monster trucks Tom watched on TV. The size helped to keep the chair from sinking into the sand. Abbie wondered if she should have gotten permission from Alex, but she wanted to surprise them both. Abbie told Sam about the chairs she had bought Andy.

"Wow, Abbie. That's an expensive gift. Those chairs cost thousands of dollars. Do you expect Alex to be okay with you spending thousands of dollars on his son?"

"Why not, Sam! Alex said he'd help me with the money. It is sitting out there, multiplying as we speak. I've got to spend it and spending it on Andy makes me happy."

Sam shook her head.

"But don't you think you should have asked? That's an extravagant gift, Abbie. He might not see things the way you do."

"Do you think he'll be upset, Sam? If I donated a hundred chairs to the children in your therapy program – that might be extravagant. But one chair? You are overreacting."

"Okay, Abbie. But I hope I don't have to say I told you so."

Abbie and Sam worked with Kohl for another thirty minutes. Then, on their way home, they stopped to grab takeout food and headed back to the hotel. Alex sent her a text after they went back to the hotel.

"Can you come over to the house? Andy got his gifts from you."

"Sure," Abbie replied. "I'm finishing dinner. I will be over soon."

Abbie arrived at Alex's house thirty minutes later. When she walked in, the tension in the air was thick. Andy looked teary-eyed, and Alex looked angry. Abbie looked from one to the other.

"What's going on, Montgomery?"

Andy answered first.

"Dad says I can't keep the chairs, Abbie, but I love them. Kohl and I will have so much fun. The one chair has the same tires as the monster trucks I watch. Dad's angry, Abbie, and I don't understand why?"

Alex spoke up next.

"He's correct, Abbie. I am angry. These chairs cost thousands of dollars. You can't buy him gifts in this price range without asking first. I told him we cannot accept them, and he is upset."

Abbie looked from one to the other.

"Andy, can you take Kohl outside and play ball while your dad and I discuss this issue?"

"Can I go play, Dad?"

"Yes, Andy. You and Kohl can play in the backyard, but don't go elsewhere."

Alex and Abbie both watched as the pair went out the door. Abbie turned to Alex.

"I don't understand, Montgomery. Why can't he have the chairs? And I didn't ask you because they were to be a surprise."

Alex took a moment before answering.

"Abbie, I said they were too expensive, which is why."

"Really, Montgomery? You promised to help me with the zeros. This is helping me. There's so much freaking money. I need to spend it, or it will grow, grow, and grow."

They stared at one another.

"What's the price of freedom, Montgomery?"

"What are you talking about, Abbie?"

"I asked, what's the price of freedom?"

"How would I know, Abbie? And what does that have to do with any of this?"

"Because Montgomery, those two chairs give Andy the freedom to move around his environment much better than he can now. The beach chair with its monster wheels – as Andy calls them – gives him the freedom to move on the beach without sinking into the sand. He can play with Kohl and his friends. The electric wheelchair means he and Kohl can go ahead of us when we are at the zoo. We don't always need to be on top of him. So, the few thousand dollars I spend out of the billions lying in my bank account are the price of his freedom, Montgomery. And know this! I would spend every cent if it brought him the ability to stand and walk again. I love your son, Montgomery, more than every freaking penny in that account, and I thought I was doing something good for him, but obviously, I was wrong. If you don't want them, give them away. Perhaps, I've been wrong about other things, too, Montgomery, starting with us. We need a break. This was moving way too fast, anyhow. I'm going to my car. I'll get my dog on the way out."

"Abbie, wait. Can't we at least discuss this like two adults?"

Abbie put her hand up to stop him from talking.

"I can't do this, Montgomery."

And Abbie walked out the door. She gave Andy a big hug, told him she loved him and would visit him soon, loaded Kohl into the car, and drove away.

Andy came back into the house, tears streaming down his face.

"Where's Abbie going, Dad?"

Alex chose his words carefully before answering.

"She's angry with me, Andy. Abbie wants a break from me. Not you! Abbie loves you, Andy, and so does Kohl. She said we are moving too fast in our relationship, and she is grieving for her husband. And she is right when she said we are moving too fast."

Andy raised his voice, which he seldom did.

"You are both wrong. She loves us both. We bought this house for her to marry us and have sisters and brothers. How can you just let her leave, Dad? Do you think she will come back? Can I still see her and Kohl? Can't you go after her? Go tell her you're sorry, Dad. I want her to come back to us."

Andy was sobbing. Alex picked him up, walked out onto the deck, and sat on the rocking chair. They both cried for a long time.

Andy fell asleep in Alex's arms, but Alex held on. He felt as if he had lost everything again. They sat together for a long time. Alex stood up, locked the deck door behind him, and put Andy in bed with him.

Tomorrow, he'd find a way to fix the mess he had caused. Abbie was right. She was giving Andy something he hadn't had for a long time. And he had just ruined everything.

CHAPTER 18

Alex and Andy both woke up the next morning, tired and weary from a restless sleep. Finally, Alex gave in and let Andy have the wheelchairs. Abbie's intentions were honest, and the chair allowed Andy to move about his surroundings. However, if he gave in to Andy, it did not mean he was not angry with her. She had overstepped her boundaries by not asking him first, but punishing Andy for his anger with her was not the right thing to do.

Alex plugged the wheelchairs into the electrical outlets for charging before making breakfast. By the time he helped Andy shower, hang the curtains in his room, and put up the shelves and other decorations they bought yesterday, the chairs would be charged. Then, he would ask Andy about a ride when lunch was finished.

Andy helped Alex grill hamburgers with the new grill, and Alex used the new air fryer to make French fries. Abbie would not consider this a healthy lunch, but today, since it was just the two of them, they were eating burgers and fries. When lunch was finished and the dishes cleaned up, Alex asked Andy if they should try the beach chair.

"I thought we weren't keeping the chairs, Dad? What made you change your mind?"

"I thought about the chairs last night, Andy, and decided that Abbie was thinking of the freedom the chairs would give you if she bought electric chairs. I was angry because she did not ask me first, but she was right. The electric chairs will offer more freedom to move around at school and at home. "

"I plugged the beach chair in' this morning, and it's charged and ready to go. What do you say? Should we give this monster chair a go?"

Andy let out a resounding whoop. They reviewed the instructions aloud to make sure Andy understood the safety information. He repeated the instructions three times to drive home the concept of being safe when riding. He did not want Andy or anyone else to sustain an injury and told him with practice, his comfort level maneuvering the chair and his knowledge of how the chair responded and moved would improve.

They made their way to the beach, and Alex walked beside Andy's chair to help correct Andy's direction if needed. Andy appeared timid at first, and the chair moved slowly. Alex reached over and showed him how to increase the speed by placing his hand over Andy's. They smiled at each other, and Alex hoped his first reaction to Abbie's gift had not caused too much more damage to Andy's emotional status.

It was low tide, so Alex led Andy to the solid sand. Few people were on the beach this afternoon, so Andy had room to practice with the wheelchair.

"Okay, buddy, give it a go!"

Andy nodded and pushed the control stick forward. The chair started forward at a slow pace, and he laughed.

"This is fun, Dad. I wish Abbie and Kohl were here to see how great the chair works in the sand. Kohl would be walking right beside me, Dad. He would love racing me down the beach."

"Yes, Andy. Kohl would have a blast with you, and Abbie would smile from ear to ear."

Alex reached for the phone and took pictures. He needed to call Abbie this evening and apologize to her for his reaction.

"Dad, look. The chair can go in circles. This chair is awesome!"

Alex was having as much fun as Andy.

"It sure is, Andy."

Abbie woke up hours ago. The rental owner gave her keys to the house, so she checked out of the hotel and moved everything to the house. After a quick trip to the store for groceries and supplies, the house was ready. After she argued with Alex, Abbie remained restless and tried to read a couple of chapters in a book, which frequently put her to sleep, but it was futile.

Abbie got out of bed and took Kohl for a walk on the beach, hoping that the ocean air would make her sleepy. Then she turned on a boring movie when they returned and curled up on the sofa. But that didn't work either. She had too much on her mind to sleep.

Abbie talked to Sam earlier today but did not mention her argument with Alex because she did not want to admit to Sam that she was right about buying the wheelchairs.

Montgomery's attitude made her so angry. People thought they needed to tell her why she was wrong throughout her life. Not until she moved in with the Wilsons did anyone consider her thoughts valid.

Abbie grew up assuming that being a foster child made her less valuable than those around her. No parents – she must have driven them away. Poor Abbie. No home – no brains. The kids at school teased and demeaned her daily. She spent her time alone. Her foster parents would not include her in activities or holiday celebrations because they did not consider her part of their family.

Something about the way Montgomery spoke to her yesterday brought it rolling back, and she became furious. Her offer of the chairs for Andy was her way of showing affection. He shared how the other kids at school often treated him, and she wanted to do everything possible to protect him.

Abbie understood the loneliness of not having a mother to go to with concerns or when she became afraid or sick, and she kept everything to herself. She did not want Andy to grow up the same way. Alex was a loving father, but there were days when he looked wrapped up in his own loss.

Abbie planned to tell him last night that she rented a house down the beach from him, but when they argued over the chairs, she forgot to mention the rental, but it was better that she didn't. Andy might want to see Kohl, and she did not want him to assume being this close gave him an open invitation to use his new beach chair as a straightforward way to visit.

Abbie stood up from the desk in front of the beach's window and stretched. Then, it was time for another cup of coffee. When she was restless last night, she started working on a proposal to add canine water therapy to Sam's current therapy offerings.

Kohl met the requirements for a therapy dog. He needed to perform a test swim to prove he could do the work and give rescue services should someone get into trouble in the water. Abbie had no doubt he would pass with flying colors. She scheduled Kohl's test and reached out to Tom's commanding officer and crew for letters of recommendation for Kohl. Once she received copies of his certifications and the recommendations, she'd add them to her proposal and present them to Sam.

She had a solid plan, but getting Sam's company and the hospital board to accept the plan might be a struggle. Her proposal included a budget for the first year she arranged to fund. She did not plan to tell who the money was coming from other than there was an anonymous donor.

Her biggest challenge is to get Kohl back in the water again. She and Sam planned to meet at the pool again this afternoon to continue the work of getting Kohl to swim again. Physically, he was fine, and he appeared to be healing emotionally. She needed to thank Andy for Kohl's progress so far. Abbie returned to her desk to draft an email to Tom's commanding officer and glanced out the window. There she saw them. Alex walked beside Andy. Andy was sitting in his new chair. He figured out how to make the chair go in circles, making Abbie chuckle. Alex and Andy laughed as he continued to make circles. Why did Alex change his mind about chairs?

The way he behaved in front of Andy annoyed Abbie. It thrilled her that Andy appeared to be enjoying the chair, but it did not change her choice to end things with Alex for now. She was serious when she said they needed time to think about their relationship.

Abbie should not have gotten involved with someone so soon after Tom's death, and Alex still needed to come to terms with his demons over the accident.

Abbie hoped that Alex would talk with Andy about his mother. Death was difficult for adults but much more challenging for children, who rarely had the maturity to understand their perceptions about events. Andy needed someone to help him understand that the accident was not his fault. In her opinion, Andy and Alex might both benefit from counseling.

Shortly after Tom died, Julie gave Abbie the name of a psychologist that was a friend of hers. She picked up the piece of paper with the phone number. The time had come for her to make a call as well. She did not know if she and Alex would get back together, but she needed therapy.

The afternoon flew by, and her phone pinged as she gathered up Kohl's equipment—another message from Alex.

"I'm sorry. I realized I was wrong. Can we talk?"

Pictures of Andy on the beach with his new chair followed his message.

Abbie smiled at the photos but refused to answer Alex. They both needed the space, and she would not let his pictures pull her back into a relationship that needed work. It took every ounce of her willpower to ignore him.

Alex and Andy returned to the house, and Andy talked non-stop. He had so much fun doing circles and learning how to use his chair. Then, he told his dad he wanted to call Abbie and thank her for the chairs.

Alex ignored Andy's request and did not tell him he sent her photos. He did not want to tell him she did not reply. Presumably, she is busy house hunting. She'll look at the text later.

They made dinner and watched a movie Andy wanted to see. After that, Alex helped Andy shower, got him into bed, and went out on the deck to relax and recheck his phone—still no messages from Abbie.

Alex sat watching the waves for a while but was restless. He had become used to talking to Abbie every day, sometimes multiple times, and his evening always ended with a call or at least a text. He needed to do something.

Alex walked into the house, cleaned the kitchen, did a load of laundry, dried the dishes, emptied the last of the remaining boxes of books, and arranged them on the shelves in the den. When he looked at the clock, it was after midnight. He rechecked his phone, and still no message from Abbie. Alex sighed. What had he said that made her so angry? He sent another message.

"You still awake?"

An hour passed and Alex still had not received a response. He knew there had to be more to this argument than he realized. So, he turned off the lights and went to bed, hoping tomorrow's outcome might be a little brighter.

Abbie heard her phone ping. She was in bed, tired, and ready to sleep. After reading Alex's text, she laid her phone back on the nightstand, vowing to distance herself from him and fix herself. Then, she turned off the light and drifted off to sleep.

CHAPTER 19

Abbie and Kohl took an early morning walk on the beach, and Abbie was thrilled when Kohl walked into the edge of the water. Baby steps. That was all he needed to overcome his fear.

Abbie drove to the Charleston house to find the paddleboards and other supplies for the rental and sent Dana a text about meeting her for lunch. Dana agreed to meet for lunch at the hospital cafeteria.

The house was in decent shape, and she checked for any mail, opened the windows to let in the ocean breeze, cleaned the fridge, took out the garbage, and called a cleaning company to do a bi-monthly cleaning.

On the way to the hospital, Abbie stopped at her favorite café and bought shrimp pot pies for lunch with Dana. How had so much happened since her lunch with Alex? He had eaten the same thing the day they met for lunch.

She texted Dana and told her they were in the cafeteria's outdoor section. Dana joined Abbie and gave her and Kohl a big hug. Kohl sat beside Dana with his head on her lap.

"How are you and Kohl getting along, Abbie? Is Kohl making any more progress with swimming? Sam said you were working to get him in the pool."

"We've made a little progress in the pool. We walked in the surf this morning but didn't go far. At least we made progress in the ocean as well. The paddle boards are in the car, and we may try that tomorrow morning."

"Wow, that's great. Sam also said you're working on a plan for a canine therapy program. What's that all about?"

Abbie explained the program and the proposal.

"Do you think it will pass? The stuffy hospital boards can be a real bear to work with for new and innovative ideas."

"It's going to be a struggle, but it might help that we are not asking for any money." Dana looked up at Abbie.

"Who's going to fund the program, Abbie? What's the chance insurance companies will pay?"

"We have an anonymous donor. Sam and I are going to track the results and will present those results to the hospital, the therapy company, and the insurance companies after six months. We will also track similar injuries using traditional therapies and compare the results. Insurance companies are historically difficult to work with when they deal with new treatment concepts. In the meantime, we will work hard and pray for the best."

Dana laughed. "I'm impressed. You've been quite busy, Abbie. Who's the donor?"

"Can't say, Dana!"

"Interesting concept, Abbie, and aren't you full of secrets lately?"

Abbie shrugged.

"The articles I read on water therapy for animals show impressive results. There was one about canine therapy with autistic children that has shown success. The advantage we have and need to keep in mind is this program involves Kohl, who has already proven his skills to the community."

"In the eyes of the community, he is a hero because of the rescues performed. He received the highest award that the coast guard gives out. And I'm certain he'll get back in the water and be prepared to do a live swim for the decision-makers. There is nobody that believes in him more than I do, Dana. I'm aware there might be a bit of prejudice to that belief, Dana, but he's impressive, no matter who's judging."

Dana nodded.

"He is impressive, and I'll help any way I can."

"I would love to use Andy and Kohl during the live swim, but since I am not speaking to Montgomery, that option is out."

Dana's head snapped up.

"Whoa, whoa, whoa! What do you mean you and Montgomery are no longer on speaking terms? What happened?"

Abbie told Dana about the wheelchairs and arguing with Alex. Abbie explained her side of the argument, and Alex's attitude about the chairs caused her to be angry. She admitted Sam had said to talk to Alex before buying the chairs, but she ignored the advice. When everything blew up, she had not wanted to admit to Sam that she was right.

"Abbie, I'm sorry about the argument. Perhaps, dating someone was just too soon. I don't blame you for being angry with Tom, but everything with Alex moved so fast."

"Frustrated is what I feel about the events that have taken place. I broke down and called a therapist to work on myself.

I should have done that long ago, but the argument with Alex pushed me over the edge. He sent me a text yesterday. It was a picture of Andy riding on his new beach chair, but I didn't bother to answer his text."

"It is a tough decision to call it quits with him, Abbie. Have you considered all the options before deciding to call it off? Does he know you are selling the Charleston house?"

"The argument over the chairs occurred before I had an opportunity to talk about the beach rental. I'm just three doors down from his place. When I was working on the proposal yesterday, I looked up and in front of the window overlooking the beach; what do I see but Andy in the new chair I bought, doing circles on the beach. Andy and Alex were both laughing. I wanted to run outside and wrap my arms around them, but I sat back down. I'm so torn, Dana. I needed a therapist more than I realized."

Dana and Abbie walked back toward the ER. They said goodbye before they approached the corridor to the ER unit. Kohl made progress this week and forcing him to enter the ER could cause a setback from memories caused by Tom's death.

Sam said she was available this afternoon for another session in the pool, and the two arrived at the pool at the designated time. Kohl trotted over to Sam and entered the water's edge. She threw two short throws, then a long one that bounced and landed in the water.

When Sam told Kohl to get the ball, Abbie was already in the pool. When she noticed his reluctance, Abbie commanded him to come, and he walked into the water without further hesitation. Finally, Abbie gave the command to get the ball. Kohl swam into deeper water, retrieved the ball, and returned the ball to Sam. Sam threw the ball repeatedly, which landed in the water, and Kohl retrieved the ball every time.

Kohl walked to his water dish and took a long drink. Then, he lay on the floor to rest. Abbie wrapped her towel around her body to dry off and get warm. Kohl was done for the day. She was proud of him. Sam looked at her, and they smiled at one another, hopeful that their patience had paid off.

Abbie sat on her bench near the window and looked out toward the ocean, nervous about the proposal and worried that Kohl would never get back into the water again. On the other hand, she was excited about Kohl's future and the opportunity to provide therapy to the community. Both she and Sam were aware of the tough road ahead; convincing the decision makers, they knew that pulling this off and proving Kohl's ability would not be easy.

Abbie and Sam juggled schedules to allow time for training skills and maneuvers and prep for the presentation. The program's goal was to help clients improve not only their motor skills and joint movement but also to help clients who needed to improve self-esteem, social skills, verbal communication, and interaction with others.

At the end of the presentation, they would ask for recommendations from the specialty physicians. As providers, their knowledge of the patient's history was the best way to determine who might qualify for the program. In addition, she and Sam were used to collaborating with the providers, so mapping out a recovery plan would be easy and provide the best outcome for the patients.

Sam put together a list of pain specialists, orthopedic practitioners, cardiac rehab services, and neurosurgeons at the hospital that they would target first. Then, once the program was off the ground, it would be time to determine the next steps.

Her dream was to have Alex and Andy be part of the initial program, but she needed more time before approaching the subject. Sam might reach out to Alex because he knew they were best friends. Abbie had given him a brief dissertation on the program she was trying to put together.

Alex knew that she and Sam were using Kohl to promote the program, and that would require her to be present for all the meetings and advertising that would take place. She wanted him to say yes to Andy being part of the program because he believed in what they were doing and not to use it as a ploy to get her to talk to him.

Abbie promised herself she would be civil with Alex, but they would need to keep their hands off one another. Ugh, Abbie thought! That was not likely to happen but staying away from Alex proved to be one of the hardest things to accomplish. In addition, she had to concentrate on the program.

The next few weeks flew by as Sam, Abbie, and Kohl worked to get the program together. Abbie felt exhausted and nauseous from a lack of sleep, trying to ignore Alex, and the personal therapy sessions.

Alex had sent countless text messages, begging her to call, but she ignored his messages. Andy missed her, and he missed her, too. He was sorry. What could he do to make things right?

When Abbie woke up this morning, there was yet another message from Alex. Andy was crying for Kohl. Was there any way possible to have Kohl for the weekend?

Abbie missed Alex, but her focus was on getting the program running. Kohl and Andy deserved a break, and she agreed to let them see each other. Kohl was ready for his demonstration to the board members. He had worked hard, and he deserved a break. She would call Sam and see if she would meet with Alex. She picked up her phone and sent Sam a message.

"When you have a few minutes, could you call me, please?"

Her phone rang immediately.

"Good morning," Abbie answered. "Am I interrupting your work?"

"No, Abbie. I just wrapped up with a patient and poured a cup of coffee. What's up?"

"Alex sent a text asking if Kohl could stay with him and Andy for the weekend. Andy is crying for Kohl, and I thought Kohl needed a break from training. If I give you Alex's number, would you meet him and drop off Kohl?"

"Why don't you do it, Abbie? It would allow you and Alex a chance to talk."

"I can't, Sam. If I call, I'm going to give in, and right now, my focus needs to be on this program. I don't need the distraction. I'm not mad at him anymore. The sessions with my therapist helped, but I can't get distracted. Please, Sam? I'll beg if I must."

"Alright, Abbie. I'll call him, but this goes on your tab. The favors are adding up, and you are going to owe me. What do you want me to tell him when he asks how you are?"

"Makeup something, Sam. Tell him I'm fine. That's a lie. I am not fine. Say I'm seeing a therapist and trying to work through all the changes in the last couple of months. He'll understand. Tell him, I'm trying to figure out if I should go back to work or look for something else. I don't want him to know too much about our program right now. We keep this between the crew and us until the initial meetings are over and we get approval."

"Fine, Abbie. I'll call him. What's his number?"

CHAPTER 20

Alex's phone rang. He did not recognize the number but answered anyway, in case it was someone from the hospital.

"Hello. Dr. Montgomery speaking."

"Hi, Alex, it's Sam, Abbie's friend. How are you?"

"I'm good, Sam. Is Abbie all right?"

"She is doing okay, but she asked me to call you. She received your text asking if Kohl could visit with Andy. I'll be happy to meet you or drop him off."

"Why can't she drop him off herself?"

"Look, Alex. She's seeing a therapist and trying to get her head straight after the accident and the inheritance Tom left her. There were too many big life changes, and she is not managing them well."

"Abbie asked me to tell you she is not mad at you, but she needs time to work through all the changes. She's also trying to decide if she should go back to the hospital to work or look for something else to do. Kohl is a big part of that decision. The bottom line is that she doesn't want to leave him alone for hours on end if she returns to work. Honestly, Alex, I think she doesn't remember she is wealthy, and she could take going back to work off her mind. I know she has worked since she was old enough to get a job, but she doesn't even consider her current financial situation. She's so stubborn, Alex. To make this work with her, you must understand her need for independence. Give her time, Alex. She loved being with you, and she adores Andy."

"I appreciate the information, Sam. I shouldn't admit this to you, but I am crazy in love with her. And that's between us, Sam. So, please don't tell her I admitted that to you."

"No problem. I know how to keep a secret, Doc."

"Great. So, when do you think I can get Kohl?"

"Are you working tomorrow? I can have Abbie drop him off at the therapy building, and you can pick him up when you leave work. Does that work for you?"

"That will be perfect because I can surprise Andy with Kohl when I pick him up from school, and in the meantime, I need to buy a bigger vehicle. I've tried getting him in the one I have, and that didn't work."

"Have fun car shopping. See you tomorrow, Alex."

Alex hung up the phone, grabbed his keys, and headed out the door to find a bigger vehicle. He was not telling Andy. This would be a great surprise.

He located a car dealership and told the salesperson he needed to trade his vehicle for one that would hold a one-hundred-fifty-pound dog and an electric wheelchair. The guy looked at him like he had two heads, but in the end, they settled for the biggest SUV in the lot. It came with all the extra features which would make Andy happy. He would see TV commercials and tell him they should get a new car with all the fun stuff.

Alex told the salesperson he needed it today. So, they sent the car to be cleaned while Alex signed the paperwork and wrote the check.

He went to Andy's school and waited outside. He leaned against the vehicle. Andy looked around, saw his dad, and wheeled himself to the vehicle.

"Where is our car?" Andy asked, looking perplexed.

"You're looking at it, Andy," Andy's eyes got big.

"When did we get this? Where's our other car? This is so cool. Why do we need this big car? Can it fit in the garage, Dad? Can we go now? I can't wait to ride in it."

Alex smiled and helped Andy into the car. He showed Andy all the extras that were included in the SUV.

"That's so cool. We are riding in style now, Dad."

"Yes, we are. How about we go grab burgers and fries for dinner tonight?"

"That would be very cool!"

Andy gave his dad a list of all the places they should visit with their big car and was almost to wound up to sleep, but he finally settled down and drifted off to sleep. Alex had trouble falling asleep as well. He was excited to have Kohl this weekend. If he couldn't have Abbie around, having Kohl would help Andy feel better.

The following day, Andy asked what they would do for the weekend.

"I hadn't thought that far ahead. What would you like to do?"

Alex had a tough time not revealing to Andy that Kohl was staying for the weekend.

"I'd like to ride my beach chair, Dad. I would also like to return to the zoo, but it won't be the same without Kohl and Abbie."

"I understand how you feel, Andy, but we can't stop doing things we enjoy because they are not with us."

"But I miss them. Do you think Abbie is going to be mad at us forever?"

"Andy, I want you to understand that Abbie is not mad at you. She was angry with me because of how I reacted to her buying you the electric wheelchairs. Abbie loves you, and so does Kohl. However, she needs time to manage the loss of her husband. She is meeting with a doctor friend who can help her get over her loss."

"You're a doctor. Why can't you help her with her loss?"

"I'm an emergency doctor, Andy. I treat people who get injured or sick and need help immediately, like when you fell and skinned your knee. We had to clean it up and get ointment on it right away so that it would heal and not leave a scar. Abbie is meeting with a doctor to help her not be sad. When her husband died, she was sad. So, the doctor she meets with helps her by giving her advice to help her not be so sad."

"Is it okay if I miss them, Dad?"

"It is okay. I miss them as well. Now, let's get you to school. I'll pick you up in our cool new car after work, and we'll have a fun weekend."

Alex met Sam, and Kohl greeted him without huffing or showing his teeth, and he hoped they got through the weekend without problems. Alex looked at Kohl.

"I need to pick Andy up at school. Do you want to go with me? Then you can spend the weekend with Andy?"

Kohl looked at him, then turned to look at Sam.

"It's fine, Kohl. Abbie said for you to have fun, and she will see you on Monday."

Kohl looked back at Alex with his tail wagging and let out a sharp bark.

"You can drop him off here when you come to work on Monday if that is more convenient. Abbie will pick him up."

"I don't know how to thank you, Sam. Andy is going to be so excited when he sees Kohl."

"No problem, Doc. I hope the three of you have a great weekend."

Alex loaded Kohl into the vehicle and talked to him on the short ride to the school. They got out of the vehicle, and Alex and Kohl stood waiting for Andy to come out of the building.

Alex was eager to see Andy's face when he realized Kohl was with him. He spotted Kohl at the same time Kohl spotted him. Kohl looked at Alex.

"Go get Andy Kohl."

Kohl took off running to Andy.

Andy wrapped his arm around Kohl as Kohl licked tears of joy from Andy's face. The kids gathered around Andy and Kohl, and there were non-stop questions. Parents joined the chaos, eager to discover what the excitement was about.

Alex decided he had better intervene before the school asked him not to bring Kohl back again. So, he got Andy and Kohl sorted out of the crowd and started maneuvering them to the vehicle. Once he got them both in the SUV, Andy started his nonstop line of questioning.

"Where's Abbie? Did she come too?"

"No! It is just us three guys for the weekend."

"Did you say Kohl is staying with us for the entire weekend? Can we go to the zoo tomorrow? When we get home, I want to show Kohl my beach chair. We can do circles in the sand. He'll like that, Dad. Can he sleep in bed with me like we used to do? Do we have food for him, Dad? We can stop at the store if we don't."

"Yes, he is staying for the weekend, we have food for him, and yes to everything else you asked as well, Andy. I think the zoo would be fun tomorrow."

Andy let out a whoop, and Kohl barked along with him. Alex smiled. Even if he didn't want Kohl to sleep in bed with Andy, he was sure there would be no way to stop him.

The weekend was a whirlwind of activity. Andy and Kohl had a blast on the beach with his new chair. Kohl barked, ran up and down the beach, and ran in and out of the water. When had he started doing that again? Alex wondered.

Sam hadn't mentioned that Abbie had gotten Kohl back into the ocean, but he was glad he was making progress because it was essential to Abbie, and it showed that Kohl was healing from the trauma of losing Tom.

Andy thought it was hilarious and encouraged Kohl to run back into the water. Of course, they drew a crowd of people, and Andy managed it like a champion. He learned enough about Kohl's habits to answer questions. He told them how Kohl used to rescue people from the water, about what they did for fun, and how Kohl slept with him, and because he was so big, almost as big as the bed, it did not leave him room, but he didn't mind. Alex's made a mental note to buy Andy a giant bed.

They spent Saturday at the zoo and had a full day of fun. Unfortunately, it exhausted Andy and Kohl by evening, and they both fell asleep soon after they got home. Alex would need to work something out with Abbie to have Kohl stay more often.

Abbie took her weekend to get caught up on things she wanted to get done. She found a hairdresser who could work with curly hair and got her hair trimmed, then went shopping for new linens for the rental and put the owner-supplied ones into storage.

She was fatigued from the work and long nights she had spent on the proposal and stretched out on the sofa with a movie and a blanket. She slept for four hours. When she woke up, she gasped when she realized how long she had slept.

She didn't want to eat but made toast and tea and stretched out on the sofa again. When she woke up the next time, it was 7:00 am. Now, she was certain she was getting sick. The only time she ever slept like this was when she was coming down with something. She stood up, and the room spun, causing her to want to vomit. She sat on the sofa and thought of probable causes for nausea and dizziness.

She decided she was getting an inner ear infection. They had been in the water almost every day. There was no ear pain, but she would need to get an appointment soon. There was always an urgent care nearby, and she searched the map on her phone for someplace close.

She curled up with her blanket and watched the news, but nothing was happening that weekend. She stood up. No dizziness this time. Slight nausea, but manageable! She showered, dressed, fixed a cup of tea, and planned her day.

It was a perfect day to be on the beach. The water was calm, and there was not a cloud in the sky. She still had not told Alex where her rental was located and did not want to run into him today. She hoped Kohl did not just decide to stroll home from Alex's place.

Abbie looked for the nearest urgent care center and scheduled an appointment online so she would not have to sit in the waiting room forever. When she left for the appointment, she allowed adequate time for traffic. When she arrived, she noticed only one other person was in front of her this morning. She still felt a little queasy and sipped on a water bottle, hoping that might help quell the nausea.

The nurse called her name, and Abbie walked back to the exam room. Funny how being a patient often made her nervous. As a nurse, she was always at ease talking with patients and explaining their plan of care. But, as a patient, she was nervous.

The doctor came in and talked to Abbie about her symptoms. He checked her ears, listened to her lungs, palpated her stomach, and listened to her bowel sounds like any other healthcare provider would.

"Abbie, your ears look fine. Let's run a couple of simple blood tests here at the office. You may be coming down with the flu."

"I agree to whatever test you think is necessary, but is it okay if I just stretch out on the table and rest while we wait for the results?"

"Sure! It's not extremely comfortable, but you are welcome to lie down. The nurse will be right in, and we'll have the test results in about ten or fifteen minutes."

The nurse drew her blood, and Abbie curled up on the table. Before she realized it, the doctor woke her up.

"Well, Abbie. Your lab results are excellent. The only positive thing was your pregnancy test." he said, smiling.

Abbie sat straight up.

"My, what test? Did I hear you say pregnancy test?"

"Yes. I take it this a surprise for you?"

"That doesn't even begin to describe my feelings now."

"Do you want to talk about it? I have time," the doctor offered.

"It's complicated! The condensed version is that my husband died in an accident three months ago. After his death, I discovered he was not the person I had known and been married to for years.

So, I reached out to a doctor I worked with to help me deal with the grief. One thing led to another, and we had sex twice. Well, more than twice, but only two nights. Dear God. Neither of us thought about protection. How were we that stupid?"

"It happens more often than you can imagine."

"Do you need the name of an OB doctor in the area?"

"It was the last thing I would have imagined I needed today, but yes, I would appreciate your recommendations."

CHAPTER 21

Abbie walked out of the urgent care with the OB/GYN recommendations in one hand and a prescription for prenatal vitamins in the other. Is there a prescription for the courage to tell Montgomery we're having a baby? Abbie asked aloud. Or a prescription for motherhood? Dear Lord. How was one person supposed to manage so many life changes alone until the negativity affected your life? She did not know how anyone else felt, but she had reached her limit for this year, got in her car, and drove to the rental.

Abbie laid the prescriptions on top of the kitchen counter, put the teapot on the stove to heat, reached into the cupboard for a tea bag, and realized she had no decaf. Sighing, she turned off the stove, took a bottle of water out of the fridge, and went for a walk on the shore, hoping she might find a peaceful place to think. The sound of the waves always soothed her.

Abbie walked north along the shoreline, found a quiet spot near the pier, and sat on the sand. She watched the waves and relaxed. Glancing at her watch, she realized an hour had passed since she left the rental, so she finished her water, got up, and walked back to the house.

When she returned to her house, too many thoughts were still rolling around in her head. She thought of going for a run, and as she was changing her clothes, she stopped, wondering if she was allowed to run while pregnant. There were other pregnant women running. Dear Lord! How did she call herself a nurse when she was unable to answer a straightforward question?

Locating her purse, she found the list of the Ob/Gyn physicians she had received, chose one, and then picked up her phone. Her hands were shaking. Abbie took a deep breath and dialed the number.

There was no doubt in her mind Alex was the baby's father. Her last period had been barely a week after Tom's funeral, and since she had no intention of having sex with anyone, she had gone off her birth control medication. Montgomery said it had been a long time for him, as well. Neither of them had prepared for what happened during the first night she stayed at his house, nor were they thinking of protection the second night.

Abbie was angry at herself for being so forgetful, but they were both to blame. Now that she was over the shock of finding herself pregnant and had her first prenatal appointment scheduled, there was nothing more to do than eat right, get enough sleep, take her vitamins, and figure out how to tell Alex. She also needed to tell the rest of the crew, but for now, she was keeping this information to herself.

The day she had asked Alex to help with her financial plight, she never imagined he would now be the father of their baby. How was she going to tell him? He was a reasonable person. He'd be as shocked as she was, but he deserved to know. Maybe she should wait a few days, then call him and schedule a time for them to talk.

Today was Sam's day off from work, and Kohl was spending the weekend with Andy and Alex, so Abbie took advantage of the quiet, stretched out on the sofa, napped for a while, and gave the project one last review.

The basic equipment needed for the demo had arrived. Sam finished the sample therapy schedule to present to the board members and physicians attending the meeting. They planned to divide the presentation responsibilities, and her responsibilities would include introductions and their backgrounds, including Kohl's. Then she would present the basic format of the program. Sam's responsibilities would include finishing the presentation by providing specifics on the therapy, research findings, and the potential start date of the program.

They had a PowerPoint presentation ready to go, as well. Abbie would discuss their expected findings and when reports would be available for review. She'd review the budget and the donor, then finish the presentation with the audience's questions.

Abbie added an hour to their schedule to answer questions. Sam and Abbie would respond to the questions while Sam's assistant took notes. She would provide Sam and Abbie with a list of any follow-ups needed.

Once the program was underway, they would offer an open invitation to the board members and physicians, giving them the opportunity to view the therapy sessions. However, the offer was contingent on receiving permission from the patients.

Abbie and Sam had reviewed their lists, and they decided this weekend was off-limits for any work related to the program.

Abbie fell asleep again and woke up as she heard her phone ding. Alex was sending pictures of Kohl and Andy, and she laughed when she noticed they had taken the pictures on the beach in front of her rental. Setting her phone down without responding to Alex made her feel guilty. She knew he could tell she had read the text, but she was not ready to talk with him.

Organizing the hydrotherapy project kept her so busy she wasn't even angry with him anymore. She had put him on the back burner, which wasn't fair to him or Andy. Once she and Sam got this program underway, she would call him about the pregnancy.

She tried to find more information on Tom and his family and ran into roadblocks. She put that on the back burner as well. Nothing she found changed the outcome. Mr. Walker said she was the only one left, and that wasn't going to change either.

The next morning, Abbie decided she would sell the Charleston house. Even though she had the money to keep both houses, she was tired of driving back and forth between the two. She planned to donate the furniture and other minor items she no longer needed and would put the rest into storage until she decided on a permeant home. She talked with a realtor and scheduled an appointment at 11:00 am to meet at the Charleston house.

Kohl wagged his tail and leaned against her when she walked into the therapy department to pick him up from his stay with Alex. Once in the SUV, he laid his head on the console to be closer to her.

She and Kohl met the realtor, signed the contract, called Habitat for Humanity to schedule a pickup, and marked items for donation. She loaded her vehicle with the items she wanted to keep. If she ran out of space, she'd rent a storage unit.

Abbie decided not to return to work for Memorial and picked up her phone to call Dana.

"Hey, Dana. Are you busy? I was hoping to talk to you."

"Now is good, Abbie. We are not busy right now, so it is a good time to catch up with each other."

"I'm calling to let you know I am going to resign my position at Memorial and move to the North Myrtle area."

"Why Abbie? I thought you loved your job?"

"I do, but Kohl is making progress and overcoming his fear of the water. He likes the pool and working with Sam. And honestly, I am tired of driving back and forth from Charleston to North Myrtle. I'll send an official resignation letter later today, but I wanted to tell you first. Hitting you up with that news via email wouldn't be fair."

Abbie did not offer Dana information about the baby. Alex should be the first to know, and then she'd tell the rest of their friends.

CHAPTER 22

Alex arrived at the ER, which was quiet this morning. He was still not sure what was going on with Abbie. When he dropped Kohl off, Sam only told him she was fine and that they were working on a new therapy program they'd announce soon.

"Do you think you could convince her to call me? I realize she is angry with me over my response to the wheelchairs, but I told her I was sorry."

"Look, Alex. You need to give her space. It was your point of view over the chairs that made her angry. She's had too many things to manage and depended on you to be her friend and safe place. You were at fault, too. Just hang in there. She's had to fight for things her entire life. She likes you, Doc, which means she trusts you, but if you break that trust, she may never take you back."

"Thanks for the info. I'm not planning to hurt her. I'd like her to call me."

"Got it. I'll see what I can do."

Alex examined patients, ordered tests, reviewed results, and time crawled. He sighed! Dr. Damon Parker heard him.

"What's going on, Alex? I never hear you sigh. Something I can do to help?"

"No, not unless you are an expert on women!"

"Ha-ha. I am not touching that one with a ten-foot pole. Why do you think I'm still single? I thought you were single as well?"

"Damon, I'm a widow. The husband of one of my nurses at my prior hospital was a rescue swimmer with the Coast Guard. He died in an accident. I offered to be her sounding board of sorts if she needed something. It turned into more than that, and now she's ghosting me, and I'm not sure why."

"Yep, see. That's why I stay single. I ride a motorcycle. There's room for two, but I let everyone know there's only room for me, and that's it. I own a saddle bag. If I can't haul it in there, it doesn't ride."

"I just bought the biggest SUV on the lot because she has a one-hundred-fifty-pound dog that my son is in love with, and since she isn't speaking to me, I pick up the dog next door at the therapy place, and he stays with Andy and me for the weekend. Otherwise, Andy is angry with me as well. I can't win. Samantha, or Sam as everyone calls her, is one of her best friends, so she has become her dog's drop-off spot."

"I've met Sam. She rides as well. I see her ride her bike to work almost every day. Small world, Alex. I hope that works out for you. We should grab a beer one evening."

"Sounds good, Damon. I've got a house on the beach if you want to kick back at my place rather than a bar. I'll grab the beer and throw a couple of burgers on the grill as well."

"You have a place on the beach? You don't give off the vibe of a beach bum, Montgomery, but I'm always in for a burger and a beer."

They shook hands.

"I'm out of here for today. See you in the morning, Montgomery."

Damon got his helmet out of his locker and headed out the door. Sam was getting on her bike when Damon threw up his hand and said, "How are you doing, Sam?" And pulled out of the lot.

Sam watched Damon Parker ride away.

What is he up to now? She wondered. She had been working here for several years, and he had never spoken a word to her. His reputation at the hospital preceded him, but it was not great. He was one of the hottest-looking doctors on staff, and Montgomery was number two, but Parker was a player and not someone she planned to date.

The nurses were always flirting with Parker, but he paid no attention to most of them, and the ones he paid attention to always ended up with a broken heart.

Today was presentation day, so Abbie set her alarm to wake up early. She had minimal morning sickness and needed time for it to pass if this morning was the one. She did not want to walk into the meeting today, being shades of green. Luckily, she felt good.

Abbie was getting a baby bump, too, but others might not notice if she wore the right clothes.

Today's attire was a business suit and heels. She pulled her curly hair into a low bun. There was no doubt her curls would find a way to escape, but she hoped she would stay together long enough to get through the presentation.

She gave Kohl a bath yesterday, trimmed his fur, and brushed him. There was no beach walk this morning. She wanted to keep him clean and shiny.

Abbie made a video of Kohl and Sam in the pool making therapy moves, and she and Kohl doing rescue maneuvers. The video was to be part of the presentation this morning. This was the best way to show his skills until they did a live presentation.

She and Sam stood by the door at the entrance to the boardroom and greeted everyone by name as they entered.

As part of their preparation, they used the internet to research everyone invited to the presentation and studied each member. They were familiar with their backgrounds, positions, and pictures and could name everyone by sight.

As they walked to the podium at the front of the room, Abbie turned to Sam and whispered.

"Who's the tall, hot guy in the front row? We didn't invite him, did we?"

Sam rolled her eyes.

"Not you too, Abbie."

"What's that supposed to mean?" Abbie whispered.

"Dr. Damon Parker, Emergency Room physician! The women fancy themselves in love with him. He's known as the bad boy in the hospital. He rides a motorcycle and anyone else he wants. They fall at his feet."

Abbie smiled, put on her business face, and turned to the crowd.

Abbie noticed what appeared to be doubt on the faces of the hospital board members, many of whom were not physicians. The physicians appeared to be on board.

During the presentation, Sam and Abbie smiled at one another once when they noticed the whispering between the neuro and orthopedic surgeons.

They answered question after question for nearly an hour after the presentation. Every single doctor came up to thank and assured the two of them they planned to send a list with their first patient recommendations.

The presentation was a hit.

Dr. Parker came up and introduced himself to Abbie and said hello again to Sam.

"Thank you, Ms. Foster. Great presentation and great ideas you and Sam have put together!"

"Please, Dr. Parker, call me Abbie." Abbie turned to Kohl.

"Hey, Kohl. Come over here and say hello to Dr. Parker."

Kohl approached the doctor, sat, and raised his paw to shake.

Damon shook Kohl's hand.

"Nice to meet you, Kohl, and you and Abbie can call me Damon."

"Ladies, I'm aware you did not invite me, but I overheard the other doctors talking. I had time before I needed to start my shift in the ER. Sorry, but someone needs to be the party crasher."

"No worries. Dr. Parker. Who better to crash a party than you?" Abbie and Damon laughed.

"Very nice to meet you, Abbie. See you around, Sam."

And Damon gave Sam a two-finger salute and winked at her before leaving the room. She shook her head. The confidence he exuded made you think he owned the place.

"Oh my, Sam. You better watch out," Abbie said, smiling at her.

"He'll have you falling at his feet next."

Sam watched him walk away.

"It will be a snowy day in hell before that happens, Abbie. Let's get out of here and grab lunch. I'm starving."

Damon left the meeting thinking about Abbie and Sam.

Both were stunning women and had the brains to go with it, and that was a rare combination around here. Sure, the nurses were smart and did their jobs well, but these two had a whole different vibe.

Damon arrived in the ER and ran into Alex.

"Hey, Alex. Listen, I just crashed a presentation that was going on in the grand rounds' theater. Any chance the stunning woman putting on the presentation named Abbie is your lady? She had a big Newfoundland dog with her."

"She's here?"

"She was six minutes ago. You need to find her and get sorted out whatever is going on with the two of you, Alex. Someone that stunning and that smart won't be single long. Someone is going to come along and take her away from you." Damon said. "I may even get in line for her myself."

Alex chucked.

"Just try it, Parker, and if that crazy dog of hers doesn't take you out, I will."

"Noted, Montgomery."

Damon gave Alex a fist bump.

"Go see if she is still here. I've got this covered."

Alex walked down the long hallway to the theater on the first floor. It was empty. He walked to the snack bar and up to the cafeteria on the second floor, but she was nowhere to be found. He sent her a text.

"Hey, Abbie. I heard you were at the hospital for a presentation. You still here? Stop in the ER if you're still in the building."

Abbie ignored his text messages. He'd stop and see her if he had any idea where she was staying, and he wondered if she had gone back to the beach house in Charleston.

He and Andy could go for a drive this weekend. He was sure Andy was going to ask for Kohl to stay again this weekend, but there were places he couldn't take Kohl. He needed a copy of his rescue certificate and made a mental note to get a copy from Abbie.

He walked back to the ER.

"Thanks for covering Parker, but she must be gone. She is nowhere to be found."

"Sorry, man. Tell me, is every one of her friends as gorgeous as she and Sam?"

Alex smiled.

"Every single one. The crew, as they call themselves! The five of them are the most stunning women I've ever seen. I don't think they are aware of how they appear to others when they are together."

"You'll need to bring your sunglasses the first time you meet them together. They spend time together when they are not busy. They are all single. I'll invite you over if Abbie and I ever get back together, and I know when that's happening. Each of them is in the healthcare field. Every one of them is brilliant, according to Abbie. They call Kate the brains. She's a physician who engages in gene therapy."

"They put us both to shame, Parker. I'll fill you in on the details over that beer we discussed, but they are also fierce and protective of one another. I'm telling you, Parker, do not get involved with any of them. They'll make you fall in love with them, then just disappear."

"Noted, Montgomery!"

Abbie and Sam were relaxing at an outdoor table after their presentation.

"Are you going to have a glass of wine to celebrate our early success?" Sam asked Abbie, "Or could we order a split of champagne?"

"Thanks, Sam, but I'll pass on the alcohol. I talked too much this morning, so I am sticking to water for now, and I need to run to Charleston this afternoon because I put the house up for sale."

"Abbie, you love that house. What made you decide to do that?"

Abbie sighed. "Kohl is doing so much better up here, and to tell you the truth, Sam, it's the memories we made in that house. Wonderful memories, Sam. But it's hard to be there without Tom. I donated the furniture and small appliances that are still good. I donated Tom's clothes, too. The rest is being moved into storage up here. The realtor will let the paint contractors in today, and I want to see how that is going, so Kohl and I are making a trip after lunch."

"Wow, big decision, Abbie! Did you tell Alex you are selling your house?"

"No, Sam. I still haven't talked to him, but I will. I haven't told him I have the rental. It's only three houses from him. I try to time my walks and our time on the beach when I don't expect him to be there. It's inevitable that we will run into one another, or he and Andy will have Kohl for the weekend, and Kohl will rat me out by running to the door to be let inside. I resigned from my position at Memorial as well."

"Dana said you might do that now that you have the means to do what you want and not have to work."

"The decision to resign had nothing to do with the money sitting in my account. It's for Kohl. I have nobody to leave him with except you and Montgomery, and you are both working, but that's still not why I quit. Kohl has so much talent. If we get this program off the ground, it's hard to tell where it might go. This is an exciting opportunity for both Kohl and us. I need to do this for him while he can still swim. Newfoundland dogs live around eight to ten years, and he has so much to offer the community. I could retire him since Tom's gone, and nobody would think twice about my decision, but he's an extraordinary dog. Isn't that why we are doing this, Sam?"

"It is an exciting venture, Abbie. We need to consider training another dog or two. If this program takes off, Kohl can't be the only dog."

Abbie laughed.

"Oh, my, what did we get ourselves into, Sam? Do you have space at your apartment for a dog that big?"

"I'll make it work. Should we get two? Do you have the name of Kohl's breeder? He's so mild-tempered. Do you have room for another dog, Abbie? We can get our own dogs, and by our own, I mean the ones we own. I don't trust anyone else to train them correctly."

Abbie nodded. "We can look, but any puppies we buy need a certified exam proving they have good hips. Otherwise, they won't be able to swim for the time it will take for a therapy visit."

"I'll follow your lead on this, Abbie. If they are Abbie-approved, then that's good enough for me."

CHAPTER 23

Late Friday afternoon, Abbie received an official letter from the hospital and therapy company boards stating they had received permission to move forward with the program and were looking forward to reviewing the results.

The board was not seeking an official demo or live demonstration. The video provided during the presentation was enough for them to understand the capabilities Kohl brought to the program and Abbie and Sam's ability to pull this together.

Abbie picked up the phone and called Sam.

"Can you do something for me, Sam?"

"Sure, Abbie. Name it!"

"Can you set up a call with the crew so that we can tell them we received permission to start our new therapy program?" Abbie shouted and started laughing.

"We did it, Sam." But Sam hadn't heard her over the screaming she was doing on the other end of the phone.

"Oh, Abbie. I'm so happy they approved it. I assumed we were going to battle this for months. Let's bask in the glory of their decision for a couple of days, and we can then get a marketing plan together. We should do a press release to get this whole thing moving."

"That's a great idea. I need a couple of days to oversee the moving and storage of my stuff, but after I'm done with that chore, I will be ready to go."

"I hope you have a good weekend, Abbie. I'll set up something with the crew for Sunday evening. Talk to you soon."

Sam had no more patients for the day, so she was going to slip out early. She grabbed her purse, swung it over her shoulder, and danced to her bike.

Damon Parker sat on his bike and was getting ready to put on his helmet when he noticed Sam and chuckled.

"Hey there, Sam. Do you always dance on your way out of the building or only on Friday evenings?"

Sam laughed.

"This, Dr. Parker, is a special celebration dance. Reserved for only the best occasions!"

Damon got off his bike and walked over to Sam.

"Did you get approval for the hydrotherapy program? I've never known them to do anything that fast. It takes months."

"Yes!" Sam shouted. Damon picked her up and spun her around in the air.

"That's fantastic." He smiled at her as he placed her back on the ground.

"Do you want to celebrate tonight?"

Sam hesitated. She looked him in the eye.

"Hell, yes. I'm in the mood to celebrate."

Damon grabbed her by the hand.

"Let's take my bike. I'll bring you back later to get yours."

They walked hand in hand over to his bike. Both were so caught up in Sam's celebration that they did not notice Alex leaning against the exit door, smiling at them as he watched them ride away.

"Good choice, Parker," Alex mumbled. "Abbie is mine."

Alex picked Andy up at school. "I miss Kohl, Dad. Can he come over this weekend?"

"Not this weekend, Andy. I planned to take a drive along the coast and check out the old neighborhood tomorrow. We can grab breakfast on the way, then go to your favorite place for lunch. How does that sound?"

"That sounds fun, but it would be better with Kohl."

"I realize you miss him and Abbie too, Andy, but we need to be patient until Abbie works through her list of the adult tasks she needs to finish. I'll contact her and see if we can have Kohl next weekend, and we can plan to do something fun."

"Okay, Dad. If I can't see him every weekend, I will plan something fun for our next weekend together."

"We might have him stay over every other weekend. What if we invite your new friends over from school and they can meet him, too? I'll invite a couple of my doctor friends. That will be a fun guys' night out on the beach. We can set up games, cook burgers, and finish the night with s'mores."

"That sounds great, Dad. Can I invite ten friends?"

"Let's stick to five, and you will make six."

"I can't wait!"

Abbie was looking forward to a quiet weekend. She slept late, which was becoming a habit, and then she and Kohl took a walk on the beach. When they returned from their walk, they sat on the deck in the afternoon sun and jotted a list of marketing ideas for her meeting with Sam next week.

Abbie was looking forward to talking with Dana, Julie, and Kate the next night. They had missed their weekly calls for the past three weeks. Now that they had approved the program, they could get back to their routine.

The painters had completed the work on the Charleston house, which looked great. It looked clean and beachy, and the realtor expected it to sell fast, which was great—one more thing off her list before the baby was born.

Her Ob/Gyn appointment was on Monday, and she was also looking forward to getting that off her to-do list. Once she had official information from the doctor that she could pass on to Montgomery, she'd text him and set up a meeting.

Sam woke up in a strange bed, confused for a moment, then remembered where she was and that she and Damon Parker had gone out for food and drinks to celebrate the approval of the hydrotherapy program. The bar was four blocks from his place, so they parked the bike in his garage and walked.

Their plan to drink one or two beers went haywire when a friend started buying shots. They both had enough common sense to realize that neither of them could get behind the wheel of a car or on a bike. So, Damon offered her his spare room.

He made no advances toward her last night, and she was unsure if that made her happy or sad, but it didn't matter for now. The smell of coffee propelled her to grab her clothes, and she headed to the shower. She could shower again after she got home and find clean clothes. For now, the smell of coffee motivated her. She showered and dressed, and Damon held out a cup of coffee as she exited the bathroom.

"Ah, coffee. You might be okay, Parker, despite what the rest of them say."

He chuckled. "I bet they say a lot about me, don't they?"

Sam took a long sip of coffee and sat on the stool at the kitchen counter to delay answering him.

"Does it matter what anyone says? You know the rumors are made up by women that can't get your attention. If you're doing something you don't want to share, that's on you."

"Well said." They both laughed.

"Last night was fun, Damon."

"Thanks for letting me crash. I don't drink very often, so those shots went straight to my head. Good thing there was a lengthy list of greasy food to choose from on their menu. Please remind me to share my hospital bill with you when I need triple bypass surgery. I hope you are friends with a good cardiac surgeon."

"Of course, I am, and if we decide to do other crazy things, I am friends with plenty of doctors to take care of us."

"Great. That makes everything so much better. Excellent coffee."

"Thanks, Samantha. Special beans that I grind myself. If being an ER doc has taught me anything at all, it's that life is too short for terrible coffee."

"I could not agree more."

Damon sat next to Sam.

"Let's take a ride up the coast. It will be a wonderful day to ride, and we can grab lunch along the way."

Sam took another swig of coffee and turned to face Damon.

"Look, Parker. We can be friends, and that's it, so if you have any other ideas of where this friendship might go, other than up the coast, you need to rethink your plan."

"Sam, I'm offering to take you riding today. You also own a bike, which tells me you like to ride. Sometimes I enjoy having someone to ride with for the day that doesn't have an ulterior motive."

"Alright. I'll go, but can you take me back to the hospital to get my bike and give me an hour to shower and change clothes?"

"That works for me, but let's take my bike. It will be easier for us to talk and easier to find parking as well."

Alex and Andy took a drive through their old neighborhood. Andy asked questions about the new family who bought their house, but Alex told him he didn't know enough to answer his questions.

When they passed Abbie's place, it shocked Alex to see a for-sale sign and the sold sign on top. What was she up to now? Sam made him think everything was still okay. He'd trust her for now but still wondered where Abbie was staying. She apparently found a rental in town.

He had heard late yesterday that the board had approved their program, and he was also proud of her and Kohl and Sam. Hospitals approved nothing as fast as they approved this one, so it must be one hell of a decent program.

And abruptly, it hit him. She had the money Tom left in the trust. Did she bribe the board? Although he had not known her for long, that was not who she was. He'd ask Parker if Sam had said anything about where the money was coming from, but he doubted he would get anything out of her. That group was tight-lipped and loyal to a fault.

Alex wondered again about the money. There was money coming from somewhere. The board never gives their blessing this quickly. Abbie was a good person. Wasn't this why she walked away from him? She said he didn't trust her.

Alex groaned.

"What's wrong, Dad?"

"Nothing, Andy. I remembered something I was supposed to do."

"Is it something I can help with, Dad?"

"Maybe, Andy. We'll talk when we get home."

After they got home, Alex made snacks and poured lemonade for him and Andy, and they went out on the deck.

"How do you like the new house and your new school, Andy?"

"I love it here, Dad. I love my school too. The kids are much nicer here than at my school in Charleston. They don't tease me for being in a wheelchair or not having a mom."

Alex took a deep breath – a perfect opening for the subject with Andy.

"Andy, do you remember the day I came home, and you and Abbie were sitting in the rocking chair?"

"I remember, Dad."

"Abbie told me you were sad about your mother dying. Why don't you tell me about that, dear?"

"It was nothing, Dad. She asked me how I had my bedroom decorated at our Denver house because we were discussing ways to decorate my room here. I told her that sometimes I get sad because it was my fault that mom died."

"Why do you assume that is your fault?"

"Because I yelled at you to watch out for the dog in the road and scared you. When you moved the steering wheel so fast, we slid, flew over the guide rail, and rolled over the hill. Mom and I would be okay if I hadn't yelled and scared you."

Andy was trying not to cry, but tears were leaking from his eyes and running down his cheeks. Alex got up and picked him up and sat again with Andy on his lap.

"Andy, the accident was my fault. I'm the one to blame. I was not paying attention to the road. I looked at a text on my phone from the ER, and I know better than to read a text while driving. Not one thing that happened during the accident is your fault, Andy. I didn't want to hit that dog, so I jerked on the steering wheel, which caused us to slide on the ice. Once we started sliding, I couldn't get control of the car again. I don't know where the dog came from that evening. I wanted to look for him after the accident but didn't have the time."

"Is any of this making sense to you?"

Andy nodded.

"You and your mother were both injured. I was trying to help the two of you. I asked the police officer later if they saw him near the accident scene, and they told me they noticed his tracks in the snow but did not see him. They don't think I injured him in the accident. They think he walked away from the accident scene. But Andy, none of this was your fault. I'm sorry I did not realize you thought the accident was your fault. Can you ever forgive me, Andy?"

Andy nodded.

"It was probably the dog's fault, Dad. Is that why you won't allow me to get a dog?"

Alex nodded his head.

"Yes, Andy, that's part of it. I did not want to be reminded of that dog on the road, and it makes me miss your mother."

"But you love Kohl, don't you, Dad?"

"Yes, I do, Andy. Kohl is a great dog who has done much good for our community and saved numerous lives."

"And you love Abbie too, right, Dad?" Alex hesitated for a moment and nodded.

"Yes, Andy. I love Abbie, as well."

Andy hugged him tightly.

"Will she come back to us, Dad?"

"I believe she will, but she needs time."

"Andy, I have an idea. A doctor I work with meets with people who've lost someone they love. I will schedule an appointment for the two of us, and she will help us understand our feelings and why we have not shared them with one another. It should help us understand each other and help us understand Abbie as well. She is going through the same things we went through since she lost her husband. If we understand ourselves better, it might help us get back together."

"That's a great idea, Dad. Sometimes, I get sad when I see the kids at school with their mothers. I know not everyone has a mother and a dad because the kids told me their parents got divorced and are always fighting. They might need to visit your doctor, friend, too."

"They might, Andy. My friend will want to talk to us together sometimes at our appointments, and other times she will want to talk to us by ourselves. Will you be okay doing that?"

"Sure. Are you okay with that, too?"

"I am fine with it. We might need to see her for weeks or even months. We have a lot to tell her since we have been keeping this to ourselves for a long time."

Alex got up to pour each of them another glass of lemonade.

"Let's find a pool to go swimming in this afternoon, Andy. The weather is perfect, and we haven't gone swimming for a long time. We are due."

"I agree, Dad. I have an idea. Let's get our own pool, and Kohl could swim with us."

Alex grinned.

"That is a perfect idea, Andy. Kohl would have a blast with you in the water."

"And he's a rescue dog, so you don't need to worry that I might drown."

Alex shook his head.

"Let's not discuss drowning right now. Let's get our trunks, towels, and whatever you want for a float, and I will call a pool company tomorrow and get this started."

CHAPTER 24

Abbie and Sam hired a marketing firm to announce the program to the public. Doing this helped free up time to focus on the patient recommendations. There were dozens of applications coming in from the doctors who attended the presentation. Sam took over the scheduling, and Abbie took over the job of finding another dog or two to add to the staff.

Abbie took a break this morning to attend her doctor's appointment but was nervous going in the door. The staff and the doctor greeted her.

The doctor did her examination and calculated her pregnancy to be close to ten weeks. Abbie answered her personal and mental health questions but hesitated when the doctor asked for the father's medical history. The doctor waited for her to answer.

"Abbie, do you know the father of the baby? Is this something you don't want to discuss?" The doctor asked.

"I know who the father is, but I haven't told him yet."

"That's okay. Take your time and do it when you are ready."

"Thank you. I appreciate the advice."

"Well, since you are at ten weeks of gestation, let's do our first sonogram and look at the baby."

Abbie lay on the table as instructed. The doctor moved the sonogram wand over her stomach and said everything looked great.

"Hum, just as I expected." The doctor said.

"What does that mean?"

"Well, your measurements were on the higher end for your current ten-week pregnancy. I can single out at least two fetuses, Abbie."

Abbie's head whipped around to the sonogram screen.

"What? Where? Are you sure you're counting correctly?"

The doctor smiled and asked her to turn to the right so that she could get a better picture.

"Look right here, Abbie. There is one there and the other there, and there's another right there. Congratulations, Abbie."

"Damn you, Alex Montgomery. Now what? What am I supposed to do with three babies?"

"Abbie." The doctor spoke her name to get her attention.

"Is Alex Montgomery the father of these babies? Alex is a friend of mine."

"You aren't pregnant with his babies, too, are you? We were only friends when this happened."

The doctor laughed.

"No, Abbie. Apparently, your friendship and my friendship with Alex are two distinct types of friendships."

"Well, thank goodness for that little piece of good news."

"Abbie, neither I nor my staff is permitted to say a word to him, so don't worry, nothing will get back to him. You need to tell him when you are ready. Please call me if you need my help with any of those discussions. But I will say you could not have picked a better person for a father than Alex."

"I know he is a good person, but I am supposed to be mad at him. I stopped seeing him because we both needed therapy. My husband died not too long ago, and Alex was a friend I thought I could trust. But there's something between us that neither of us understands. How much longer do you think I have until the entire world knows by looking at my stomach that I am pregnant?"

"Maybe a couple more weeks, Abbie, but that's probably it. I will need to meet with the two of you so that you both understand the risk associated with triplets. I realize he's a physician, but he is of course not a specialist in high-risk pregnancy."

"I think we might need to go back and revisit those mental health questions." Abbie chuckled.

"You'll be fine, Abbie, and I'll give you and Alex my phone number. I rarely do that, but he is a colleague and friend, so I trust you will use the number only if necessary."

"I promise we will only use it for an emergency. Montgomery may have a heart attack when he finds out, so we may need a referral."

Abbie walked to her car with information on triplets provided by the office staff. My life is out of control, she thought. How do I tell him all of this? She might have a couple of weeks to plan this out, but if she ran into him before, he'd most likely figure it out on his own.

Tomorrow she and Sam were to see puppies, and she'd have to convince Sam that they should only pick one dog for now. Once Sam knew she was pregnant, she'd understand.

Abbie decided that since she was out, she had better find clothing to fit her growing belly. Luckily, she was not working a full-time job that required dress clothes. Some cute summer dresses might help hide everything for now, and leggings and long tops should work as well.

Dear God. How was she supposed to manage three babies? She needed help and needed to keep her therapy appointments. She'd never survive three babies without someone to talk with about the changes in her life.

Alex and Andy had been meeting with the therapist together and had started their appointments two weeks ago.

Andy had an appointment with the therapist, which should be over soon.

Alex waited outside the office and was sitting on the bench under the porch when Abbie walked up. She was looking at her phone and did not know he was sitting there until the last minute.

"Abbie. What are you doing here?"

Abbie stopped in her tracks. This was not how she envisioned this entire conversation taking place.

"Hey, Alex. I started therapy and have been trying to work on myself. I wanted to call you; no, I needed to, but the new program has kept me busy. How's Andy?"

"He's good, Abbie. We had that long-needed discussion on Maria's death, and I also decided I needed therapy, so we came at the same time."

"That's great, Alex. Andy is such a great kid. He's going to be fine."

"Thanks, Abbie, but we need to discuss what happens next with us."

As Alex made that statement, the wind blew Abbie's dress against her growing stomach. She reached to grab her dress, and when she looked up, she saw the anger on Alex's face.

"Montgomery, there are several subjects we need to discuss."

"Is that my baby or Tom's? And I want an answer now."

Neither Alex nor Abbie heard the office door open. Andy and the therapist stood watching the interaction between the two.

"If you insist on knowing, Montgomery, these babies are mine."

Abbie paused and wondered if Alex had noticed she had exposed there was more than one baby.

"And they are yours as well. If you even care enough to claim them someday!"

"Abbie, did you say we are having babies? Does that mean we have more than one? Can I have a sister and a brother at the same time?"

Abbie glared at Alex.

"This is not how I wanted to do this and not how Andy deserved to find out."

She turned to Andy and stooped to his level.

"What would you say, Andy, if I told you we are having three babies? One for each of us?"

Abbie turned her head and watched Alex Montgomery turn as white as a sheet.

"I will see you real soon, love," she said to Andy, kissing him on the forehead. She stood up and looked at her therapist.

"I'll wait for you in the office."

Alex sat on the bench. Andy and the therapist were still staring at him.

"I'm so happy, Dad. Three babies. Isn't that great?"

Alex was still as white as a sheet, and the therapist tried not to laugh at him.

Alex looked up at Andy's smiling face.

"Yes, Andy. Three babies, and if they are as wonderful as you, everything will be great."

The therapist said goodbye to Andy, then walked over and put her hand on Alex's shoulder.

"I suggest you get it together, Alex. She's going to need you. But knowing her, she will do this by herself to prove she does not need your help."

And with that, she turned and walked back into the office. Abbie looked up when her therapist entered. She smiled at Abbie.

"Good job with the announcement. That news ought to keep him up for a night or two at least."

And they laughed until Abbie started crying. She took a drink and wiped her face with the sleeve of her dress.

"Abbie, you need to talk to me. I can't help if you're silent."

"I haven't told anyone yet. Before I told him, I wanted things to be better between Alex and me, and I never wanted Andy to find out this way."

"Andy will be fine. He might be better than the two of you put together. He's excited that he's having brothers or sisters or both. I'm sure you are becoming overwhelmed, Abbie, but you will figure it out. Every mother does! You might need more help than mothers with single births, but from what you have shared with me, you can afford to hire the best. There is a reason that money fell into your lap. This might be it. I realize I'm supposed to be the voice of reason, but motherhood is tough. Get help before you are so exhausted from carrying three babies, you forget to ask."

"I'll do that tomorrow. I wonder how Kohl will react to this?"

"He's a dog, Abbie. When life gets messy, he'll walk away and be asleep in the corner somewhere, ignoring you. You need to call Alex and get this mess sorted out."

"I'll call him."

Abbie stood up and walked to the door.

"Thank you. I'm going to need you for the next twenty years. Don't even think of retiring."

Alex dealt with Andy's questions on the ride home. Abbie's confession had blindsided him, and he was having trouble thinking beyond the next breath.

He got dinner ready, cleaned up, and helped Andy with his shower. Andy watched his favorite show on the TV, and Alex sat beside him on the sofa.

He looked around the room and wondered if this house was big enough for four kids. They might need to sell the house and search for something bigger. He better call tomorrow and put a hold on the pool.

What was he thinking? Abbie could decide to do this on her own. How did he make her understand he loved her and wanted to marry her? He had since the moment they realized each other existed.

The two of them were alike in so many ways and well-suited in the bedroom, but if she got pregnant with three kids every time they had sex, they were in big trouble.

He picked up his phone and sent Abbie a text.

"Can we talk?"

This time, she responded.

"Not tonight, Alex. Find a time when Andy is with friends. We have things to work out."

"Thank you, Abbie. I'll get back to you tomorrow. Sleep well!"

Abbie had one more text to send before she went to sleep.

"Hey, Dana. Can you set up a call for tomorrow? I need to talk to my crew."

"Sure. Is everything okay?"

"Yes. Thanks. Talk tomorrow."

CHAPTER 25

Alex walked into the ER, tired and still anxious from the run-in with Abbie the day before at the therapist's office. Dr. Parker took one peek at Alex and was shocked at the way Alex looked this morning.

"Where were you when that truck ran over you?"

Alex laughed.

"I was sitting on the porch at the therapist's office waiting for Andy when Abbie walked up for her appointment."

"How did that go?"

"Not well. No, horrible! It depends on your perception of the situation. Andy thinks it's great. But the jury is still out."

"It sounds like there might be more to that story."

"Oh, there's more. So much more!" Groaned Alex.

"Abbie is pregnant with triplets."

Damon turned around so fast the room spun, and he caught himself from falling.

"Wait. What? Did I hear you say the word triplets?"

"We were talking when she arrived at the therapist's office. She was wearing a summer dress. The wind blew, and she grabbed her dress to keep it from flying up. However, when she grabbed the dress, it caught the shape of her stomach. It was obvious she was pregnant. I asked if it was my baby or Tom's. At first, she said the babies were hers. I caught the plural of baby when she answered. Neither of us realized that Andy and the therapist had come out of the office and were watching us. She went over to Andy and told him that there were three babies. One for each of us."

"Dear lord, Montgomery. Have a seat before one of us passes out. I will sit too because that news would weaken any man."

Alex started laughing and couldn't stop. Dr. Parker started laughing too, and the two sat there doubled over laughing until the whole ER staff were staring and started laughing as well, which made the whole scene that much funnier, and they couldn't stop. Ten minutes later, Damon pulled it together.

"Dang, Montgomery. I'll give you my bike if you want to get on and ride into the sunset."

Alex almost started laughing again but took a big breath to calm himself down.

"It is 7:15 a.m. That would be one long ride."

"Darn straight, Montgomery. So, start now!"

Alex got up, walked over to the coffee pot, and poured a cup for both.

"I'm afraid to check the patient board this morning."

"We are safe. For now. No big surprises out there. Nurse practitioners should be able to manage everything. If not, they'll find us. You need to get that coffee in before we find you in the lounge passed out."

Alex sat and started drinking the coffee. He got up to pour a second cup when Amy from human resources came around the corner.

"Hi, Dr. Montgomery. I have a resume that needs to be reviewed for the open ER director of nursing position. This applicant said she knows you."

"Sure, Amy. I have time to look."

Alex reached for the resume. His first thought was, if that document is Abbie's resume, I swear I'll have her committed.

His eyes moved to the name on the resume, and he smiled. Perhaps, someone was watching out for him after all. He handed the resume back to Amy.

"Dana worked as the director of nursing at the hospital in Charleston, and she's perfect for the position. She and Abbie are best friends."

Amy took the resume.

"And Dr. Montgomery, Dana asked that you not tell Abbie. It is to be a surprise. She misses her and wants to work with you again."

"Don't worry, Amy. I will not tell her."

Dana had set up the zoom call for this morning. Abbie did not tell her what was going on, but she sensed it was essential to Abbie, so she scheduled it as early as possible. Everyone's schedules were open for an hour, and she decided to take advantage of the free time.

Abbie logged in to the call after a poor night of sleep and a bout of morning sickness again this morning. She rarely experienced morning sickness, so when it hit, it was often hours, sometimes before she got better. Everyone else logged in as well. Abbie spoke up first.

"Thanks for taking time from your busy schedule this morning. I have news to share with everyone."

Abbie took a big breath.

"I'm pregnant and Alex is the father. I had a sonogram yesterday, and while everything is good so far, the doctor discovered we are having triplets."

There was dead silence. Then everyone started talking. Abbie picked up a word or two, but there was so much excitement, she got teary again. Dang hormones! Julie spoke up louder than the others.

"Abbie, are you feeling okay? You appear tired. What does Alex have to say about this?"

"Andy is happy that he's going to have brothers and or sisters. Alex turned as white as a sheet and nearly passed out. I'm not aware if he had anything to say because I walked away and sat in the therapist's office."

They wanted the whole story, so Abbie filled everyone in on the events that had been happening. She answered their questions. When they were ready to hang up, Dana spoke up.

"Listen, everyone. Before we hang up, I have news as well."

"Dang, girl. Don't tell us you're pregnant, too." Sam said.

Dana laughed.

"No, Sam. I have a new job I wanted to announce. You are speaking to the new director of nursing for the ER at Coastal Hospital."

Once again, everyone started talking over one another.

"Abbie, I'll help with whatever is needed."

"Do you need a place to stay? Dana? I have a spare room."

"Are you sure? I don't want to add to your problems."

"You are welcome to stay with me, Dana, and If I get things worked out with Montgomery, I can turn the rental over to you. Even if we don't, that rental is not big enough for three babies. I'll need to find a new place. The spare room is empty. Bring your bed, or we can buy one."

Now that everything was out in the open, Abbie could relax. The next order of business was to get at least one puppy.

She sent Sam a text to ask if she was free after work. She'd located Kohl's breeder, and they had time to stop early that evening.

Sam replied, and they were set. She drove her big SUV and hoped they would find their next therapy dog. She took Kohl to the store and bought the supplies needed to care for the new dogs.

Montgomery was going to assume she'd lost her mind, but Andy would be thrilled, and she wanted to let him name the next dog. Sam wouldn't care, but she wanted to ask her opinion.

Abbie walked around the house searching for any area that needed puppy-proofing. Soon, she needed to baby-proof the house but was unsure what house she would land in with her three babies.

She could not put off talking to Alex any longer. They had to be together at the next doctor's appointment, and he deserved to be involved in this whole baby-raising process.

Abbie's emotions had taken her on a roller coaster ride. She was not angry with him any longer. From observing how he interacted with Andy, she knew he was a good father. Loving, fun, but strict when necessary, and she knew that he would be the same with the babies they were expecting.

Alex had no clue that life was going to involve puppies, too. Abbie paused in the middle of making the puppy's bed near Kohl's bed. What if he didn't want to be part of this crazy life they were about to start? Well, if not, I'll figure it out on my own.

She picked up her phone, and her hands shook when she sent a text to Alex.

"Sorry for making this so difficult. Do you have time in your schedule to meet this week?"

She was nervous when he didn't reply right away. What if he is trying to avoid me? Is he the type to try to pay me back with the same behavior I exposed him to for so long? What if he's not interested any longer?

Her phone dinged, and she saw Alex's name on the screen.

"How's tomorrow after I'm done with my shift? I'll find someone to stay with, Andy."

"Let me check with Sam. Andy will have a blast with her."

"That's good. And the meeting place?"

"My place where we have privacy."

"That is a good plan. I need your address."

"Walk out your front door, head north. My house is the third one." Abbie cringed, waiting for his response to her proximity.

"I'm standing here shaking my head, Abbie. You are incredibly good at being right next to me but always fly under my radar. I'll see you tomorrow."

She laid her phone on the coffee table and noticed Kohl standing by his bed. He was glancing from her to the new bed as if to ask, why do we have a second bed? Abbie sighed, determined she would not battle Kohl over this addition to their family.

"Kohl, we are getting a new puppy. You, I, and Sam will shop for a new puppy this afternoon."

He cocked his head to one side and stared at her.

"We need more dogs who can assist people, Kohl. We're going to visit your breeder this afternoon, and you can help us pick out the next great Newfie."

Abbie asked Sam if she could take care of Andy tomorrow afternoon so that she and Alex could talk.

"It's past time for the two of you to get your issues resolved, Abbie. And I'll be happy to hang out with Andy. Take all the time you need. What's the possibility of Montgomery letting me take Andy into the therapy pool? He's a handsome little version of his father and would be a great spokesmodel for the program."

"I'm sure he will approve. We need to figure out how Andy does with the two of you in the pool. If he does well, we can talk to his therapist and switch him to our program."

"He trusts Kohl, and Andy is not afraid of him, so that is a perfect idea. Let's have you approach Alex with the idea. I have enough to deal with right now, Sam. He might be more agreeable if the idea comes from you."

"No problem. I'll text him now and ask him to drop Andy off at the pool building and ask permission to take Andy to dinner. I hope Andy agrees. We can have fun, and it will give me time to see what type of help he needs to recover from his injuries. If Montgomery disapproves of Andy being the spokesperson, we will find someone else to be the model."

Sam texted Alex and offered to keep Andy occupied while he and Abbie talked. He thanked her for the offer and promised to drop him off at the pool after school. Sam replied she wanted to take him to dinner as well, so there was no rush to pick him up and offered to take Andy home and help him get ready for bed.

She wanted Abbie and Alex to have as much time as needed to resolve their issues. With three babies on the way, they had issues to work out.

"There's a lot of texting going on, Sam. What are you up to now?"

"Nothing Abbie. I am asking Montgomery if I can take Andy to dinner. You two need to take your time and get everything settled. You love him, Abbie. Get this settled. Tom's death proved to us that life is too short."

"I love him, Sam. But I worry about people's thoughts when they realize Alex and I are dating. Even Dana asked if we had something going on before Tom's death."

"Abbie, the only people that matter, love you beyond reason, and we are with you no matter what you decide. I told Parker that same thing the other morning."

"Did you? That needs more explanation, Sam. When were you with Parker? I told you he was coming for you."

"It was nothing, Abbie. He noticed me coming out of the building. That was the day we got approval. I may have been dancing on the sidewalk. He saw me and asked if I always danced on Friday. I told him we got approved, and he said we should celebrate our first success. We planned only to have one drink, and he would take me back for my bike, but he told the people in the bar, and they started buying shots."

"Oh no, Sam. What happened?"

"If you let me finish, nothing happened. We parked his bike at his house and walked to this local bar. We both had too much to drink, so I stayed in the guest room at his house. End of story. He took me to pick up my bike the next day. We took a ride up the coast and stopped in Wilmington for lunch. That's it. He waves if he sees me. Nothing else."

"Good luck, Sam. Montgomery and I were only planning to be friends, and look at what happened."

Abbie pulled into the driveway, and Kohl noticed the puppies in the yard. He let out a low bark and stood facing out the back window of the SUV. Abbie opened the back liftgate, Kohl jumped out and trotted over to the breeder.

The puppies didn't have his attention; Kohl recognized his breeders. It was a love fest between the three of them. Abbie and Sam stood back and observed them for several minutes. Then they introduced themselves.

The breeders told Abbie and Sam how they had followed Kohl's career. Tom's death shocked them, but they were proud of Kohl and glad they could meet him again as an adult dog.

Abbie and Sam filled them in on their approved program. While talking, they walked over to the fenced area, and the puppies ran toward Kohl when he barked at them.

The breeder opened the gate, and they walked into the play yard. The puppies were all over him in an instant. He let them climb on top of him. He sniffed them and got up and started jogging around the yard. They followed him every step of the way. Sam and Abbie scrutinized the interaction of the dogs with Kohl. Personalities and decent work relationships with other dogs were significant factors in successful training.

She and Sam had discussed gender pick during the drive. The males were stronger and could work with the adults much better, but they wondered if a female dog might be better with the younger clients. In the end, they decided the male dogs would be the better option. If they had a large adult client and the only dog available was a female, she might tire quickly trying to keep them afloat.

"Okay, Sam, one dog or two?"

"We should get two, Abbie. We will need at least three dogs if this program takes off as expected. If we get two now, we will not have to be training puppies constantly."

"I know you are more the expert at training, Abbie, but will you consider sharing in the training and who they stay with every day? They are so stinking cute. I want to be part of everything."

"I agree with the training. Do you think your apartment is big enough for them? We could consider getting you a bigger place. I can foot the bill, and we can write it off as a business expense."

"No, Abbie. I can't ask you to do that."

"You are not asking, Sam. I am offering. The pups need outdoor space to run and play. I can buy the place, and you can pay me rent. The program will pick up the cost of vet visits, food, and training equipment."

"Abbie, that's asking you to do too much."

"Sam, we cannot do the program without dogs; they need a place to stay. As you mentioned earlier, one of us needs to house and feed the two of them, or we share them. I will be lucky to feed myself in the next couple of months. My belly is blowing up like a balloon."

"My therapist said that things happen for a reason, and maybe I inherited that money to start the therapy program. I need to spend the money, Sam. Tom loved you and the others as though you were his sisters. Let me do this for us. For Tom. For the people out there, who may have the opportunity walk again."

"Abbie. Be honest with me. Are you the anonymous donor?"

Abbie stood still and looked away.

"Why didn't you tell me?"

"I wasn't trying to hide anything from you, Sam. I know how the hospital budgets work and decided we might receive approval if the money came from a source other than the hospital budget. The money Tom left allows us to do good things. I may never know who made this money, but I guarantee you, I am putting it to beneficial use."

"Geez, Abbie. How can I say no to that?"

The breeders took the female puppies inside the house. That left four males. Two of them showed more interest in Kohl, which helped them decide. They could not have a shy dog.

They chose two, and Abbie paid half the cost of the dogs and the money to have a thorough medical examination to prove they were fit for the work. The breeder would deliver the dogs if their health check came back clean.

Abbie called for Kohl, but he stood and stared at her.

"Let's go, Kohl. We need to go home." He didn't move.

"I am going to get that puppy crate out when I get home, if you do not start listening to me."

Sam and the breeders tried not to laugh, but it was proving difficult.

"Now, Kohl, or I'll leave you with these puppies to crawl over you day in and day out."

Kohl huffed at her and started toward the car.

"And we are going to stop that annoying habit as well. I will not have three of you huffing at me every time you disagree."

Kohl jumped into the back of the car. Abbie and Sam thanked the breeder and started the drive home.

"What's next on the to-do list, Abbie?"

"House hunting, Sam. We'll make a cash offer and ask for a fifteen-day closing. If everything goes right, we should be able to get you moved into the new place before the dogs are ready to come home."

"Why do I feel like everything is out of my control, Abbie?"

"Welcome to my world, Sam."

CHAPTER 26

Abbie was nervous about meeting Alex later today.

She needed to get puppy supplies for Sam, but first, they needed to find a house. Abbie fixed a cup of tea and started looking online for houses. Sam said she was not particular about choosing a specific type of house. All she needed was a bedroom, a bath, and a kitchen. Abbie looked at her and asked how much room she thought she would need for three dogs.

Sam groaned.

"Tell me, Abbie, how much room do three dogs need?"

"As much as they want."

Sam rolled her eyes. She asked why she was saying three dogs. They had only picked out two.

Abbie reminded her that Kohl would be right by their sides, and Sam asked again what had just happened to her life.

Abbie found two houses she thought might work. She sent them to Sam to look over. They all had back yards, and it would be easy for a fence company to install one that would keep the puppies corralled until they learned to listen to their owners.

Sam sent her the rolling eyes emoji. This was going to be more challenging than she thought.

Abbie called the realtor she had used to find the beach house, filling her in on their requirements. She scheduled an appointment to look at the houses. One house was close enough to the therapy building that Sam could walk to if she wanted, and the house was immense, bright, and airy and had a large backyard with a covered patio. It would be a big plus if she did not need to get two puppies in a vehicle every day.

Sam had not even considered she would need an SUV or van. There was no way she would get those dogs into a regular car, and when Kohl was with them, it would be impossible.

Abbie and Kohl took their afternoon nap. Then she got ready to meet Alex. After her shower, Abbie put on a dress, did her hair, and put on makeup. Earlier this afternoon, she had fixed a marinade, and the steaks were marinating in the fridge.

She wanted to show him she would always consider his needs as well, and she knew he liked a good steak. There would be baked potatoes and vegetables for her, and she hoped she had no evening sickness. The morning sickness had resolved now that she was past the first trimester, but she wanted to be prepared for anything. She looked at the clock and decided to go sit on the front porch and watch the waves until he arrived.

Alex gathered his things and locked them up in his locker in the doctor's lounge. Parker was there, as well.

"Do you have any big plans for the evening, Montgomery?"

"Yes, I do. I am picking up Andy, then dropping him off next door with Sam. Abbie and I are meeting this evening to discuss what is next for us. Sam is going to take him in the pool for a little while, then they are heading out to dinner, and who knows what else."

"Really? Maybe I will stop and see him and Sam on my way out. I am waiting for labs on one more patient, and if everything is okay, I'll discharge him and get out of here."

"What's up with you and Sam, Damon?"

"What's that mean, Montgomery?"

"I saw the two of you talking the other day when I was leaving. I also saw you pick her up and swing her around, and the next thing I knew, you two were holding hands and leaving on the same bike."

"That was not what you were thinking. She was dancing down the sidewalk. It was the day she and Abbie got approval for their program. We left to go celebrate with a couple of drinks. We had a couple too many, and she stayed the night in the guest room. That's it."

"That's cool, Parker, as Andy would say."

"Is it going to be necessary for me to report everything to you since she and Abbie are best friends?"

"No way, Parker. I do not want to know what you two might be doing."

Alex went to the school to pick up Andy, and when he got in the car, he reminded him he was going swimming with Sam.

"I can't wait, Dad. Did Sam say where she and I are going for dinner?"

"She didn't tell me, but I'm sure she has somewhere fun planned."

"Do you think Abbie is still mad at us, Dad? I want to see Kohl and the babies."

"Andy, Abbie is not mad at either of us. She and I are going to talk about everything this evening and get it all worked out. You will see Kohl and the babies. Those babies are your siblings."

"Okay, Dad, but can you tell her I love her and want her to come home?"

Alex nodded his head. He needed a moment before answering Andy without getting emotional.

"I'll tell her we both love her and want her and Kohl to come home to live with us. I'm going to ask her to marry us as well. Are you okay with that, Andy?"

"Yes, Dad. Do you think she'll say yes? I miss them both."

"I hope so, Andy. But if she says no the first time, I will just keep asking until she says yes."

"That sounds like a good plan. Dad, I still love mom too. Do you think she will be okay with us marrying Abbie since she can't be here?"

"I still love your mother too, Andy. That's never going to change. But I am sure she will be okay with us marrying Abbie. I bet she will love all those babies just as much as we will."

Alex dropped off Andy and headed home to shower and change before meeting Abbie. He was eager to see her again and knew their relationship was on the line with her. Sam told him to take his time; if he wanted, she would take Andy home and get him to bed on time, and he gave her the code to open the door.

Alex sent Abbie a text to let her know he was on his way and walked the short distance. Knocking on the door, he overheard her give Kohl instructions and smiled. He had hoped they were beyond that point, but he was unsure.

She opened the door, and it amazed Alex how beautiful she looked. The pregnancy had only enhanced her looks, and she looked amazing.

"Hi, Alex. Come on in. Kohl's on notice to be replaced if he doesn't behave."

Alex grinned at her and Kohl.

"I think Kohl and I have settled our differences, haven't we, buddy?" Kohl barked once at Alex.

"See, Abbie. We have settled our differences."

"I see that, but he needs to prove his behavior has changed, or it's the puppy crate for him."

Kohl huffed.

"Don't put your money on him, Montgomery, or you will go broke."

Abbie walked toward Alex and wrapped her arms around him.

"I want to say that I'm so sorry things have been difficult between us, and I promise not to be so rough on you and be more understanding. I love you, Montgomery. Can you forgive me?"

Alex wrapped her tight in his arms.

"I love you too, Abbie. Andy said to tell you he loves you as well. We have been miserable without you. I'm not sure I understand how everything happened so fast, but I don't care. We need you in our lives. We don't want to live without you."

They stood holding each other for a long time. Abbie stepped back to look at him and saw the love in his eyes.

"I can see the love now, Alex, and I admit I wasn't looking close enough to see that before, and I have loved you for a while, but I thought it was too soon, so I was trying to deny it every time that feeling crept in. Life is about to get crazy, Alex. Are you sure you are ready for all this?"

"Yes, Abbie, I am sure."

Alex took her by the hand and sat on the sofa.

"Why don't we start with me meeting my babies? After that, you can tell me about your new project. Parker has hinted at it since he crashed the meeting, but I was hoping you could tell me the details of your program. I will support you and whatever comes with it."

Alex bent down, kissed her stomach, and murmured softly to the babies. Abbie swore at her dang hormones that were causing her to get emotional again.

"Let me get us something to drink, and I will tell you where we are with everything."

She poured him iced tea and grabbed a bottle of water for herself.

Once they were both seated, Abbie outlined the approved program and the marketing plan they had worked on with the company she had hired.

Abbie admitted to being the donor that was funding the program.

Alex told her it was her decision since the money was from her trust fund. He also told her how proud he was of her and her generosity.

Abbie asked him to continue to keep the whole donor part secret and told him about her conversation with her crew about the pregnancy and that they were thrilled. She let him know Dana had told her about her new position.

"If I move back in with you, Alex, I told Dana she could have this house. I will just have her take over the rental agreement unless she wants to purchase it. Then that is between her and the owner."

"Abbie, do you have any reservations about moving in with Andy and me?"

"No, Alex. Why do you ask?"

"Well, you said if you move back, I want to make sure we are honest with one another."

"Alright, Alex. When I move in with you and Andy. But there is more to the story you need to hear before you agree."

What now? Alex thought to himself. What else could she have up her sleeve?

"Go on, Abbie. We are being honest about everything. Just continue so we are clear on where we both stand."

"The program has received so many referrals already for the program that Sam and I are not sure how we are going to keep up. I called Kohl's breeders. Sam and Kohl and I paid a visit to them yesterday."

"And?" Alex prompted.

"They were so happy to see Kohl. He recognized them as soon as we pulled into the driveway and started barking. He ran right over to them when I opened the back liftgate. There were eight puppies in the yard, and he ignored them to soak up love from his breeders. When he was curious enough to go to the fence and investigate, they opened the gate, and he walked into the fenced area and lay down on the ground. Those puppies were all over him. Then he got up and trotted around the yard, and they followed him the whole time. He got back down on the ground and rolled around with them. He was great with them, Alex."

"I feel like there is more to this story, Abbie. How many puppies are you planning to bring home?"

Abbie paused before answering him. She hoped this would not undo their progress in the past hour.

"Only two, Montgomery! Sam is going to help raise them so that we won't have them all the time. They need to work with both of us so we will share the responsibility. The donor will fund the program and their care. The program will also buy Sam a house to raise and train the puppies. There is a house right across the street from the hospital, making it easy to access the pools for her and the dogs. Kohl will stay with her, too, sometimes."

Alex took a deep breath to calculate the square footage needed for all of them.

"Do you think our six-bedroom house is enough space, or do we need to sell this one and build something new?"

"You would do that for us, Montgomery?"

"Of course, I would, Abbie. You and Sam have an amazing plan put together, and that will change lives. I would also like to get Andy into the program. How do I go about that?"

"Funny that you should ask Alex. Sam and I would like to use him as a spokesmodel for the program. He loves and trusts Kohl, so he is at ease interacting with Kohl and will help others be at ease as well. You will need to be okay with him being in a couple of commercials and having his face in ads. He looks so much like you, and I bet he is going to break a few hearts growing up. He would have to agree as well."

"I give you my permission, Abbie, but we talk to Andy together. If he agrees, then it is fine with me."

"I believe this program can help him, Alex. It would be amazing to see him walk again. And don't worry. We will not speak one word to anyone about the physical advances we believe are possible with this program. It will just be another form of therapy. Of course, we will discuss how much better water is for doing exercises, but that is as far as we go with any promises."

"I understand there are no promises."

"Thanks. I made dinner. Would you like to stay and have dinner, Alex?"

"There is something else I would like more right now."

He scooped her up, started down the hallway, found her bedroom, and kicked the door closed so that Kohl would not come in and interrupt them. He laid her on the bed. "

"With your permission, I would like to show you how much I love you and our new babies, Abbie."

"Well, get busy, Montgomery. We need to make up for the lost time."

Kohl was standing at their door when they got dressed and opened the door to come back out to the living room. Alex almost tripped over him.

Abbie threatened him again with the puppy crate, but he just ignored her.

"I need to give these hungry babies food, Alex. Would you turn the grill on to heat, please, while I finish the salad and veggies?"

"Sure. Any cravings I need to be aware of? I do not want to get caught at 2:00 a.m. without the right combination of foods."

"I have had no cravings yet, so I can't prepare either of us. What did Maria crave?"

"She craved ice cream, so that was easy. I made sure we had it on hand and prayed that the electric did not go out."

"Well, you may get off easy. I am starting my fourth month, and cravings usually lessen by that point. And that reminds me, we need to see the OB/GYN. She wants you there as well. I'm seeing Andrea Jeffers. She said you are friends."

"We met at the welcome reception at lunch one day right after I started at Coastal. I call her from the ER often. How did you find her, and how did she know I was the father?"

"When the doctor at Urgent Care told me I was pregnant, he asked if I needed recommendations. He gave me her number. I must tell you that when she told me there were three babies, I kind of swore at you aloud. She asked then if you were the father. I told her we were friends that found ourselves in bed. When she said she was also friends with you, I asked her if she was pregnant, too."

"Abbie! Is that what you think of me?"

"No, Montgomery. I was just angry and alone with three babies. She told me you were not that type of friend. But she said to make sure you are at these appointments because we need to know what to expect, and while you are a doctor, you are not a specialist in multiple births."

"I'll be with you for every appointment, Abbie. Isn't her office in the building right next to Coastal hospital?"

"It is, which will make it easier for you to be at the visit and return to work."

"Just schedule the appointment. I will be there. Parker will cover for me."

They finished eating and cleaned up the kitchen. Abbie sat on the sofa and put her feet up.

"How about we get your stuff together, Abbie? I want you and Kohl to stay with me tonight. Andy was worried about how this would all work out tonight. If Kohl crawls in bed with him tonight and he sees you in the morning, it will make him one happy little boy."

"That sounds good, but we better hurry. If I don't get to bed soon, I'm going to be sleeping on the beach with the rest of the beach bums."

They got her things together and walked the short distance back to his house.

Kohl searched for Andy and crawled into bed with him. They overheard Andy say hello, and that it was time to go to sleep. Abbie agreed with Andy.

They thanked Sam for helping Andy and told her they would talk tomorrow.

Abbie got through her nighttime routine and crawled into bed. Alex got into bed when she was almost asleep and cuddled up to her. She was out within seconds.

Abbie did not hear him get up the next morning. When she woke up, Kohl was in bed with her, and she found a note from Alex on the nightstand.

Abbie fleetingly remembered Andy coming in to kiss her goodbye. She read the note from Alex. See you later, love. Stop in if you are up this way.

Abbie sent a text to Sam, letting her know Alex had given his permission to have Andy join the program and be the spokesperson for the program. They needed to talk to him, of course, she told her, but she did not think he would refuse.

She let Sam know that she and Alex had worked out their problems, and that, for now, everything was okay.

She was going to stop in later today, and they could go through their checklist.

Sam asked if there was any word from the breeders, and she told her it would be days before she expected the results to be completed.

The realtor had time this afternoon if she wanted to look at the house. Sam agreed they should, and Abbie told her she would schedule the showing.

CHAPTER 27

Abbie sent Alex a text asking if he could call the school and let them know she would pick Andy up from school today.

Abbie and Sam wanted to talk with him regarding the spokesmodel's role.

She sent him the link for the house they had found for Sam and the new pups and asked if he wanted to meet them to view the house. He responded with a yes. And said he'd contact the school, but he preferred keeping the news of the new puppies as a surprise for Andy.

She put Kohl outside while she showered and dressed. There was no morning sickness today. And she hoped she had seen the last of that nuisance.

Abbie sent Sam a text and filled her in on her plans and wandered around the house. Alex had asked if they needed to build a new house to fit everyone. She looked at the bedrooms. They had enough bedrooms, including one for a full-time nanny. If they put doors between the rooms, the nanny could have her own sitting room, and the babies could all sleep in one room. As they grew and the nanny was no longer needed, they could turn one room into a playroom. When they were older yet, they could each have their own room and bath.

Abbie preferred to stay at the beach. Finding an empty property to build a new house on was impossible. The other choice would be to find a large piece of property with a small house they could tear down and start from nothing. Abbie sighed. They'd be retired before they found a piece of property, and the cost would be exorbitant.

She sent Alex another text, reminding him to ask Andy's doctor if Andy could take part in the hydrotherapy program. She also sent Alex the email where the application needed to be sent.

Alex replied to her text.

"I'm on top of it, Abbie."

"Sorry, too many things are running through my brain this morning. And thanks for letting me sleep this morning."

Alex replied again, this time with a heart emoji.

She texted Dana asking when she was moving in and letting her know she had moved in with Alex.

She called the moving company and scheduled a date to move her things from the rental, then called the owner of the rental to check on changing the lease from her name to Dana's.

Tomorrow, she needed to clean out her storage unit before her belly was too big, and she could reach none of her belongings.

Grabbing a bottle of water, she sat on the deck and started a list. It became a lengthy list, which included fencing the backyard to keep the pups from wandering away.

Abbie needed to discuss the fence with Alex and check online for any zoning restrictions and permits they might need. Add to the list, find a nanny service!

Abbie opened the door of the refrigerator, then looked in the freezer. Was this refrigerator even big enough to hold food for four growing kids and two adults? Alex was right. They should build a new house. She was getting overwhelmed.

Abbie sent Alex another text asking him for advice on a local fence company, a contractor, a nanny service, and a bigger fridge. Her phone rang, and she saw Alex's name and answered.

"Abbie, what's wrong this morning? Did the refrigerator stop working? And why do we need a contractor?"

"I started making a list of things I needed to get done, and it just keeps growing and growing. I don't know where to start."

"Have you showered and dressed to go out in public yet today?"

"Yes, I'm dressed, Montgomery. It's almost noon."

"Great! Meet me in the ER. We can have lunch together on the cafeteria patio and discuss your list. You can bring Kohl. I've checked, and his certification allows him in the building."

"Are you sure? Is the ER slow this morning? We can do it another time, Alex."

"We are good, Abbie. Dr. Parker is here, and he will cover. See you in ten minutes!"

Damon overheard the end of Alex's comment.

"Is it you that needs coverage, Montgomery?"

"Yes, if you don't mind. Abbie has been texting me this morning with questions. She's asking about contractors, nannies, fences, and a bigger refrigerator."

"Why the fence? The babies are small enough not to worry over a fence."

"That is not why we need a fence, Damon. She and Sam bought two new Newfie pups that are arriving soon. So, not only does the yard need to be fenced, but Sam is also going to care for the pups as well. Also, she doesn't have room in her apartment, so today, they are looking at a house for sale across the street from the hospital."

"Wow, Montgomery. How sure are you that the two of them should even talk? They have far-out ideas."

"I am well aware of their ability to conger up new projects. I wonder if either of them has considered that Sam will need either a van or an SUV to carry around four hundred fifty pounds of dog."

"Do you need me to help you find a second job? I also know people who might help you fund their projects."

"Listen, Parker. If I tell you something, I need your absolute guarantee; you won't ever tell anyone what I tell you."

"Not sure if I should be hanging out with you, Montgomery. It just keeps getting deeper and deeper, but you have my guarantee."

"I'm serious, Parker. You will put Abbie, Sam, Andy, and the babies at serious risk of harm if you let any of this slip."

"Is she in witness protection, Montgomery?"

"No, it's worse than that. When her husband died, she was the sole person to inherit his money. Abbie has a significant trust fund, and she is using it to fund this program. Her trust pays every cent of the expenses. She is the anonymous donor."

"How significant, Alex! If you are worried about her safety, it must be more than a couple of pennies."

"Hundreds of billions."

"Did you say millions or billions?"

"You understood right the first time."

Damon whistled. He sat on the chair across from Alex.

"How do you manage all that?"

"I try to ignore it, and so does Abbie. The idea for the project came from her. She and Sam believe it will work. Abbie knew they would have trouble getting funding from the hospital, so she's funding everything. Trust me, with interest; she can't spend it fast enough to make a dent in the balance."

"That must be the craziest story I've learned in quite a while. I guarantee you I am not telling a soul, and I will never let on to Abbie or Sam that you shared that information with me."

"I appreciate it. Abbie is going to be here soon. I told her to come to lunch with me so that she'd stop texting me. I don't care how much she texts me, but I read the panic starting in her text."

"This entire relationship started when she texted me that she needed my help. When I called her, she sounded drunk or on drugs or that someone had slipped something into her food or drink. It was a couple of hours after the attorney told her about Tom's trust fund. Abbie was panicking and needed someone she could talk to about everything she had learned when meeting with the attorney. She had just met me, but she said she trusted me. I could hear the same panic starting today and tried to stop it before it flew off the rails."

"Enjoy your lunch with Abbie."

Abbie arrived with Kohl, and Alex introduced the two of them to the rest of the ER staff. She had met Damon before.

They walked to the cafeteria. Alex paid for lunch, and they found a table on the covered patio. Abbie shared her concerns and got out her to-do list, checking to ensure she did not forget to mention any of the tasks. Alex asked for her list and suggested she start with groceries and the fence. Abbie nodded her head in agreement and asked him if he thought she should use a delivery service for the groceries. He agreed, and he saw her relax. He asked if she was going to continue her therapy, and she nodded her head.

"I told her I did not allow her to retire for at least twenty years. With three children the same age, I would need her."

"Why don't you and Kohl go home and take a nap? I've called the school and cleared you to pick up Andy. I'll call the fence place this afternoon, and we'll get a grocery list together tonight. Tomorrow, we'll work on two or three other things on your list."

"Thanks, Montgomery. How could I do this without you?"

"You will be fine, but I don't want to do it without you, Abbie."

She took her nap, then she and Kohl picked up Andy.

Kohl barked as soon as he saw him, and once again, chaos ensued, and Abbie had to step in and get Andy and Kohl to the car. Andy told her what he did at school during their drive to meet with Sam. She told him they were meeting with Sam at the pool.

"Are we swimming today, Abbie?"

"Not today, but your dad and I are going to talk with Sam and get you on a schedule."

"That's cool. Can Kohl swim with me?"

"We might work that out."

They let Kohl roam around outside while Sam finished with her patient, then went into the area with the pool. Andy and Kohl both made a beeline for Sam, and she hugged them both simultaneously.

"Sam, Abbie said you can get me on a swimming schedule. Will Kohl be able to swim with me?"

"Well, Andy. That's why we wanted to talk to you today. Abbie and I are starting a new therapy program. It's called hydrotherapy. Hydro is another word for water. Our plan is to have Kohl help people do their therapy in the water. The exercises you do now in therapy will be easier to do in the water, and there will be less pain. Do you have any pain now, Andy, during your therapy?"

"Not actually, Sam. But sometimes, my legs feel like they need different exercises."

"I'm glad that you do not have any pain, and we will give your legs the exercises they need."

She described the program in a language that a seven-year-old understood, and Andy agreed to take part.

"Have you heard the word spokesperson, Andy?"

"I'm not sure, Sam."

"On TV, you have seen people selling things. They try to convince people how much better that item might be than other items they buy. Right?" Andy nodded. "Abbie and I were hoping for you and Kohl to be our spokespersons for the new therapy program. Your dad has given us his okay."

"Does that mean that Kohl and I are going to be on TV, Abbie?"

"Well, to start out, the photographer will get photos of you and Kohl together and use them on the website and the other paper materials we hand out. Your pictures will go up here on the walls and in the hospital where your dad works so that people who work and visit there can see your pictures, too."

"That's so cool. Thanks, Abbie, and Sam. That sounds fun."

Abbie pulled a chair over next to Andy to speak to him eye to eye.

"It will be, Andy, but it will be work, too. You still need the therapy so that we can get you up and walking again but imagine how proud your mother and dad will be that you are part of this program."

"I am going to show my mother that I can walk again, and I'll work hard, Abbie, because I want you to be proud of me, and if I can walk again, I can play with the babies."

"Your Dad and I are always proud of you, Andy." Abbie hugged him and kissed him on the cheek. "Thanks for kissing me goodbye this morning, Andy. I was exhausted, but I felt your kiss."

Alex entered the pool area before anyone noticed him. He overheard Andy's promise to work hard and Abbie's response. Abbie's emotions were contagious. He was teary-eyed as well.

Alex spoke up, and everyone turned toward him. Andy told his dad everything he and Abbie discussed and promised he and Kohl would be great spokespersons.

Sam touched Andy on the shoulder to get his attention.

"Hey, Andy. I am going to meet the realtor to see the house across the street. Do you want to go with me?"

"Yes but let me ask my dad."

"Dad, can we go?"

Alex nodded, and Andy and Kohl headed toward the door. They left their cars parked, and Alex reminded Andy of the rules of crossing the street.

The long tree-lined driveway circled in front of the house and to the left and ended at a double garage attached to the house via a breezeway. Susan, the realtor, waited on the wide front porch. It was perfect for anyone wanting to sit outside to enjoy the weather.

Sam smiled when she entered the front door, which opened to a wide hallway with a den to the right and the living room to the left. The living room had double sliding pocket doors that opened to the dining room, and the same type of door opened to an enormous kitchen.

Sam fell in love with everything she saw.

There was a bedroom and bath on the lower floor and a library, as well. Just past the den on the right was a curved stairway that led to the second floor, which held three more bedrooms and three baths. The bedrooms were huge; each had a sitting room attached and a balcony to relax and enjoy the view. Sam turned and looked at Abbie.

"This house is magnificent."

Abbie nodded. "It is gorgeous. And it has enough bedrooms for Kate and Julie to visit and still have their own privacy or if we need room for visiting doctors or investors. If Andy stays, there's a bedroom or den on the lower floor that is perfect."

"What's your opinion, Montgomery?"

"It's the quintessential southern home, Abbie."

"Sam, this house fits you and is gorgeous. The modern upgrades to the kitchen and bathrooms are great. It is not a house you should pass up. But let's check out the backyard and the heating and cooling systems."

The systems checked out and were newer than expected.

There was a generator in case a hurricane took out the power. They walked into the backyard. It was large and had sprawling oak trees, which provided shade.

Alex looked at the perimeter of the property. It was level, and the fence company should have an easy installation. He turned to Abbie and Sam.

"The backyard should be easy to fence."

"Is that so we can keep the babies in, Dad?"

Alex looked at Abbie, and she nodded her head.

"It will work to keep them safe when they are big enough to walk, Andy, but Abbie and Sam are getting us two Newfoundland puppies who are going to be trained to work with other patients like you."

Andy looked at Abbie and Sam, then back at Alex.

"Are you serious?"

Alex nodded, and Andy started sobbing. Abbie walked to Andy and stooped to his level.

"Why are you crying, Andy?"

Andy reached out to hug Abbie.

"I have waited so long for a brother or sister, and I have been asking Dad for a puppy for so long. Now I get to have everything. I'm just so happy."

"Andy, Sam and I will need help to pick names for the new puppies. Do you want to help us?" Andy nodded and held on to Abbie for a long time.

There was a knock at the back door, and they looked up. Damon Parker walked out onto the back porch.

"Are you buying this house, Sam? This is the perfect southern home. If you don't buy it, I will. Can someone show me around this gorgeous house?"

Andy volunteered.

"I will, but I can't show you upstairs, Dr. Parker. Sam can do that for you."

Damon pushed Andy and his wheelchair back into the house, and Andy gave him the details as he understood them. Once they were done with Damon's tour, he and Alex walked outside to check out the garage while Abbie and Sam finished with the realtor.

"Do you love it, Sam? Abbie asked. Should we sign for it?"

"I love it, Abbie, and I say get those papers signed before Parker walks back in here and tries to outbid us."

Alex and Damon walked back into the house, and Damon couldn't stop talking about the garage and how perfect it would be to work on his bike.

He turned to the realtor.

"I will put in a bid on this place if they are not interested."

Sam beat her to the punch.

"Too late, Parker. Abbie signed the contract."

"Dang it, Sam. I'll give up my house for this charmer. How about you rent me the garage?"

"Dream on, Parker. You lost."

"My mama taught me that the loser always buys dinner. Are you hungry, Andy?"

Andy said yes, and they went out the door.

Damon grabbed Sam around the waist as they stepped onto the porch.

"You are one fortunate lady, and I am jealous."

Sam did not respond and just kept walking.

Abbie nudged Alex and raised her eyebrows as he shrugged and took her hand, not letting on that he knew they had been out and even spent the night together.

CHAPTER 28

Abbie's phone rang. It was the breeder, letting her know that the health check done on the pups came back with a perfect rating and that they could deliver them on Saturday if that worked with Abbie's schedule. She sent Sam a text with the good news.

They installed the fencing at both houses, so they were ready. Abbie rechecked her supplies and determined everything was ready so she could relax. This evening, she and Andy could discuss names.

Abbie scheduled an appointment for today with the OB/GYN. She had been feeling great, but her belly was growing so fast. Alex had found an agency that had nannies, and they would also tolerate three dogs. Then she called her friend at the cleaning company and signed a contract for cleaning services twice weekly. Once the dogs and the babies were older, they could cut back. For now, her growing belly was interfering with her activities.

When they finished dinner, Abbie told Andy the puppies were arriving on Saturday. He let out a resounding woo-hoo, and Kohl joined in by barking. Abbie got everyone to quiet down by asking Andy if he had suggestions for good names.

"Well, my friends say Kohl is as big as a gorilla. Do you remember the gorilla that can use sign language, Abbie? We learned about him in school. Maybe we could name one of them after the gorilla. My friends would think that was funny."

"Let's check the internet. It should be easy to find." Abbie and Alex both reached for their phones.

Alex spoke up first.

"I've got it. It's Koko, Andy. Is that the name you wanted?"

"Yes, that's it, and that means Kohl and Koko are names that start with a K. We need one more name with a K."

Andy pondered her question for a minute and then said,

"My best friend's name in Denver is Cody. Could we use that name, Abbie, but spell it with a K?"

"That is a wonderful idea, Andy. So, Koko and Kody? Are you happy with those names, Andy?"

"Yes. The names are perfect. Now, all their names start with the letter K, and mine, yours, and Dad's start with an A."

"Okay, perfect, Andy. Let's look at the internet and check the names. Sometimes, names have meanings, so let's check the names Koko and Kody."

Abbie typed the name Koko and found the meaning.

"The name Koko in Native American means the night. That's good, Andy, because his fur is black. The name Kody means helpful. That's perfect too. His purpose with the therapy program is to help people. Fantastic job with the names, Andy!"

"Can we call Sam and tell her the names?"

"Sure. I'll dial and let you talk."

Abbie placed the call to Sam and handed the phone to Andy. Andy talked nonstop and told her the names, what the names meant, what day they were being delivered, and ideas he had to help her with their training. Sam was sending Alex smiling emojis as Andy talked to her, and Abbie was smiling, too.

Abbie's doctor's appointment went well, and she chuckled when she noticed how nervous Alex was. The doctor was glad Alex joined her at the appointment, and they discussed hospital politics while she did her exam. Alex held her hand throughout the exam and relaxed when he had confirmation everything was fine.

"Are you interested in knowing the genders?"

Abbie and Alex looked at one another, and Alex squeezed her hand.

"I'm fine with knowing if that's what Abbie wants."

Abbie smiled at him and squeezed his hand.

"Can you tell us the genders of each of them today?"

"We will try. Abbie, I want you to look at Alex, not at the screen. If you change your mind at the last moment, you won't be able to unsee the results."

"Do you have a gender preference, Montgomery?"

"Healthy is my preference, Abbie! Gender does not matter to me. Do you have a gender preference?"

"Healthy is also my preference, and Andy won't care, either. He's just excited that he is becoming a big brother."

Alex nodded his head. "Should we let him name them, or do we keep that as a surprise for him?"

"Let's surprise him. We can agree on three names, but it might take time."

"I will not argue with you over names. Let's not tell anyone else about the genders, either. I want to surprise everyone."

"Let's decide on names; then we can reveal their genders. Are you opposed to that?"

"That sounds like a splendid plan to me."

They heard the doctor chuckle. "Are you ready? You can wait until delivery if you want a surprise."

"We're ready," Alex said, and Abbie nodded her head and squeezed Alex's hand until he expected it to break.

"We'll call this one baby number one, and that baby is a girl. Then this will be baby number two, and that is a girl. This is baby number three. Any guess on the gender of this one?" Abbie and Alex both shook their heads. "Baby number three… is a girl as well."

Alex bent over and kissed Abbie, and she wrapped him in a hug. Alex whispered into her ear.

"Thank you, my love. I would have been happy with any combination. I hope you are happy, too."

Abbie kissed him again. "I am ecstatic, Alex. I just want them to be healthy. Because they are ours, I can't imagine anything else that could make me this happy."

When their appointment was over, Alex suggested they stop for lunch. He had time before he had to be back at the hospital. After lunch, Alex suggested they take a walk on the beach. Abbie thanked him. She had been so busy that she had not left time for any walks.

Alex parked at the house, and they strolled to the beach, discussing the information the doctor had given them this morning. They discussed plans for a contractor to install doorways between three bedrooms.

One room was for the nanny. Her room would have a doorway that accessed the room with the cribs. The third room, which would connect with the crib room, would function as a playroom until the babies were older, then each would have their own room. Every room had a bathroom, and that would be perfect for busy mornings.

Alex looked at his watch, then looked at Abbie.

"There's one thing I must ask you before the chaos takes over our lives, Abbie."

She turned to him. "Anything Alex!"

Alex reached into his pocket and took out a small box. Bending on one knee, he reached for Abbie's hand.

"In the brief time we have known each other, there have been many changes in our lives. I love you, Abbie, and I don't want to miss a moment of our son's or daughters' lives without you next to me. Will you marry me, Abbie?"

Abbie looked stunned, and Alex got nervous.

She nodded her head and said, "Yes, Alex. I will marry you. And yes, to the craziness about to consume our lives. With three dogs, three babies, and a big brother, we may be old before we find peace. When we do, I want you by my side."

Alex slipped the ring he had bought onto her finger and stood to kiss her. Abbie never glanced down at the ring he placed on her finger. She was looking straight at him. He was the only one she could see and all she wanted for the rest of their lives. They wrapped their arms around one another and stood, embraced in the love that they had found.

Alex took her hand and started back toward the house.

"I'm going to have a nap. I'll fix a fancy dinner, as Andy calls them. I'll fix his favorite burgers and fries and something gooey for dessert, and you can tell him you asked me to marry you."

"That sounds perfect. Do you want a big wedding, Abbie?"

"No, Montgomery! I would prefer a simple beach ceremony with our friends and your colleagues unless you prefer something different. Do you want a big wedding?"

"No, Abbie. I have what I want with you. I need nothing big, and Andy will just be happy that we are getting married. He loves you as well, Abbie."

"And I love him as if he were my child, Alex. I hope you both realize that, Alex."

"We do, Abbie. He might want to call you Mom. Are you okay with that?"

"I'd be thrilled if he wants to call me mom."

"Great! Look at the calendar and pick a date and time, and I'll call the caterer and find someone who can provide us with a simple wedding setup on the beach. You can take your crew and find a gorgeous dress that will make Andy and me cry when we watch you walk toward us, and we can do whatever else you want."

"That sounds perfect. We can ask Andy this evening if he has any ideas that we can include."

They had burgers and fries at the dining room table with candles.

"Are we celebrating something again, Dad, since we are using candles? When we light candles, it makes me wonder if we are celebrating."

"Yes, Andy, we are celebrating. I asked Abbie to marry us today, and she said yes."

Andy's eyes got big, and he looked back and forth between Abbie and his dad.

"Abbie? Did you say yes? That means you're going to be my mom. Isn't that right, Dad?"

"I said yes, Andy, and if you want me to be your mom, then that is what I will be."

"Yes. Of course, I want you to be my mom. I love you, Abbie, and I love Kohl, too. You make Dad and me happy."

Andy sat for a moment.

"Abbie, if I call you mom, does that mean my actual mother is no longer my mother?"

Alex spoke up first.

"I'll take this, Abbie. Andy, your mother will always be your mother. Nothing on earth will ever change that relationship. Even though she is not here, your mother is your mother forever. You can refer to Abbie as Mom; it changes nothing between you and your mother. Or you can continue to call her Abbie. We leave that decision up to you."

"Abbie, I want to call you Mom. Would that be okay with you?"

"It would honor me to be your mother, Andy."

Abbie got up and walked over to him and stooped to his level.

"I can never replace your mother, but I promise to be a good and loving mother to you." They hugged one another, and Abbie kissed his head.

Abbie turned to Alex. "I need your help to get up. The babies are too heavy, and I can't get up by myself."

Saturday rolled around, and they waited for Kody and Koko. Abbie received a text from the breeder when they were about a mile away. They went outside to wait in the backyard. Kohl followed, not knowing what was happening. He just followed Andy when they were together.

The breeder arrived and opened the back gate to the SUV, and the puppies jumped from the vehicle. They got excited as they spotted Kohl and Andy. They ran to Kohl first, who met them halfway to the gate. Andy rolled his wheelchair next to Kohl, and the puppies jumped all over him. They were trying to crawl up on his chair, so he picked each one up and held them as they licked his face. Everyone was excited and laughing. Sam pulled into the driveway, soon after the puppies arrived, and she was excited like everyone else.

Abbie spoke up to get everyone's attention.

"Okay, everyone. If we can find Andy beneath the pile of puppies on his lap, it's time for him to tell us which puppy is Koko, and which one is Kody."

Andy had both puppies on his lap. He peeked around the puppies and waved at Abbie. "Okay, Abbie, I am going to ask them."

Andy turned the puppies around on his lap.

"Which one of you wants to be, Koko?" The puppy with the green collar barked as if to acknowledge Andy's question.

Andy hugged him and said, "You are Koko, and you," he said, looking at the puppy wearing the red collar, "will be called Kody." That puppy acknowledged Andy by barking as well.

"Well, that settles it," Sam said. "We will need to remember them by their collar color until they learn their names and develop their own looks and personality."

Everyone agreed! They thanked the breeders, and Andy hugged them. "We will call you when we are ready for more puppies."

Alex groaned at Andy's statement, and Kohl let out a bark. Abbie wondered if she had lost her mind for agreeing to take on all this responsibility. Sam looked over at Abbie and laughed.

"Do you think we can take care of them and the triplets, Abbie?"

"I am uncertain of everything, but we will figure out how to do it. The dogs will be easy to train, and the babies will grow in time. We need a routine, and it needs to start tomorrow. Right now, I'm taking the pups inside. They need to get acquainted with us and the house. Are you coming?"

"We should let them get used to you tonight, Abbie. Tomorrow, we'll introduce them to the water and pool. We need to figure out if they can swim. I think we will stick to that routine for several days; then I'll take them to my house. I want Kohl to stay with them at my place. He will be familiar to them and provide them with comfort in a strange place."

"That's a good plan. Okay, we're going inside. Wish me luck!"

Abbie found the puppies running through the house, and Kohl kept a close eye on them. Andy tried to follow in his wheelchair, but they were everywhere, and he could not keep up with the two of them. Andy picked them up one by one and took them to their water and food dishes. They drank and had food, and then he showed them their bed.

Alex was glad Andy was taking the lead on what they needed. He would be collaborating with them, as well as Abbie and Sam. They would grow fast, and Andy could not pick them up from his chair.

Even though he and Kohl had a contentious start, they had gotten used to each other, and he did not huff at him any longer. There were still times he huffed when told to do something he did not want to do, but that would not likely change.

Abbie joined him on the sofa and watched the chaos unfold. "Are you sure you want to marry me and this craziness, Montgomery?"

"I do, Abbie. You will have Koko and Kody trained before long, and our babies are going to sprout. I pray that life will settle into a routine, and we will survive."

"I just said the same to Sam. We are going to introduce them to the water tomorrow. Can you and Andy join us after you pick him up from school? He enjoys swimming with Kohl, allowing us to see if they can swim and keep pace with Andy and Kohl."

"We can do that, Abbie. Parker asked earlier today when we were getting the dogs. He may stop at the pool, too. Would you and Sam be okay with him stopping?"

"I don't mind, and I doubt Sam will, either. Damon likes her, but she is determined not to date him. I don't understand what she has against him. He stopped by the other day, and I said I thought he was interested in her. She says he's a 'love them and leave them' guy, and she doesn't want to be involved. He is very handsome. They would make a great-looking couple."

"I overheard the nurses talking the other day. The rumor is that he's with someone new. Apparently, he has asked no one out for several weeks. Chances are he likes her more than she realizes."

"That may be true. Time will tell!"

Abbie helped Andy prepare for bed and put the pups in their crate. Andy was unhappy that Kohl was not sleeping with him. Alex assured him that Kohl was looking after the puppies until they adjusted and didn't keep everyone up, crying through the night.

Abbie snuggled up to Alex in bed and started laughing. "What's so funny, Abbie?"

"I was wondering if this could be the last night we have any peace before everyone's away at college?"

"If that is true, I am going to show you how we are going to spend the night," Alex said as he rolled Abbie closer.

CHAPTER 29

Kohl woke everyone up the next morning. He and the puppies needed to go outside, and they were hungry, too. Alex and Andy got ready for their day, and Abbie fed the puppies and prepared breakfast for everyone else. Once Kody and Koko had their morning nap, Abbie loaded everyone into the SUV and headed to the pool. Sam was free to work with Kohl for a couple of hours this morning, and she also had an hour after work this afternoon. Sam had received permission to use the pool for training the puppies if nobody else was on the schedule to use the pool.

Kohl walked in and greeted Sam, and the puppies followed his lead. Sam called them by name and walked around to the sloped entry to the pool. Kohl waded into the water, and the other dogs followed. They jumped and barked at the water, and Kohl barked at them, and they hushed. They waded deeper into the water.

Sam took Koko, and Abbie took Kody and walked beside them, encouraging them as they swam into the deeper water. They had the pups turn around and swim back to the pool's shallow end. Once they had accomplished that routine, they put their therapy vest on them to acclimate them to their equipment's feel, weight, and buoyancy. They were cooperative, and Kohl watched over their every move.

The pups had been swimming for about an hour, wearing them out. They said goodbye to Sam. Abbie headed home to feed them, and then they would take naps before meeting Alex and Andy later this afternoon.

Everyone finished their meals, including Abbie, and she put the puppies in the crate, and they fell asleep. She stretched out on the bed and set the alarm. The babies were making her exhausted, and Abbie appreciated the freedom of not having a full-time job. She thanked Tom and his ancestors for their generous gift.

Kohl woke her just before her alarm sounded, and Abbie took the pups outside, and they played as the neighbors watched. A couple of tourists stopped and asked questions, and Abbie explained their role as therapy dogs. She made a mental to-do list and added calling the marketing department to discuss introducing Koko and Kody to the public and the board of directors.

Alex and Andy changed into their swim trunks while Abbie put on Kohl's therapy vest. Sam worked with Andy on his exercises after Alex took Andy into the water.

Abbie filled Alex in on their progress this morning and their easy adaptation to the water. Abbie reminded him that they were water dogs with webbed feet, and they were born to work in the water. The pups played while Kohl and Andy worked on his exercises. He was determined to walk again.

Damon Parker entered the pool building and chuckled when he saw the three dogs and four people in the water. He had changed into his trunks as well. *Why not?* He needed the exercise and wanted to meet the new pups. Sam looked up, and surprise registered on her face. Damon gave her his two-finger salute and entered the pool.

Sam shook her head. *What was he doing here?* She needed to concentrate on Andy's therapy and did not want to become distracted from her work. She watched him enter the pool. He walked through the water to where Alex and Abbie were standing and picked up both Koko and Kody.

Damon asked the pups what their names were. Abbie introduced him to the pups by name. He placed the pups back in the water and swam. They followed him around the way his female fans followed him.

Sam remained distracted by Damon. *Why did he need to be so handsome?* He played with the pups, and they acted as though he had raised them himself; they followed him everywhere. If she ever needed someone to watch the dogs, he was the first one she would call.

Sam told Andy if he wanted, he could try swimming on his own. Initially, he was nervous, but Sam reminded him that the vest would keep him afloat. He kicked his legs and swam over to Damon.

Abbie and Alex watched Andy swim over to Damon. He couldn't swim on his own a week ago. Abbie wrapped her arms around Alex and attempted to wrap her legs around him, but her belly prevented her from accomplishing her mission. Alex lifted her legs to the side, and he walked toward Andy and Damon.

"These little guys are getting tired out, Andy. You ready to head home?"

"Sure, Dad. You're right. The pups look tired, too."

Alex helped Andy get out of the pool, and they went to the locker room to change into dry clothes. Abbie and Sam dried the pups off, and they continued to play with Damon.

"We should take a break and grab some dinner."

"I'm not sure, Parker. I'm worn out myself."

"Perfect reason to go somewhere and have someone else cook, or I can cook for you at your amazing house."

"Good point! I guess we both need food, but you pick the place while I get changed."

Abbie and Sam walked to the changing room together while Alex and Andy tried to keep the pups from returning to the water.

"What's up with you two, Sam? I saw him put his arm around you at the house showing."

"There's nothing going on between us. He's jealous because he didn't look at the house before we bought it, and he missed having that fabulous garage space. Mark my words; he'll figure out a way to con me out of garage space."

"Are you sure the garage is the only thing he's interested in, Sam? He likes you!"

"See, that's the problem, Abbie. Parker is used to getting what he wants. The nurses and other women around here fall at his feet. I don't do that. I respect myself, and he needs to respect my wants and needs, but he somehow manipulates everyone into doing what he wants."

"Montgomery told me he overheard the nurses saying that he must be dating someone because he pays no attention to them any longer."

"I don't know, and I don't care!"

"Okay, Sam. Would you care if I asked you to be my bridesmaid?"

"Of course, I would. Did you tell the others yet?"

"Not yet. We need to set up a Zoom call, so I can tell everyone and check their calendars. Alex is good with whatever date and time we choose. We are planning to do something simple on the beach in front of the house and have everything catered. Dana is moving next week, so we also need to check her schedule. I'm hoping it won't be too difficult for them to get the same weekend off."

"I'll text everyone this evening. Are you free tomorrow, Abbie?"

"Other than being buried under three dogs and contractors, I'm good."

"Okay, I will include you in the text."

"Perfect. Have fun at dinner with Damon, Sam. And you need to pay attention to the signals he is giving you. You're missing all the fun stuff. And by the way, we need to order bedroom furniture, or Julie and Kate may need to sleep on the floor. Send me pictures of what you want, and I will order everything. If you are working on the day of delivery, I'm available."

Sam locked the doors on her way out. She looked for Damon's bike but did not see it anywhere. "Where's your bike, Parker?"

"No bikes tonight, Sam. I brought the truck. Any preference for dinner?"

Sam shook her head as Damon opened the door and helped her into the truck. He made a left out of the hospital drive and headed toward the beach. They waited in line for the swing bridge to turn and discussed the program's progress. Sam told him how Andy was doing and discussed how he was progressing. His legs were getting stronger, and he was having so much fun in the water with Kohl that she bet he didn't realize he was participating in therapy. They discussed the marketing plan that was moving along well and the photo session they had set for the following week.

"Did Alex tell you he asked Abbie to marry him?"

"Yes. He asked me if I could be one of his groomsmen. He is going to ask Andy tonight to be his best man. They are taking him to dinner, and he will ask him there. He also said that Abbie would insist on the four of you to be her bridesmaids, and he was trying to line up his four."

"Who else did he ask?"

"Coastal has a new cardiologist that we see in the ER. Good guy. Conor O'Brien. Moved here from Chicago! Says he can't stand the bitter winds of Chicago any longer. He came here from Ireland for med school and stayed. Alex is going to ask him. He thought it would be an effective way for Conor to meet people. He is trying to decide on one more, but I'm uncertain who is on his list."

"It should be fun no matter who he asks. Alex and Abbie are a fun couple. It will be interesting to see how they manage everything they have on their plate."

They chose a steak house that was popular on the beach, and Sam was glad Abbie was not here to start questioning Damon about his nutrition classes and the effects of red meat on one's cardiovascular system. She hoped the cardiac surgeon attending her wedding wasn't fond of red meat.

Damon shared with her the laughing episode that occurred when Alex found out Abbie was expecting.

"I was ready to panic for him. I offered him my bike to ride into the sunset and disappear."

"Is that what you'd do, Parker? Disappear and take no responsibility for your actions?"

"Whoa, whoa, Samantha! I said no such thing. I would not just run off."

"And why are you calling me, Samantha?"

"Because that's your name, and I enjoy the sound of it. It's sexy, and it fits your personality."

"Are you ready to order? We need to eat and get out of here. It's getting so deep; we won't be able to move."

"What's your last name, Samantha?"

"Why do you need my last name, Parker?"

They stared at one another, waiting for the first one to react.

"It's D'Alessandro!"

Damon smiled and continued to stare.

"Damon. I can't tell what is going on in that brain of yours, but you better spit it out before I call an Uber and leave you here to eat alone."

"I needed a moment to think. Your last name is sexy as well. Samantha D'Alessandro. Perfect!"

"You should have told me I needed boots, Parker. My flip-flops will suck me into the muck that's rising fast."

The server approached and took their drinks order. Damon changed the discussion to the new pups and the therapy program. He did not want to push his luck with her. Sam stood her ground and made known what she wanted. The other women he had dated did anything they assumed might make him happy. Sam considered everyone's needs, not just her own.

They discussed a variety of subjects over the next hour while they were eating. Damon was not ready to end his evening with Sam.

"Let's take a walk on the beach, Samantha. I know you need to get your place ready for the pups, but we can keep it short, and I will help you do a detailed walkthrough."

"A short walk sounds good, but I need to get the house ready soon. The dogs are already big enough to get into things they shouldn't."

Damon took her hand as they stepped onto the beach.

"You are aware this isn't going anywhere, Damon. Correct?"

"We can change directions, Samantha. Your call."

Sam smirked at him.

"You are smarter than you are acting, Parker. I mean us. This can't go anywhere."

"And why not, Samantha? I like you! You're gorgeous, intelligent, and caring. That's a rare find these days. I want to learn everything else about you, as well. So, why are you against us dating?"

"I'm not into playboys, Parker. Just not into the love them and leave them scenario."

"I've dropped that antic, Samantha. I was bored. The other ladies I dated were shallow. All they wanted was for me to buy them things and take them places. They were looking for a husband and a bank account they hoped was full of money. They only wanted the title of a doctor's wife. I can't figure out why they think that is a title and why it is so important. I saw right through their BS. The reason it seems like I dated so many women was that nobody was worth a second date."

"Do you consider this a date, Parker?"

"I'm not sure how to answer that with you, Samantha. If I say no, it's not, I don't want you to think you are not worth it. If my answer is yes, then I worry because I'm not sure you are ready to call it a date. So, I call it dinner because we both need to eat."

"Understood! I am not trying to be difficult. That's not my intent. If I do agree to date you, we need to go slow."

"Understood as well! I can go as slow or as fast as you need."

Sam shook her head.

"Somehow, I believe there's a double meaning in that statement, but I agree to have dinner, and/or a bike ride or two with you."

"Thank you, Samantha. Now, let's get the house ready for your pups."

Abbie and Alex dropped her car and the dogs off at the house and took Andy to dinner at a nice Italian restaurant.

"This is a fancy menu, Dad. I need help to understand what everything is and decide what to eat. Are we celebrating something tonight?"

They placed their order, and Abbie nodded her head at Alex.

"Andy, Abbie, and I would like to have our wedding on the beach. After the ceremony, everyone can come to the house for dinner and drinks. We will hire someone to play music, and we can all dance and have fun. I am trying to decide on who should be my best man."

"Ask Dr. Parker, Dad. He's your friend. What does a best man do? I'm sure Dr. Parker can learn whatever you need him to do."

Alex tried not to chuckle. He was not sure what Parker's response would be to Andy's description of him.

"A best man helps pick the suits to wear and helps the groom get everything ready for the wedding ceremony. He also holds on to the rings until the ceremony and greets guests when they arrive and shows them to their seats."

"That job doesn't sound too hard. I bet Dr. Parker could do that for you."

"I was hoping you might be my best man, Andy. Let's make this official. Andrew Montgomery, I am asking you to be my best man when Abbie and I get married. Will you be my best man?"

"Are you serious, Dad? I would love to be your best man. Do you think I can remember everything I need to do? That's so cool!"

"You will be perfect. And you will have Dr. Parker and Dr. O'Brien to help you remember everything. We'll use your beach wheelchair that Abbie bought while we are in the sand, then you can change to your other electric one after the ceremony."

"I guess we should have Kohl be another groom's man. What do you think, Andy?"

"Can a dog be a groom's man, Dad.?"

"Yes, he can, Andy! He will be just like Dr. Parker and Dr. O'Brien. He can show people to their seats. I don't think the pups are old enough to attend a wedding. They will need to stay in their crate during the ceremony."

"Kohl and I will help you with everything that needs to be done. I'm so excited. Wait until I tell Kohl. He'll be excited too."

Abbie reached for Alex's hand under the table. "Thanks for including Kohl. Although he may do nothing other than huff at you for whatever unknown offense, we met because of him."

"Not having regrets, are you, Abbie?"

"None! I get sad sometimes because of how Tom died and how quickly his death changed so many lives. But you, Alex Montgomery, and these four children are my future, and I am absolutely in love with every one of you."

CHAPTER 30

They had managed to settle into a routine. Abbie looked forward to the wedding, which was this weekend. Andy continued to do great in school and therapy. The pups settled into a bit more of a routine at the pool and adjusted well to their home routine and established a routine at Sam's house as well. Sam took on three new patients for the hydrotherapy program, and they were doing well, too. Her assistant took copious notes and documented everything into a computer program that Kate recommended from her research experience.

The marketing department scheduled the photo shoot for last week, and Andy and Kohl, and the pups did an excellent job posing for the ads. They would distribute the ads next week, and Sam brought in an additional therapist to assist her with her busy schedule.

Abbie and Alex explained to Andy that the ads would make him and the pups extremely popular. So, he should expect to get the same response and questions from community members he answered when he and Kohl went out in public. They were cute, and they, too, would draw fans.

Construction in the bedrooms for the babies was done, and furniture ordered for Sam's house was delivered. Julie and Kate made their travel plans for the wedding, and Dana moved into the beach rental. She had her schedule to start work at Coastal next week.

Abbie and Alex asked Andy to help them choose the cribs and other furniture and necessities for the babies, and everything arrived as scheduled. The room for the nanny had new decor and looked bright and beachy.

She thought it might be too early to furnish the nursery, but Alex and Dr. Jeffers reminded her that multiple births sometimes came early. Dr. Jeffers also reminded her to rest and not drive.

Sam helped Abbie pick out her wedding dress and the dresses for her bridesmaids, and they looked elegant but casual and would keep them cool if the temperatures spiked.

Abbie wanted to look sexy for Alex on their wedding day despite her ever-growing belly and chose an off-the-shoulder gown made of a smooth crepe satin that would offer her comfort yet still have enough structure to drape. The sweetheart neckline and gathered empire waist would show off her growing breast yet keep them from falling out of the gown. With her curls pulled up, it would give her a touch of formality but still be beach appropriate.

The food and music selections were made, and the deck would be set up with linen-covered tables with simple beach-themed centerpieces. Andy and Alex picked out matching suits, and Drs. Parker and O'Brien completed their choices as well. Andy had even purchased a bow tie for Kohl to wear during the ceremony.

Abbie let Alex pick the music for the procession, and he would not give her one clue about what song he chose. She reminded him of her emotional pregnancy and warned him not to make her cry during her walk to the altar. He smiled, kissed her, and told her she would be fine, but he did not tell her he planned to have an extra handkerchief or two in his suit. He talked to Dana; she would be available to touch up Abbie's makeup before their official photo session.

Abbie sent Dana a text and asked if she wanted any help. She said no to the help but yes to the company. The three dogs were training with Sam at the pool, so Abbie took advantage of a day to herself and walked over to Dana's rental. Dana's decorating style was more imaginative than Abbie's. When Abbie walked in, the place looked different.

"Wow, Dana. This place looks fabulous. Alex won't even recognize it."

"Do you think he was ever here long enough to remember what it looked like?"

"No, but it looks fantastic anyway."

Abbie sat at the kitchen counter and opened boxes of kitchen items, then Dana put them in the dishwasher. Dana wanted to have everything put away before starting her twelve-hour shifts at the ER next week. She would work with Alex again. He'd changed so much since his time at Memorial. He and Abbie were perfect for each other, and from what she saw, Andy also appeared to be thriving.

Dana and Alex discussed the episode with Kohl when Tom passed away and agreed that those attitudes were to be left in the past. They also agreed there would be no more lies about ER activities.

Everyone had busy lives right now, but Dana was getting organized and would soon have a routine. Maybe, she would get lucky, like Abbie, and find someone who made her laugh. Dana enjoyed being single for a long time, and the dating scene was fun, but now, she wanted more of a relationship. When Abbie moved up here, she realized how much they did together and missed those times. With Sam here as well, and all the babies and pups, Abbie would be busier than she expected.

"Okay, Abbie. I think we have done enough. Let's go grab lunch. Since you can't drive, I will play chauffeur. You can pick the place based on your cravings."

"I have had no cravings, but let's pick something outdoor. The weather is glorious, and I want to relax with you and discuss anything other than dogs, baby furniture, and wedding plans. Let's talk about your latest hot guy. How do you do it? You're like a magnet for them."

"Get in the car, Abbie, and I'll fill you in after we order. Do you need help with the seat belt?"

"Dana. I'm pregnant, not ninety years old. But don't let me get down on the floor because you may need to call in the reinforcements to get me back up."

They had to wait for the staff to find a table with enough room for Abbie to fit behind. Once they were seated and placed their orders, Abbie asked Dana who she was dating.

"Okay, Dana. Tell me about your love life."

"Nothing to tell! I needed to take a break. The past few relationships got boring and were not going anywhere, so I worked on myself. I've missed seeing you almost every day at work, and I needed a change. After Tom died, I thought about how quickly life can change. We are supposed to know that, right? We are ER nurses! Almost every day, we watch death happen. But Tom's death struck home with me. It made me realize I need something more than one fling after another. The hot guys are fun, but I'm so over it."

"I understand, Dana, and I loved Tom, but my relationship with Alex is different. He makes life seem more secure. Safe for once! I no longer worry that I will be out on the street again. That fear gets ingrained in you when you have no family. That emptiness is gone. It tries to rear its ugly head, but now I can chase it away. When you spend years of your life with no one to love and no one to love you, the emptiness can be overwhelming. But on a happier note, I can't wait to marry Montgomery. We are excited about the babies, and here I am talking about babies again."

"I'm not talking about babies either, Abbie, but I can't wait. And I am excited about the wedding, as well. Is everything set? Anything I can help with?"

"We have completed everything down to the bowtie Kohl is wearing. The only thing I need to do between now and the wedding is to rest. I know everything will be perfect."

"Let's finish up this food and get you home for one of those naps."

Saturday arrived, and Alex got up to take out the dogs and let Abbie sleep. He and Andy left to go to the barbershop, and when they returned, they planned to relax and take the dogs for a walk on the beach.

Sam offered to take Andy and the dogs to her house tonight, so he and Abbie had the night alone. He did not know who was more excited, he or Andy.

Marrying Abbie was exciting. He and Maria enjoyed a good relationship and a good marriage, but loving Abbie was different. When he held her for the first time after their lunch, days after Tom died, it made him feel like she belonged to him. That they belonged together, he felt a little weirded out by the intensity and tried to blame it on her recent loss. It felt different. He listened to so many people talk about things happening for a reason and did not believe in that garbage. But now, he understood what they meant. Things moved swiftly with the two of them, and the unexpected pregnancy moved it along a little faster, but she became the one he wanted. And honestly, his life had become more fulfilling in the past several months than in the past.

Alex and Andy got their chores done and laughed at the funny things the dogs did on the beach. As usual, everyone stopped to ask questions, and Andy told them about Kohl's past and the project they became involved in.

The pups loved the waves and barked and jumped in the water. They made everyone around them laugh, and Alex smiled. This is what Abbie brought to their lives. Happiness and joy that made him want to jump in the waves like pups. He'd laughed more at life with Abbie than ever before. She brought light, laughter, and joy to everyone around her, and her generosity with Tom's money allowed her to bring hope to people as well.

Abbie's crew arrived, and the house got loud. They turned on music, opened a bottle of champagne for the four of them, and poured ginger ale for Abbie.

Andy looked at his dad and asked, "Dad, are all girls this loud and noisy?"

"Well, Andy! Abbie's friends like to have fun, and today they are celebrating us getting married. Sometimes, they are loud and messy, and sometimes, they cry for no reason, but they are fun to have around."

"I don't know how much of that noise I can stand, Dad. They are noisy. I'm going to think about all this as I get older. I'm not sure I can take all this for the rest of my life."

"You have plenty of time to figure out what you like, Andy. Abbie's loud friends love you, and you can always trust them if you need anything. They are all smart, beautiful women. Maybe being smart and pretty makes them louder, but I don't think you will want to go without them for the rest of your life."

All the details for the wedding were done, and Dr. Parker and Dr. O'Brien arrived on time. Alex offered them a beer and gave Andy a soda, and they walked out to the deck to wait until the minister arrived.

Abbie and the other ladies finished dressing and were also ready to go. The photographer arrived on time, and the flowers arrived earlier. Andy put Kohl's bow tie on, and they looked in the mirror so he could make sure they looked perfect for the wedding. Alex took a couple of pictures and sent them to Abbie via text. She responded with multiple heart emojis.

The guest arrived, and Damon, Conor, and Andy greeted everyone. Andy changed over to his beach chair and showed everyone to their seats. The photographer continued taking photos, and Alex, Andy, and his groomsmen took their places. Abbie and the ladies started their walk to the altar. Abbie and Kohl walked together.

Once the ladies took their places, the music started for Abbie's walk to Alex. Sam saw Abbie get teary-eyed. She glanced over at Alex and noticed the same. When she looked at the crowd, there did not appear to be a dry eye there, either.

Sam glanced over at Alex.

"Damn you, Montgomery. Do you realize how long it took us to get our makeup on?" Everyone laughed, and her statement helped to stop the tears.

Alex stood staring as Abbie walked toward him. She looked stunning on a typical day and even more so with the pregnancy. Today, he failed to find the words to describe the vision before him. He would have to thank Sam for swearing at him. She was observant and noticed the emotions running through him, Abbie, and the guest, and she saved his reputation at the hospital.

If not for her crack at humor, everyone would be in tears. He was only sure of one thing today. He loved Abbie; if those baby girls were as beautiful as her, he would never let them out of the house.

Abbie and Kohl arrived at the altar, and Kohl walked over to stand beside Andy. She handed her bouquet to Sam, then took Alex's hands. She struggled to control her tears, but Dana guaranteed she would fix her makeup if needed. In her eyes, Alex was the most handsome guy and shamed all the cover models. He was unaware of his looks, but she melted when he smiled at her. She fell head over heels in love with him and Andy. Andy had his father's good looks; she knew he would break hearts once he was older.

The pastor spoke and caught their attention. He spoke all the familiar words a couple hears and repeats when married. During their first meeting with him, he asked Abbie if she wanted to write her own vows, and she declined. She told him the only one who needed to hear her inner thoughts was Alex, and she shared those with him during their time alone. Alex said he felt the same. His thoughts were for her only, and anyone who looked at them together would recognize that they belonged together.

Once the minister pronounced them husband and wife, Alex gave Abbie a slow, sexy kiss, and the photographer snapped photos. The sun would set soon, and she was eager to get images before the sunset. They accepted congratulations from their friends and sent them up to the house for appetizers and drinks.

The photographer took pictures with Andy and their attendants first, sent them to the house and posed for photos of the two of them. Dana touched up her makeup while the guys were being photographed, but Dana assured her she needed no makeup at all. When the photographer finished their outside photos, Alex and Abbie took a few minutes to themselves.

"You take my breath away, Mrs. Montgomery. I am so glad it is you who I am spending the rest of my life loving."

"Ditto, Dr. Montgomery. I have no terms to describe the love I have for you and all our children. Loving you has given me everything my heart was missing."

They watched the sun go down below the horizon together and walked up to join the guests. Abbie complained of starving as usual and said the babies wanted food. Alex chuckled. She might be the only woman he knew who was unafraid to say she wanted to eat. Besides her pregnancy belly, she maintained her perfect shape, and Alex loved her no matter how she looked.

They ate, cut the wedding cake, danced, and enjoyed the evening with their friends. Abbie noticed Sam and Damon talking together and noticed that Dana and Dr. O'Brien looked a little cozy at the table near the far end of the deck. Interesting. She hoped Dana would fit in with the guests, who would be her coworkers at the hospital.

Sam and Damon approached her and Alex, and said it was time to take Andy, Kohl, and the pups and head back to Sam's house. The day's excitement took its toll on Andy. He wore himself out and was ready to sleep.

"Abbie. Would it be okay to call you mom now that you and Dad are married?"

"I would love you to call me mom, Andy, if that is what you and your dad want."

"Dad, do you think it would be alright?"

Alex bent down to his level. "Andy, I am fine with you calling her mom. Abbie and I said we left that up to you. If you are ready, help yourself."

Abbie reached out to give Andy a hug. "If you get to call me mom, then I get to call you, my son. Are you okay with that, Andy?"

"Yes, you can call me your son."

Abbie hugged him again. "Be good for Sam and Damon, son. We will pick you up tomorrow. Love you!"

"I'll be good, Mom, and I love you, too."

Alex reached over to hug Andy as well and hid his tears until he could blink them away. He helped Abbie to a standing position. Everyone else cleared out too. Kate and Julie left with Sam. Dana and Conor O'Brien gave her a hug as well. As she said goodbye to the other guest, she noticed Dana and Conor walking toward the beach rental and smiled. *That doesn't look like taking a break to me, Dana*, and Abbie wished her luck.

"Listen to the quiet, Abbie. It could be years before we hear this again. I am ready for our lives to be filled with the crying and laughter of our beautiful children and words of love between all of us. Every day will not be perfect, but I don't want it to be. I love this craziness. It makes me excited about what might come next."

"Do you want to know what excites me, Montgomery?"

"Tell me what excites you, Abbie?"

"You do, Montgomery!"

And with that, Alex picked her up and walked to the bedroom to spend the first night of their married life together.

CHAPTER 31

A ndy was home from school on a school holiday today, so he and Abbie had fun things planned for the day. She prepared pancakes for breakfast, which were Andy's favorite.

Abbie's due date was four weeks away. So, the doctor had instructed her not to do anything more than shower, dress, and take short walks. They had decided to keep Ms. Helen, the nanny, who had previously worked for Alex and Andy, and she had been to the house and set up her room. She agreed to move in when Abbie or Alex notified her of the homecoming.

Abbie and Andy finished breakfast, loaded the dishwasher, and took the dogs for a walk on the beach. She leashed the pups when Alex was gone. Neither she nor Andy could chase a running pup, and she did not want to worry that they might wander into the street. They were expecting rain later today, but the sun was out this morning. They took their time during their walk and let the pups socialize with the beachgoers. Koko and Kody had outstanding personalities like Kohl's. The three dogs played but listened when given a command. In addition, Kohl kept them in line with a quick bark.

They returned to the house, and Abbie set up the Trouble® game, and they played several rounds. She lost to Andy every time. Next, they played with Andy's Xbox® and challenged one another to several rounds of motorcycle racing. They fixed lunch and let the dogs out in the backyard for their playtime. Andy asked if he could watch a movie after lunch that Abbie had bought him, and she said he had a great idea. Abbie planned for them to rest on the sofa while they watched the movie.

Her back was hurting this morning from toting around three babies, and she needed to rest. Abbie brought the pups in, and they went to their crate to rest. Andy laid on the sofa, and she took the recliner. Both fell asleep soon after the movie started. Abbie woke up, but Andy was still asleep. So, she closed her eyes and fell back asleep.

When she woke up again, Andy was awake and playing Xbox®. Kohl and the pups went out again, and she fixed Andy a snack. She'd prepped a roast earlier this morning, and it was cooking on low in the slow cooker. Abbie added potatoes and carrots, poured a glass of water for herself, and fixed Andy a glass of lemonade. He was still playing his game when she walked into the living room.

"Are you winning that game, Andy? You're good at all the games we play."

"Yes, I'm winning, but I'm going to put this one away and get a different one. I'll find one we can both play."

Abbie sat in the recliner and adjusted the controls to find a comfortable position. Yet, it seemed that every time she got comfortable, she had to pee. She stood up, and a cramp hit her so hard, it knocked her to her knees and took her breath away. She took a couple of deep breaths to calm herself before calling out to Andy for help. Another one hit her, and she lay on the floor. She was getting one after the other.

Kohl and the puppies ran into the room. Kohl sat next to her, and the pups sat right beside him. Kohl laid his head on her leg.

"I'm okay, Kohl. Andy will get us help."

Kohl huffed at her and laid his paw on her hand.

"Andy. I need your help. Can you grab my phone for me?"

Andy wheeled himself into the living room, where he saw Abbie lying on her side on the floor.

"Mom, are you okay?"

"I need my phone to call your dad, sweetie. Can you get it off the kitchen counter?"

"Sure!"

Andy turned toward the kitchen when another severe cramp hit Abbie, and she screamed.

"Mom, you're scaring me. Are you okay?"

"I need my phone, Andy. We need to call your dad."

After getting her phone, Andy returned to the living room.

"Mom, can you give me your passcode? I'll call Dad."

Abbie gave him the passcode and felt another wave of cramps hit her. Her water broke, and now she became really frightened.

"Mom, Dad's not answering his phone. What do you want me to do.?"

"Hand me the phone, Andy. I'll find the number to the emergency room."

Abbie found the number, hit dial, and handed the phone back to Andy as another wave came upon her.

"This is Andrew Montgomery speaking. May I speak to my dad, please? Okay! I understand he is with a patient. Is Dr. Parker available? Can I speak to him? Thanks, I'll hold."

Within seconds, Abbie could hear him talking to Damon.

"Dr. Parker, it's Andy Montgomery. I tried to call my dad, but he was with a patient. Abbie needs help. She's on the floor and can't get up, and she keeps grabbing her stomach, and I bet it hurts because she keeps screaming. She told me to call my dad, but can you help us since he is busy?"

Abbie didn't hear the conversation but knew Damon would get her the help she needed.

"Andy don't hang up the phone. I am sending the nurse to get your dad. I need you to tell me everything that's happening with Abbie."

"She's lying on the floor and is holding her stomach. Maybe the babies are coming, Dr. Parker. We need help!"

"Yes, Andy. You are going to be a big brother today. I am getting you help. Here's your dad, Andy. I'll see you soon."

"Andy, I need you to tell me what is happening?"

Andy described everything that had happened to his dad.

"Hold on just a second. Do not hang up the phone."

Andy overheard his dad telling someone to call Dr. Andrea Jeffers and let her know they were coming in with Abbie in an ambulance. Then he told someone to have security call the operator at the swing bridge and request them to keep it open. It was the fastest route to get to the house. He told Damon to call the NICU and get the incubators and delivery team ready.

"Andy, I need to hang up this phone, but I am going to call you right back on Abbie's phone via FaceTime. You need to answer her phone when it rings so that I can see Abbie and talk to her at the same time. Talking to you and Abbie via FaceTime will help me figure out how to help her."

"Okay, Dad. I can do that for you."

Andy hung up, and when the phone rang, he answered immediately.

Alex's face appeared on the screen.

"Andy, I am on my way home. I am coming with the ambulance. Thank you for being so brave and finding someone to help Abbie and your sisters. Now, I need to talk to Abbie!"

Alex heard her groan in the background.

"Andy, I need you to hold the phone, so I can watch Abbie. In the lower right corner of the screen, there's an icon. It will look like two arrows making a circle. Touch that icon. It will give me a broader view of Abbie."

Andy did everything Alex asked him to do.

"Abbie, I'm on my way! Dr. Jeffers and the NICU are aware we are coming in and are fully ready. Tell me what you are feeling."

"Wave after wave of pain, Alex. It just won't stop. My water broke a couple of minutes ago when Andy was talking to Damon. It's too early for the babies. Can we stop this and give them more time? I'm scared, Montgomery!"

"I'm scared too, sweetheart, but it's unlikely we can stop the birth, Abbie. Dr. Jeffers will figure it out once we get you to the hospital. Remember, both you and the babies are healthy. We only have four weeks until your due date, which reduces the chance of any complications. I'm so proud of you for hanging in there this long."

Abbie listened to the sirens in stereo, which meant they were close. "Abbie, we are pulling into the driveway now. I'll be there in a second."

Alex ran up the stairs, skipping steps, and the ambulance crew used the elevator. He stopped to give Andy a hug and kissed his head.

"Andy, thank you for being so brave. I am sure we are going to get to meet your sisters today."

"That's what Dr. Parker said, too."

Alex knelt next to Abbie and took her hand. He kissed her and said she was doing a fantastic job. He gave Kohl a quick pet on the head and thanked him for staying with Abbie. Kohl huffed softly at him and moved to a sitting position.

She grabbed her stomach again and moaned.

The paramedics arrived and asked questions. They loaded her onto the stretcher and used the elevator to reach the ground floor. Alex put the pups in their crate, and he and Andy followed. Alex put Andy in the front seat of the ambulance, aware that it was illegal, but he did not have time to worry about breaking laws. He'd pay the fine if needed. He placed Andy's wheelchair in the back of the ambulance and sat on the bench. Andy was busy asking the driver questions, and Alex smiled to himself. Once the paramedic got Abbie's IV started, she took Alex's hand.

"I guess we're doing this, Montgomery. You've done this once before. How can this be so frightening, yet exciting – all at the same time?"

"It's hard to explain, but it is a life-changing experience, Abbie. It's one of the most splendid events you will experience in your lifetime."

They arrived at the hospital, and Alex helped Andy out of the front seat. They walked behind the gurney with Abbie. Dr. Parker met them as soon as they entered the ER.

"How are you doing, lovely lady? You ready to give us those cute little ladies?"

Sam showed up next and used her relationship with Damon to get her through the door. Dana was working and came out from behind the nurse's station. They walked with Abbie to the delivery suite. Abbie kissed Andy and told him he should have his sisters soon. Sam took Andy with her to the waiting room.

Dr. Jeffers met them in the labor room. She checked Abbie and assured them that everything was okay, and she had the delivery room set up and enough staff to take care of their daughters.

"It's still too soon, Dr. Jeffers,"

"Abbie, you may take the record for the longest gestation time for triplets. I expected you weeks ago, but that means we have babies who are bigger and more developed, and I don't think we will meet any problems. I need to scrub in, then we'll get these little ladies delivered."

Alex looked at Abbie. "I'm head over heels in love with you, Abbie Montgomery. I know this can be frightening, but I will be right here with you when our little girls enter this world. Tomorrow, I am buying a big steak for Kohl. He was the one responsible for introducing us, and if not for you and Kohl, I might still be a miserable, sulking mess."

Abbie grabbed her stomach again. Alex bent over, placed his mouth near her stomach, and spoke to the babies. He rubbed her stomach to help relieve the pain. Dr. Jeffers came back into the room.

"Alex, go put on scrubs, and meet us in the delivery room. We'll be in room two. And hurry, we don't have time to waste. This may be the only time in your life these girls are on time. And believe me; you will not want to miss it."

Alex laughed at the doctor's remark and took off running to change into scrubs.

Alex changed and entered the delivery room. Dr. Jeffers was correct, and everything moved rapidly. He held Abbie's hand and whispered to her through the pain.

Abbie gave one long push, and their first daughter's cry filled the room. Abbie and Alex were both crying as baby number two started crying, as well. Baby number three entered, and the five of them were crying.

The nurses and doctors were busy checking everyone, and Abbie and Alex fell in love with three little girls when Dr. Jeffers handed them their daughters. Abbie held their three daughters first. Alex wanted her to enjoy the first feelings of motherhood. The babies looked up at her as she spoke to them. They looked identical. Neither he nor Abbie asked that question. He turned to glance at Dr. Jeffers.

"Are they identical?"

"Yes, Dr. Montgomery. I wondered how long it would take before either of you asked. Good luck with that as well."

"You say it like you have experience, Dr. Jeffers."

"Two sets of identical twins, Dr. Montgomery. One set male, one set female. What one set doesn't conjure up, the other set will! You'll have moments when you will not be certain of anything. They believe they can fool you, but you are the parents. And they forget you notice every one of their peculiarities. But don't let me scare you. There's nothing better in this world."

Alex held his daughters and inhaled the smell of babies. He loved that smell.

"Abbie, love! Do we have names chosen yet? How long will it be before we can tell them apart?"

"We'll use some type of color scheme until they develop their own personalities, and we can recognize their differences. Let's get everyone upstairs in the nursery. Andy is eager to meet his sisters."

Andy was being entertained in the waiting room by Sam and Dana. Alex let them know everyone was okay. They would be on a Zoom call with Julie and Kate within minutes. Andy wanted to check on his mom and his sisters. Alex explained they were getting the babies set up in the nursery, and the nurses were getting his mom into her bed. He told them his sisters weighed within an ounce of each other. Five pounds, four ounces, and they were healthy. They had their mother's blue eyes, but the staff could not tell hair color until it grew.

They needed to settle on names. Abbie insisted she did not want to rush to pick out names. She wanted their names to fit their personalities and asked Alex if he could hold off that discussion for the next day or two, insisting she needed to spend time with them before deciding. Alex could make a list, and she would make one, too.

Andy led the procession to the nursery, followed by Alex, Dana, and Sam. Andy was having a tough time seeing, so he grabbed onto the handrail below the window ledge and pulled himself into a standing position. Alex smiled and backed up, so Andy had room to move without tripping over anyone. Alex, Sam, and Dana were astounded at Andy's recovery.

The babies had Andy's attention. The nurse walked over to the observation window and turned on the microphone to speak to Andy.

"Hi, Andy. I understand you have three brand-new sisters. Do you want to peek at them?"

"Yes, please!"

The nurse pushed the three bassinets in front of the window. Alex observed as Andy took the first look at his sisters. Andy held the handrail and walked back and forth in front of the window. He smiled and spoke to each of them. They opened their eyes. He turned and looked at his dad.

"They are so tiny, Dad. They all look the same. How are we supposed to tell who's who?"

"Your mom is planning to use a color scheme until they develop their personalities and other things that will make it easier to single out each baby. We will figure it out. So, is this what you were expecting?"

"They are the best thing in the whole wide world, Dad!"

"I agree, Andy. You and your sisters are the best things ever."

Andy realized he was standing. "Dad. I'm standing!"

"I was watching you, Andy, and you took steps, too. You are walking again. I'm proud of you for the work you and Sam have done."

"That wasn't work, Dad. That was just having fun. Can I surprise Mom by walking into her room?"

"Do you feel strong enough to walk to her by yourself? If so, she would love it, Andy."

Alex wheeled Andy back to Abbie's room and left him in the hallway with Dana and Sam.

"I'll tell her you are bringing her a surprise. Then I'll get you."

Abbie turned when Alex entered the room. "Where's Andy? Isn't he with you?"

"He's waiting in the hallway with Dana and Sam. He has a surprise for you. I wanted to see if you were ready for visitors."

"I'm great, Alex. Tell him to come in."

Alex walked to the doorway and summoned Andy. His mom was ready for her surprise.

Abbie saw Andy enter the room and realized he was walking. She sat up in bed and threw her legs over the side. Andy was grinning from ear to ear. Abbie opened her arms and said to Andy.

"Come here, my strong, brave son! I am so proud of you. When did this happen?"

Alex spoke up first.

"The nurse brought his sisters over to the windows. Andy was having a tough time seeing them from his wheelchair. So, he grabbed onto the handrail, then stood for a better view. He walked in front of the window using the handrail, but he didn't realize he was standing and walking."

Andy took a seat in a recliner chair to rest, while Dana and Sam hugged Abbie and asked how the babies were doing.

Alex wanted to let Sam and Dana have time alone with her.

"Andy and I are going home to feed the dogs. Then we will go feed ourselves."

"Alex, there is food in the slow cooker. You don't have to eat it, but could you please turn it off?"

"Thanks. We will eat at home and spend time with Kohl and the pups. I'm sure Kohl is worried about you. When we return, I'll check on our girls and try to get permission to have the nurse bring them to your room, so we can hold them for a little while. I'll ask the nurse to help us get photos as well."

Alex and Andy returned to the hospital a couple of hours later. Abbie had slept and was sitting up in the chair reading a magazine. Alex had stopped at the nursery, and since he was a physician and the babies were stable, they permitted him to bring the girls into Abbie's room and introduce them to Andy.

They brought them in, and one nurse stayed with them for security reasons. Alex took them out of their bassinets one by one. He handed Abbie one and sat on the sofa next to Andy. He gave Andy specific instructions on how to hold the babies. Andy nodded his head in understanding. Alex placed the baby in his arms. Andy smiled, and the baby looked at him. Alex picked up the third baby and sat back on the sofa next to Andy. Andy was talking to her as if he had known her forever. Alex switched babies every few minutes, so they could hold all three.

Alex asked the nurse if they would permit them to take photos with his phone. She agreed, and they moved to the sofa with Andy. The nurse took photos, and they were beaming in each photo. The girls had their eyes open, and they had their first family photo.

The next several days comprised the same routine. Julie and Kate flew in, and Dana and Sam joined after work. Abbie remembered Dana walking away with Conor O'Brien and changed the conversation.

"By the way, Dana. How was your night with Conor O'Brien?"

Everyone turned to look at Dana.

"I do not know what you are talking about, Abbie."

"I noticed the two of you walking toward your house after the wedding. Spill it, as Sam likes to say!"

"There's nothing to tell. He walked me home. End of story!"

Sam spoke up next. "I think this book has a few more chapters you are leaving out."

Kate wasn't letting Sam off, either.

"Why don't you read a couple of your own chapters to us as well, Sam? We understood there's more to your story, too."

"I don't understand why Abbie needs to spread lies!"

"Don't blame that on me. Dana works in the ER with him. Ask her where she is getting her info. It might have come right from the horse's mouth."

Alex and Andy stopped outside of the entrance to Abbie's room.

Alex did not want to interrupt their conversation. Andy was walking and stopped, as well. He whispered to his dad.

"Dad, do they always talk like this?" Alex nodded his head and tried not to laugh aloud.

"Are you referring to Parker as a horse? He won't appreciate that reference, Abbie."

"Dear Lord!" Julie said. "I don't care who you are or who needs what, but you need a little happy juice. Then you will feel better and not be concerned about who is doing who."

Alex decided he needed to stop this conversation before Andy learned things he was too young to learn.

"Hey, ladies. It sounds like you're having fun here, but Andy and I could understand everything you said at the end of the hall."

They apologized to him and Andy and got up to give a round of hugs and congratulations.

"I ran into Dr. Jeffers in the hallway, Abbie. She said you and the babies are stable and can go home tomorrow."

Alex turned his attention to Abbie's crew. "Since every one of you is staying in town, and at least one of you is a pediatrician, you can bond with our babies."

"Were you aware Alex was this bossy when you married him, Abbie?" Sam said.

"There's a lot I'm aware of, Sam, and there is still a lot I need to learn. But occasionally, I don't mind him being a little bossy."

The five of them laughed, and Alex rolled his eyes.

"The lot of you are incorrigible. And forget bonding with babies! I don't want you anywhere near my girls."

Abbie got up, kissed Andy, and then whispered something in Alex's ear. He turned six shades of red. He looked Abbie right in the eyes.

"I've decided you must be the leader of this pack. And after hearing that statement, there might still be things I need to learn, as well."

Thank you for reading *Guarding My Heart*. If you enjoyed this story, read on for a preview of the next book in the My Heart Series, *Mending My Heart*.

BOOK 2

Chapter 1

D r. Damon Parker finished the day shift in the ER, grabbed the first available elevator, and got off on the floor that housed the nursery. There was laughter coming from the room near the end of the corridor; he recognized Samantha's laugh almost instantly. The florist had delivered five bouquets of flowers earlier this afternoon, and he carried an armful of flowers to the ladies and a new baseball mitt for Andrew. He knocked on the open door.

"Sounds like a celebration going on in this room, ladies, and look, here is the new momma!"

Walking over to Abbie, she stood, and Damon wrapped her in a hug and held out the biggest bouquet. Turning to the other ladies in the room, he handed each a smaller version of the bouquet that Abbie received. He said hello to Kate and Julie and asked how they had been doing since the wedding.

Stopping before Sam, Damon took her hand, pulled her to a standing position, and wrapped her in his arms. Abbie winked from across the room, and Samantha rolled her eyes.

"And last but not least, darlin, I hope these brighten your day!"

Samantha didn't know if she should thank him or spout out a smart mouth answer, but she decided to be nice and not embarrass him in front of her friends.

"Thank you, Damon. The flowers are lovely."

Damon turned toward Andy and gave him the new baseball mitt.

"This is for you, Andy. If you ever need a break from all these ladies, give me a call, and we'll toss the ball."

"That would be great, Dr. Parker. Sometimes, they talk about things I don't understand. Dad says the prettier they are, the more they talk."

Everyone in the room laughed.

Damon shook Alex's hand, and the conversation turned to the new babies.

"Andy, I haven't seen those new sisters yet. Should we go to the nursery, and you can tell me who is who?"

"Mom and Dad haven't decided on names yet, Dr. Parker, and I don't think it is viewing time in the nursery right now."

"Let's see if I can fix that, Andy."

Damon walked over to the phone on Abbie's bedside stand and dialed a number. Everyone was quiet while Damon talked to the nurse.

"Afternoon, darlin. Dr. Damon Parker here. I understand there are three identical little beauties hanging out in the nursery that I haven't had the pleasure of meeting yet. Their brother is willing to introduce me. Can we get a quick peek? Thanks! Be there in a moment."

Damon hung up the phone and saw Samantha do another eye roll.

"Are you going too, Samantha?"

"Thanks, I'll pass this time, Parker. It is easier for you to get what you want from the nurses when you aren't toting another lady with you."

Alex smiled, but Abbie couldn't contain her laughter, and the others started laughing as well.

"I don't know why you find that funny, Abbie. Or the rest of you, either!"

"Dr. Parker, we better go before someone gets in trouble with my dad. Do you want to go with us, Dad?"

"Yes, Andy! I'm not sure I should be here right now, either."

Andy stood up and ambled toward the door.

"Hey! You're walking, young man? When did that happen?" asked Damon.

"The day my sisters were born! I can't go fast yet, but Sam is going to keep helping with therapy. Someday, I'll be able to run."

"Yes, you will, Andy. Congratulations on your accomplishments!"

As soon as the men had time to get to the end of the corridor, Sam turned toward Abbie.

"Abbie. What do you find so funny?"

"Are you blind, Sam? That man only has eyes for you. He may know how to charm the nurses to get them to do what he wants, but he is not going to give up on you."

"Well, Miss Know-it-all, I've already agreed to date him. Well, not date, but I agreed to a bike ride and an occasional dinner."

"Have there been any more nights at his place?"

"What are you, Abbie? My mother?"

Julie spoke. "Are we going to have this same conversation again? I thought we settled on the idea of getting whatever is needed to keep you happy?"

Samantha smiled and turned to Julie. "And who is keeping you happy, Julie?"

"I don't believe we were talking about me, Sam. We are consenting adults. Why does it matter?"

"I'm changing the conversation. Abbie, I'm going to your place and getting the pups this evening. Koko and Kody can stay at my house until the six of you get settled at your place. I'll ask Damon if I can use his truck to transport them to my place. Once you are back on your feet, we should consider getting a vehicle big enough to take everyone back and forth between the houses."

"My SUV is not being used right now, so you can use mine, Sam."

"Thanks, Abbie, but moving three baby seats from vehicle to vehicle all the time will be too much work. Once the seats are in correctly, it is easier to leave them alone. The car will stay cleaner, too."

"Just take mine, Sam. There is not room for everyone to fit in the SUV. I think I'm going to need a van. Dear Lord! The girls are not even a week old, and I've already turned into a soccer mom."

The guys returned, and Conor O'Brien walked in, right behind Alex. Conor said hello to Dana first, then said hello to the other ladies. He gave Abbie a hug and gave her flowers and chocolates. There was a new game for Andy's X-Box®. Abbie and Alex thanked him for everything and for thinking of Andy, too.

Alex spoke. "Julie, Conor's brother, Tobin, is a renowned orthopedic surgeon in Ireland. He is en route to the United

States from Ireland to visit for a couple of weeks. I invited him over to the house. He is interested in moving to the States, and I thought maybe the two of you could find time to discuss the requirements for getting licensed here in the States."

"I'd be happy to do that, Alex. Kate and I are staying until next weekend, and I'd love to hear about the latest treatments happening in Ireland."

"Damon, I have a favor to ask," said Samantha.

"Anything, darlin. What's up?"

"I'd like to get the pups this evening and keep them at my place for a while. Unfortunately, I can't take them on my bike, and my car is also too small. Can I borrow the truck?"

"I'll help with the pups, Samantha. I've nothing planned this evening."

"Thanks. Abbie, should we leave Kohl at your place, so he can get to know the girls first? He will keep the other two in line if they get too excited when they meet the girls."

"That sounds great. Sam!"

"Damon, I don't want to rush you, but would you be willing to leave now? I'll cook dinner for us as payment for your help."

"Ready when you are, darlin. We need to drop off the bike and get the truck."

Samantha dropped her bike at the house, grabbed his truck, and went to Abbie's house. Kohl and the pups greeted them when they came through the door. Sam let the three outside, gave Kohl fresh water, and filled his food bowl.

"I swear the pups get bigger every day. How long until they are fully grown, Samantha?"

"According to the breeder, a dog reaches adult status around two years old, but we should plan for them to weigh around one-hundred-twenty pounds in one year."

Sam let the dogs back in, and Damon sat on the floor. Koko and Kody went straight to him, and Kohl went to Sam.

"We don't need to take anything other than the dogs. I have duplicates of their belongings at my place. But, if you plan on eating dinner before midnight, let's get these two leashed and loaded."

Sam bent down to give Kohl a hug and explained she was taking the pups so that he could meet the new babies tomorrow. Kohl responded with a soft bark. She gave him a treat while Damon loaded the pups in the truck. The pups were walking back and forth in the back seat area, and Damon gave them the command to sit. They stopped pacing and sat at once.

"Well, look at that, Samantha. They listen very well."

"Their training has been great, and the program receives new referrals every day. We may need to expand beyond one pool. Once Abbie gets rested and released to start doing work again, she and I need to have a serious discussion about expansion."

"She's going to be one busy lady, and those daughters are beautiful!"

"Yes, they are adorable. She and Alex are lucky."

Damon pulled into the driveway. "Okay, boys. Let's get inside the house."

Samantha went to the kitchen while Damon went out to the backyard with the dogs. Earlier today, she had prepped food, thinking about asking Damon for dinner. Now, he was here, and she was nervous because she was as bad as the rest of the women who couldn't resist him. She, too, was falling for him.

Sam took the steaks out of the fridge, so they could come to room temperature before putting them on the grill. All that would need to be done was to toss the salad and prepare the asparagus. There was a bottle of red wine for dinner, and she opened the bottle to let it breathe.

Damon walked into the kitchen with the dogs and smiled. *Dear Lord*, she was in trouble. How did she imagine she could resist him? He thought of trying to outbid her on the house when she and Abbie were with the realtor, but honestly, the house looked like it was built for him. He looked perfect here. Reaching for the wine, she poured two glasses and held out a glass to Damon.

"I opened a bottle of red wine, Damon. We can sit on the front porch and enjoy the wine until the steaks reach room temperature."

They stood in the kitchen and took one sip of wine from the glass. Damon took both glasses and placed them on the counter. He picked her up and sat her on the counter as well.

"I know a great way to waste time while the steaks reach room temperature."

Placing a hand on each side of her body, Damon leaned toward Sam's face. Closing her eyes, not sure of what to expect next, she moaned as he started kissing her neck. Resisting was not on her list of options, and she gave in and mimicked his moves and heard him moan, as well.

Read More in the Next Book!

About the Author

Kathleen Nelson Tellish is a Registered Nurse with an MBA in Healthcare Administration, and a Professional RN Wellness Coach.

She was raised in the Tri-State area spanning Pennsylvania, Ohio, and West Virginia and currently resides in Fargo, North Dakota, and Myrtle Beach, SC, with her husband, Gary. Kathleen is a former dog owner and credits her beloved Newfoundland dogs, Katie and Kohl, for inspiring her My Heart Series.

As a mother of four and grandmother to six beautiful granddaughters, Kathleen draws inspiration from her family, who have devoted themselves to serving the community through military, emergency, acute, and post-acute healthcare services. Her stories reflect her 45 years of experience in post-acute care, the stories of her loved ones, and the individuals she has met throughout her life's journey. Kathleen Nelson Tellish is a published author and a holder of both US and International Design Patents for her innovative work in voice technology.